ROYAL GAMBIT

David Kimberley

First published 2023
Published by GB Publishing Org
Copyright © 2023 David Kimberley
All rights reserved

ISBN: 978-1-912576-07-4 (paperback)
978-1-912576-11-1 (eBook)

Cover Art © Wendy Kimberley Art

CBP.
GB Publishing Org
www.gbpublishing.co.uk

For Rosie

CONTENTS

Map
Corporations and organisations

MAP

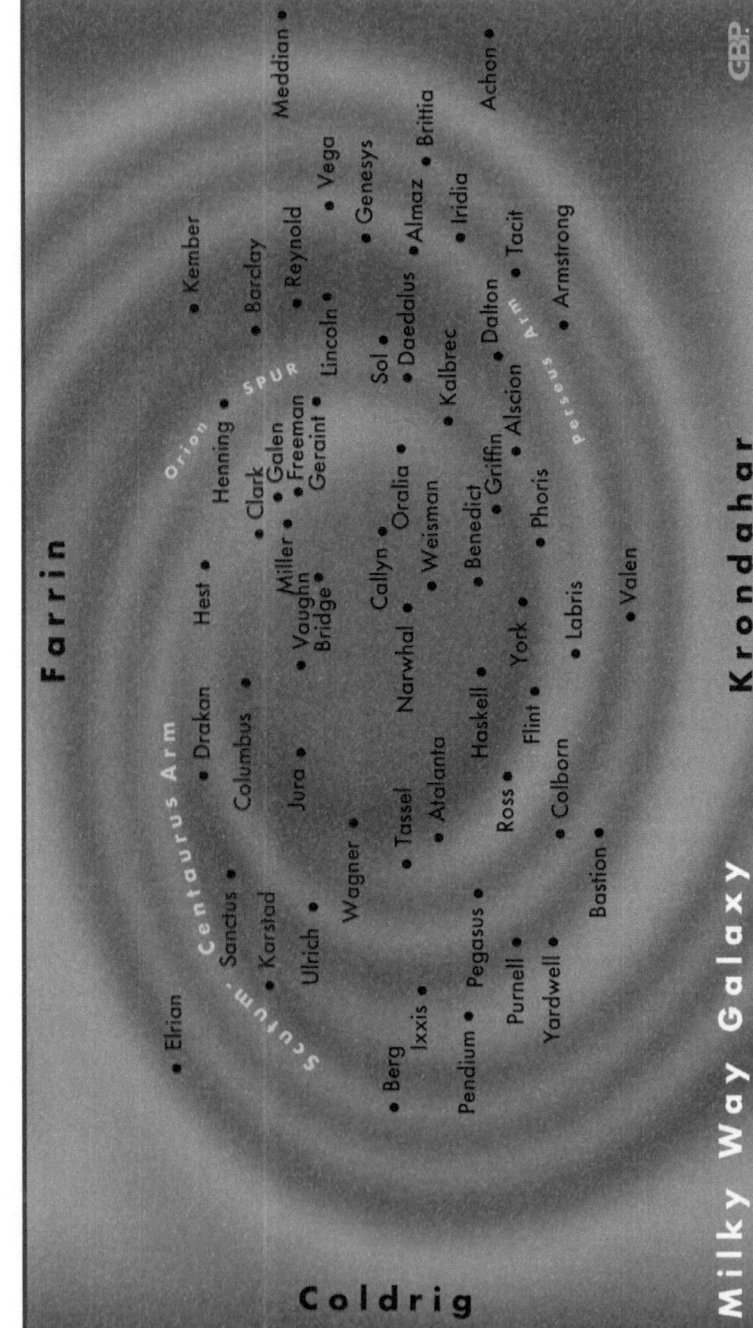

Corporations	Organisations
Taurus Galahad	Echo
Sapphire Nova	Fortitude
Libra Centauri	Jericho's Bold
Sigma Royal	Knights Templar
Impramed	Schaeffer's Nine
	Cobb Resistance
	The Kindred

Echo
Davian Kurcher – ex-Taurus enlister
Jaffren Hewn – leader of Echo
Shannon Drake – pilot of the *Falcata*
Vance Fischer – Jaffren's second
Rae Hewn – Jaffren's wife

Taurus Galahad
Karin Hayward – judicial officer
Gen. Garrett – head of military operations
Akeman – agent
Saul Winter – agent
Cmdr. Neri Ishlan – military officer
Exec. Kort – senior board member
Exec. Tench – senior board member
Exec. Marris – senior board member
Exec. Chaldevert – senior board member
Lt. Tolbert – military officer

Sigma Royal
Cmdr. Dalin Grosnik – head of board & military
Boryn Vekkerd – tech officer
Raggett – junior operations officer
Marla – junior operations officer

Cobb Resistance
Marie Butler – leader of the Resistance
Monk – member of the Resistance
Cho – member of the Resistance
Leeson – member of the Resistance
Bambridge – member of the Resistance

Additional Characters
Edlan Rane – serial killer
Sieren Broekow – ex-Taurus sniper
Morton Hurst – leader of Fortitude
Ruck – Fortitude merc
The Luminary – tech dealer
Flynn – leader of the Knights Templar
Tara Oakley – wanted killer
Hedmun Oakley – commander of the Oakley fleet & Tara's uncle
Harz – Jericho's Bold pirate
Ariana Tabb – head of Libra Centauri
Trystan Hengeveld – Libra Centauri officer
Tomas Klein – head of Sapphire Nova
Kam Bavelli – Sapphire Nova officer
Mikan Rist – assassin
Ti-Jun Niang – one of the leaders of Schaeffer's Nine
Felipe Cardozo – chief medical director of Impramed
Roman Ziegler – head of Impramed security
Clay de Bachmann – head councillor of Tidewell City

Kismet,
Genesis System

The wall crumbled impressively, breaking apart as the mech hammered relentlessly against it. Gunfire spat through the breach, bullets ricocheting off its metal frame. The mech lunged forward into the compound, disappearing from view. The panicked cries from the Sigma soldiers were music to the ears of the small group of men and women huddled in the shadows opposite the makeshift prison.

Kurcher glanced over his shoulder at the pirates. Hewn was whispering orders to them, artificial fingers jabbing in the direction of the prison. He then returned his watchful gaze to the officer standing alongside him and dug his revolver hard into the man's back. He needed to remind him he was still there.

What the hell are you doing back here? Frost's question was apt.

It wasn't so long ago that he was in Monarch City chasing Rane through the outskirts. It wasn't so long ago since that chase ended in him killing Beck and an entire Sigma enlister team. Sigma Royal wouldn't forget his face in a hurry.

The officer clenched his fists and the sound of shrikes buzzing erupted from the compound.

"Thought you didn't want to kill anyone," Kurcher said quietly into the sweating man's ear.

"I didn't." The reply was brimming with contempt. "I don't. Quickest way into the main building is to blow a hole in the wall from a distance."

I wouldn't trust this man, enlister, warned Santa Cruz. *How long will it be before he turns that mech on you?*

The thought was constantly on his mind. How easy it would be for the *linked* officer to give a silent order for the assault mech to open fire on the pirates. Then again, the man clearly wasn't stupid and knew his own life would be forfeited if he tried such a thing. Kurcher just needed to make sure he kept his gun poking into the officer's back.

"We need to make a move." Hewn appeared beside him. "If we wait much longer, we'll have the whole of Sigma bearing down on us."

Kurcher had hated this plan from the moment of its conception. It sounded so much simpler when they had cooked it up; get into Monarch, find a mech officer with access to the Link app, force him to break into the prison compound, find Trystan Hengeveld during the confusion and then get the fuck off Kismet. What could go wrong?

"Can we get inside?" he asked the officer.

"You're bound to be seen," came the sharp reply.

Kurcher exchanged a knowing look with Hewn before pushing the revolver forward again, this time getting a pained grunt in return. "Best you thin the crowd then."

At this, the officer turned to look at him. "No. I won't kill them."

Kurcher studied the man's eyes for a moment. The Link app joined the human to the mech, allowing the user to see through the automaton's visual sensors, giving them control of its actions. There were tiny shimmering symbols in the officer's eyes, which were for issuing orders, and it reminded Kurcher of the pilot app Frost used to use. Occasionally, the images in the eyes seemed to almost float and fade. It was tech unique to *The Luminary* and Hewn was still eager to find the bastard and put an end to his supply.

"What was your name again?"

The officer looked surprised by Kurcher's question. "Boryn. Tech Officer Boryn Vekkerd."

"Well, Boryn, if you don't turn those fucking shrikes on your people right now, I'll gut you, cut out your Link implant and leave you to bleed out slowly."

Vekkerd glanced down and saw the knife now pressed against his side. "If I kill them, I'll just be a piece-of-shit criminal like you. Sigma will execute me."

"You'll be coming with us," Hewn stated. "We need to study your app and how it works. Your time in Sigma is at an end no matter what. Better to stay alive, right?"

Vekkerd's shoulders sagged as it hit home he was well and truly screwed.

Hewn leant close to Kurcher. "As soon as his mech opens fire on them, we head in. The rest of our team will cause distractions so you and I can hopefully get inside without being spotted."

Kurcher snorted. "Fat chance."

"Let's just get this done." Hewn growled, checking his rifle's ammo clip.

Vekkerd needed another painful prompt before he issued the order to open fire on his own men. The moment the shrikes buzzed into action again, the pirates sprinted across the street, heading for the breach in the outer wall.

2

Vekkerd was dragged along by Kurcher.

As they neared the opening, Hewn's team split and started shooting randomly into the compound, hoping to add to the already considerable distraction.

The prison was in disarray. One of their own assault mechs smashing its way through the wall had shocked the soldiers inside, and now they were trying to make sense of what was happening while dodging a barrage of bullets. Several were already lying dead. The rest were running for some form of cover.

All Kurcher saw were the red and black uniforms flashing past in his peripheral vision as he, Hewn and Vekkerd ran for the gaping hole in the main structure. He was surprised that he hadn't had to blow anyone away yet. Last time he was in Monarch, his kill count didn't take long to start rising.

The interior of the prison was quiet. All personnel it seemed had headed out into the compound to fight off the mech. Hewn took point as he was tracking Hengeveld thanks to the codes Libra Centauri had given him to aid in the rescue. Nearby, they heard the shouts from a group of Sigma soldiers.

"The fucking thing has malfunctioned."

"Where's its user?"

"Take out the visual sensors."

Vekkerd stumbled, no doubt struggling to run through the prison while seeing through the eyes of the mech too. "Ram isn't going to last much longer."

"You named your fucking mech?" Kurcher had heard everything now. "It's not a pet."

As he pulled the officer back to his feet, Kurcher was quick to spot a Sigma soldier stepping into view behind them. Before the soldier could even raise his rifle, a single shot from the revolver took him between the eyes.

Your accuracy is improving, noted Frost.

He'll never be as good as he was, added D'Larro.

The prison was so badly thrown together that it didn't take long to locate Hengeveld. Hewn's metal arm made short work of the door, shattering the lock completely.

The Libra officer was the only person in the room, hands bound together behind his back and seated at a stained metal table. His cold blue eyes didn't even show a hint of surprise as he watched the three men enter. The look was more akin to hate.

3

"You've seen better days," Hewn commented, circling the officer.

Hengeveld's stare locked onto Kurcher. "They sent *you*? I can't believe it."

Kurcher shrugged. "What's wrong? You didn't expect to be rescued by a one-armed pirate, a wanted criminal and a Sigma soldier?"

Hengeveld's eyes shifted to Vekkerd. "I don't know how you've managed this, Hewn, but you can explain later. Get me out of here so I can contact Libra."

As the officer tried to rise from the chair, Hewn pushed him back down. "Give us something in exchange before we do."

"You've got to be fucking kidding me," snarled Hengeveld through clenched teeth.

"What've you heard since you've been here?" Hewn asked him. "Sigma are up to something and we need to know what."

"Like they would tell me anything." Hengeveld tried to curb his anger. "All I've noticed is that they have ramped up the number of mechs here and I heard them mention something about securing their other colonies too."

"You've spent all this time in their company and *that's* all you can tell us?" scoffed Kurcher. "Doesn't even look like they've been interrogating you."

"Fuck you." Hengeveld tried to stand again. "Hewn, release my hands and give me a weapon so I can shoot this murderer."

Hewn placed a metal hand on the officer's shoulder. "Libra asked us to rescue you which is a smart move on their part, making sure they don't poke the fire of war with Sigma. I agreed to this as a gesture of goodwill, for the sake of our alliance.

"Kurcher is a member of Echo and was best suited to help us get inside Monarch. I think that you should consider this vendetta of yours over."

As silence fell in the room, the sound of close gunfire echoed through the prison. Kurcher glanced at Vekkerd. "What's going on out there?"

The Sigma officer blinked as he shifted his focus from the link with his mech to Kurcher. "Ram has subdued the prison guards but scans show that reinforcements are closing in. There's no way he and your pirates can hold against the number approaching. There are also three other mechs in close proximity."

As if he hadn't heard any of that, Hengeveld instead replied to Hewn. "This man had a significant part in my brother's death. Perhaps he won't answer for this today, but I won't forget."

4

Hewn exchanged a look with Kurcher, then strode across to the door and peered out into the corridor, leaving Hengeveld to struggle to his feet unaided. "Come on, Vekkerd. Time we summon your mech and get the hell out of here."

Kurcher saw the confused looks on the faces of both Vekkerd and Hengeveld as Hewn dragged the Sigma tech officer out the door. Turning back to the bound Libra man, he gave a curt shake of the head.

"Your brother was a loyal man, like you. He was just in the wrong place at the wrong time."

Hengeveld glanced at the door. "What, you want me to say we're done before you'll get me out of here? That won't happen. I'll never forgive you for what you did."

"I don't need you to." Kurcher lifted his revolver and a single shot took Hengeveld through the eye, drawing a stunned look from the officer before he crumpled to the floor.

Let's hope that's the last we see of the Hengevelds, D'Larro remarked.

One way to end a vendetta, chuckled Ercko.

Kurcher rejoined Hewn and Vekkerd as they made their way back out of the prison.

"I don't understand," Vekkerd blurted out. "I thought you came here for him."

"We came here for you and your mech," Hewn told him.

Kurcher let the two of them take the lead. For some reason, killing Hengeveld had left a bad taste in his mouth and he just hoped that Libra didn't see through Hewn's lie when he reported that the brave officer had been shot by Sigma forces as they tried to get him to safety.

Hewn is right, Santa Cruz said. *Hengeveld was a threat to Echo's entire operation and the alliance with Libra. He needed to go. Libra will still be in Echo's debt for risking your own lives to rescue him.*

Hewn has to keep Libra on side, added Frost.

Kurcher had to admit that Hewn was much cleverer than he had thought. Their initial encounter had been a one-sided affair, with Kurcher holding all the cards and focused solely on ensuring the pirate went with him, no matter the cost. Since then, he had come to realise the man's worth and his passion for Echo's survival. Without Hewn, someone would have already collected the bounty on his head.

5

When exactly did you start relying on other people? Santa Cruz asked.

A bullet narrowly missed Kurcher's head, ricocheting off a nearby wall, and he realised that he had followed Hewn and Vekkerd through the prison courtyard and out into the streets. Just behind them, the rest of the Echo team appeared from alleyways and Kurcher did a quick headcount. Amazingly, all were accounted for, despite a few wounds between them. Still, they weren't off Kismet yet.

As they headed for the extraction point, Sigma forces closed in alarmingly fast and their retreat became an exchange of gunfire from all angles. Kurcher's revolver ammo was running dry and he looked up into the night sky, his eyes searching for any sign of salvation.

Vekkerd's mech galloped into view behind them, its blue visual sensors gleaming brightly. For a moment, Kurcher thought that the tech officer was about to attack their group, seeking some retribution for his actions. When he saw that Hewn had his weapon aimed at Vekkerd though, he knew the pirate had been thinking the same thing and instead the shrikes mounted on the mech turned on their pursuers, causing them to dive for cover.

Other blue sensors began to appear in the darkness as Sigma's mechs joined the hunt. One of them was a pursuit mech, similar to the construct that he had faced last time he was in Monarch City. Its powerful pneumatics were carrying it towards them at speed.

Just north of their position, there was a shuddering roar of an engine and the Echo ship swooped into view, descending quickly to a nearby open area among the colony buildings. The Echo team sprinted for it, finding the sleek vessel waiting for them with the cargo ramp open expectantly.

"Hurry the fuck up."

Kurcher smiled when he heard Drake's voice. She hadn't been best pleased when Hewn told her the *Falcata* was not suitable for the mission, ordering her to instead pilot the *Khopesh*. It seemed Hewn liked his ships to be named after ancient weapons.

A barrage of bullets suddenly spat at them from what felt like all sides. Two pirates were hit, tumbling to the ground, and their comrades scooped them up. Kurcher could tell that one of them was dead already, but Hewn didn't want anyone left behind.

"Move," came Hewn's deep voice above the gunfire.

Kurcher saw the Echo leader standing at the base of the ramp, beckoning his people on board. Vekkerd was being gripped tightly by the mechanical hand.

As he passed Hewn and leapt onto the ramp, Kurcher heard a loud metallic crash. The pursuit mech had caught up with Ram and the two constructs were locked in a bizarre wrestling match. Despite Ram being larger, the pursuit mech was much more agile and Kurcher tried scanning the dark streets for any sign of its human user.

"We should leave it," he yelled at Hewn. "There will be other chances."

"No.' Hewn gave Vekkerd an aggressive shake. "Get it onto the ship."

He may be clever but he's likely to get everyone killed here, Frost said.

"Drake, get us off the ground." Kurcher would deal with Hewn's ire afterwards. The pilot came back in her usual manner. "For fuck's sake."

The gats mounted on the *Khopesh* burst into life, peppering the approaching Sigma forces and laying waste to several buildings nearby.

As the mechs continued their fight, Hewn stepped onto the ramp, dragging Vekkerd almost off the ground as he did so. The pursuit mech's shrikes activated, hitting Ram point blank and sending parts of the chassis flying.

"No, no, no," cried Vekkerd.

Ram shuddered as the armour plating was torn off by the attack but, with what seemed like a futile defensive lunge, one of the assault mech's legs struck its opponent directly through the neck cavity. Kurcher noticed Vekkerd give a slight flick of his head and Ram decapitated the pursuit mech, sending oily liquid squirting into the air.

With Drake keeping the Sigma soldiers at bay, Kurcher made his way up into the ship and was joined a moment later by Hewn, Vekkerd and a sorry-looking Ram, whose exposed internal workings were leaking all over the floor. It was then that Kurcher noticed Vekkerd had also been shot, as the tech officer slumped. He had been hit in both the shoulder and the thigh.

As the *Khopesh* soared away from Monarch City, heading for the upper atmosphere, Kurcher looked around at the wounded.

Better them than you, D'Larro stated.

No more visits to Kismet, Frost muttered.

In front of him, Ram went offline, the mech's heavy head lowering as the blue sensors went dark. At that angle, Kurcher couldn't help but notice a small symbol between the sensors, visible now that the light wasn't dazzling his optic nerves. When he leant forward to get a better look, he felt his heart rate quicken and his gut tighten.

Holy shit, Frost said. *That looks way too familiar.*

Kurcher couldn't take his eyes off it. The last time he had seen something similar was at the strange console on the *Grail* but why the fuck would this mech have an alien emblem emblazoned on it?

Hewn saw the look on his face. "You injured?"

"No." Kurcher turned to glare at the unconscious Vekkerd. "He's got a lot of explaining to do when he wakes up."

Earth,
Sol system

Hayward's relief was palpable as she watched the long line of soldiers march past her, heading from the shuttles across the courtyard to the barracks. As well as the boost to military personnel, Garrett had also sent engineers whose job it was to secure and strengthen the compound defences. Heavy equipment rolled off the shuttles too. Armour plating for the walls, new long-range artillery and explosive shells were just some of the cargo she spotted.

She saw Lieutenant Tolbert near the barracks, deep in conversation with some of the new officers who Garrett had selected for this assignment. He was not the highest ranking soldier now based at the Taurus headquarters, however she had promised him continued command of his own squad.

When Hayward turned back to the shuttles, a drop of rain splashed onto her nose. She couldn't recall seeing the sun hardly at all since returning from Galt. It was almost as if Earth was weeping as the Revenants continued to spread across her surface. The fight back would commence soon enough though, with the new soldiers heading out to seize control of the surrounding territories and eradicate any of the religious fanatics they encountered.

One last figure stepped off a shuttle and Hayward couldn't help but smile as he approached her, his gait somewhat different from the last time she had seen him.

Akeman returned her smile, albeit somewhat forced. "Good to see you, Miss Hayward."

"Jesus." She laughed and shook her head. "Back to your old formal self I see. How are you?"

"Alive," he replied. "Thanks to you."

"Well, considering what you did for me, let's consider ourselves even." She glanced at the small bag he held in one hand. "You've travelled light."

Akeman shrugged. "Didn't really have much to bring apart from my HDU and data files. Figured they were more important."

She feigned disappointment. 'No vodka? Damn. I'll show you to your quarters and let you rest for a while. We're due to meet with Marris and Chaldevert in a few hours.'

9

As they headed for the main building, Hayward noticed that the agent's gun was holstered at his side. Even when surrounded by the protection of so many Taurus soldiers, Akeman still made sure he was armed. It was a trait she had been glad of that day Mikan Rist had come for her.

'How're Kort and Tench doing?' she asked him as they stepped into an elevator.

'Kort is a force to be reckoned with as always. He is the best man for the job, overseeing Kingston's rebuild operation. As for Tench, the wounds he sustained have made him slower and quieter, but he is focused on helping Kort. Galt is the best place for them.'

Hayward nodded in agreement. 'I'm pleased that both Marris and Chaldevert agreed to come to Earth. I truly believe that the Taurus board needs to be based here.'

'The general came good on his promise to supply military support I see,' Akeman commented. 'I was surprised he could spare so many. Even though Nova have recalled their remaining fleet to Valen, we still need to be wary.'

Hayward had thought the same. Sapphire Nova retreated to the outer system soon after the battle with the Taurus fleet, leaving only guardians in orbit of their other worlds. It was clear that they needed to regroup after the losses inflicted on them and she doubted they would try anything whilst still in such a state. Then again, she would never have thought they would attack Kingston so boldly in an attempt to kill off the board.

'I'm pleased you accepted my offer to come here,' she told Akeman as the elevator came to a halt. 'I'm hoping your work will be instrumental in forging the new alliance.'

He followed her out into the maze-like hallways of the upper floor. 'You do realise that I'm not friends with these people. Getting Ti-Jun Niang to agree to meet with you is not a straightforward task.'

Hayward saw Akeman clutch at his chest and grimace. She wondered whether it had been too soon to call on his services again. The medics at Kingston told her that he shouldn't have lived and she had been plagued with guilt prior to leaving the colony.

'You sure you're up for this?'

Akeman straightened. 'It's just another scar. Focusing on this work will ease the discomfort.'

She decided to change the subject somewhat. 'When was the last time you were on Earth?'

'Eleven years ago.' It was like he had been expecting the question. 'I was only here for a couple of hours, then back out to Carson. I always felt more comfortable in the Geraint system for some reason and the station had become my preferred meeting place.'

Hayward led him along a long corridor that was painted in the grey, white and black of Taurus Galahad. It was adorned with a number of ornamental swords, supposedly meant to resemble the corporation sigil. They had never looked quite right to her.

'You weren't born on Earth then?'

'No I wasn't.' Akeman seemed almost amused at the concept.

When he didn't venture any further information, Hayward tutted. 'You're such a closed book. If we are going to continue working together for the foreseeable future, I'd just like to know more about you. There's not much on you in the Taurus database. Believe me, I've looked everywhere.'

'I wouldn't have been a very good spy if my background was displayed in public records for all to see.'

'You're an agent of Taurus Galahad, not a spy.'

'There isn't much of a difference,' he said, instinctively turning his scarred face away as they passed several people. 'However, I feel like my spying days are over.'

'Just give me one piece of personal info on you,' pushed Hayward. 'Anything I don't already know.'

Akeman thought for a moment. 'I don't know where I was born. My first memory was of a family that wasn't mine; of a father figure who clearly didn't want me. That was on Bayos. He was a military man and quickly moved me on. I was a child stuck in the system, never having a true home. Eventually I grew bored of all the moving around and ended up on Aridis.'

Hayward looked surprised. 'You worked the mines?'

'Miss Hayward, do I look like a miner?' He laughed for the first time since stepping off the shuttle. 'I started out as a messenger, going from colony to colony. Later, I began working as a clearance officer for prisoners coming down from Rockland to work.'

'That must have been… interesting.' She couldn't think of another word to describe it.

'I certainly met some unique individuals. It wasn't long before I started picking up bits of intel here and there from the prisoners. Most of it was not worth Taurus' time, of course, but the occasional piece of information would warrant their attention and so I started working directly for the corporation's intelligence division.'

She had many more questions, yet knew when to stop asking. 'I feel like I know you better already.'

They arrived at the room allocated to Akeman and he gave it a cursory scan, placing his bag on the bed. Hayward watched him as he began sifting through the contents. It had been a selfish request asking him to come to Earth but one that she was glad he accepted. Already she felt safer with him there. She wondered whether he had read between the lines when he perused the description of his role at headquarters. He was smart enough to know she wanted him there as protection, not just for his vast wealth of knowledge on what else was happening out in the other systems.

'I'll leave you to rest,' she said, turning to leave.

'If you don't mind, I'd like to get to work.' Akeman pulled a bottle from the bag. 'And as if I would forget the vodka.'

Four hours later, they both found themselves seated at the long oval table in Hayward's office with the other two Earth-based board members. Once the obligatory small talk was out of the way, Hayward was keen to get down to business.

'We need to be mindful of what the other organisations are up to,' she began. 'Recent events have left Taurus vulnerable and we don't want anyone taking advantage of this. The intel that Akeman is about to share will be reported to all senior officers. General Garrett will also be made aware.'

Chaldevert gave the agent a wary glance. 'Our corporation has been plagued with traitors and double agents, including people who once sat on this board. How do we know all have been accounted for?'

'If you're concerned about where his loyalties lie, don't be. I vouch for him and trust him with my life.'

'Those who betrayed Taurus Galahad are dead,' Akeman said, his voice purposefully loud. 'Santa Cruz, Mitchell, Lenaghan, Billings, Pavleachenko, Culman. It was however a shame that most of them were killed by Sapphire

Nova as our intention had been for me to interrogate Billings and Pavleachenko to unearth more information.'

'Nova were getting rid of their loose ends,' added Hayward.

Chaldevert nodded slowly. 'Any news on the one who tried to kill you?'

Hayward looked at Akeman, who recognised the prompt to answer. 'Unfortunately the ship he took from Kingston didn't have tracking tech installed so there is no way to know where he went.'

The exploration officer's brow creased. 'Most ships are tracked these days, unless belonging to pirates or the like.'

Hayward could see that Chaldevert didn't like Akeman, but she'd had enough of his remarks. 'This one wasn't. Look, we're here to hear the latest intel so the sooner we can do this, the sooner we can all get on with our day.'

Marris cleared her throat gently. 'As long as Nova are as far from here as possible, that'll make me feel safe.'

Hayward remembered the financial officer's reaction when she had learnt of how Pavleachenko had died. Marris tended to like everyone but there might have once been some romantic link between the two. It was just a good job she hadn't been witness to the gruesome scene in Pavleachenko's office. It had taken a long time to clean what was left of him off the walls, ceiling and floor.

'Let's start with Nova then,' Akeman said, leaning forward to look at his HDU. 'After the battle against our fleet in the Geraint system, their ships returned to Flint for a time before most moved on to Valen. That is where they have remained ever since, as far as we know.'

'*Most* moved on to Valen?' Chaldevert gave him another quizzical look.

'A couple of their ships are reported to have stayed near to Straunia. Apart from their guardians defending other Nova worlds and some transports or mining vessels, Nova recalled pretty much most of their entire fleet to Valen. Tomas Klein survived the battle in Geraint and is still leading their entire corp.'

'There have been no recent news reports from Nova since they skulked off either,' added Hayward. 'They're most certainly regrouping and taking stock.'

'Do you think they will try attacking us again?' Marris asked.

'They would be stupid to do so,' replied Akeman. 'They took heavy losses. However, General Garrett has placed every Taurus ship on high alert just in case.'

Chaldevert looked wary. 'Forgive me if I don't share your optimism on this.

The general should demand their immediate surrender and disintegrate their corporation before their masterminds come up with a new plot against us.'

Hayward pointed at Akeman's HDU. 'Go on.'

'Sapphire Nova have no allies left,' the agent stated. 'The Knights Templar were aiding them but that tenuous alliance ended when Nova attacked Galt.

We do need to keep a close eye also on Sigma Royal. Since Meta was poisoned, they have been quietly building their forces on various worlds. The man who has taken control of Sigma is Dalin Grosnik, a veteran soldier with a somewhat abrasive nature. He issued orders to their entire corp to shoot on sight if encountering either Nova or Libra Centauri.'

'Sounds like something of a warmonger,' Marris noted.

'Akeman is right about Sigma,' Hayward told them. 'They seem to be gearing up for something and our belief is that it is an offensive either on Nova or on Libra, which would spark a fresh war between them.'

Akeman tapped his HDU. 'Nova wanted revenge for what happened at Straunia and came after Taurus quickly and without mercy. It could well be that Sigma are planning to avenge those who died on Meta, but they saw what happened to Nova. They won't just openly attack anyone yet.'

'Libra have clearly done something to piss them off,' said Chaldevert, rubbing at the thin layer of growth on his chin. 'Although tensions between them have been high for some time now.'

Akeman continued. 'Sigma have some sort of alliance with Fortitude, however intel is limited on this. There have been Sigma officers at Sullivan's Rest and my sources say they met with Morton Hurst. That would be a dangerous ally to have.'

Hayward stared for a moment at the window. Rain droplets were running down the glass and the grey clouds beyond threatened more bad weather.

'Are Libra making any strange moves then?' she finally asked the agent.

'Not that we are aware of. They remain in an alliance with Echo and, to a lesser degree, Schaeffer's Nine. Their board is ten-strong, headed up by Ariana Tabb.'

Marris gave a mock shiver. 'That woman has always given me the creeps.'

'Well she might.' Akeman's gaze seemed to unsettle the financial officer. 'Tabb isn't against getting her hands dirty and has quite the reputation.'

'And you invited her here?' Chaldevert directed his question at Hayward.

She could hear the disapproval in his tone. 'We reached out to everyone except Nova, Jericho's Bold and the Templars. Whether Tabb decides to come herself or send someone else, we don't yet know.'

Akeman scrolled the data before returning to his report. 'Impramed don't seem to be getting involved with the politics and are keeping to themselves, as usual. A source of mine on Summit states that there are now armed guards in Tidewell City, and there's more protection for their medical ships too on the supply routes.'

'Tidewell hasn't been the same since that incident with Nova mercs,' Chaldevert said. 'A lot of money has been lost as people chose alternative destinations for their vacation.'

'Impramed have always been very open about their personnel.' Akeman turned his HDU screen so the others could see. 'This man is Filipe Cardozo. I'm sure you all know of him. He is the Chief Medical Director of Impramed and now runs the whole corporation, following his predecessor's resignation.'

'Was there a reason for the resignation?' Hayward asked, squinting at the image of Cardozo. 'It was simply branded as being for personal reasons.'

Akeman gave a solemn nod. 'He lost his wife and daughter during a raid by the Bold. They were ambushed out in the Bridge system.'

Hayward leant back and returned her gaze to the rain-soaked window. So many had died during the last year; fathers, mothers, sons, daughters. The population of two planets gone, the colonists at Kingston who didn't survive the Nova attack, the victims of Jericho's Bold and The Kindred. When she found herself thinking about all those lost souls, her mind always returned to Rose. The girl's parents had survived, but her father had suffered a terrible head injury from a falling support and would never be the man he once was.

She remembered Rist standing over her, his cruel expressionless face illuminated ghoulishly, and the memory made her feel nauseous. Predictably, the smiling face of her son appeared but some of the features were wrong. Every year that passed meant she lost a bit more of him. Eventually he would be nothing but a silhouette, just like her husband. It had been so long since the Revenants burnt them and yet they often invaded her thoughts. The only two things that would not diminish were the love for her family and her hatred of the Revenants.

'Shall I continue, Miss Hayward?'

She blinked away the tears that threatened to flow and turned back to the table. 'Sorry, yes please.'

Akeman's eyes lingered on her for a moment before returning to the HDU. 'We've mentioned the pirate, smuggler and merc organisations briefly, however it is worth noting that they're all opportunists so are likely to try taking advantage of any weakness shown by the corporations.'

'Of course they will,' snorted Chaldevert. 'They're criminals and should never have been allowed to set up operations. Are you aware that a shipment of Eidolon was discovered on Fortuna? Most of it had already been distributed to colonists at Port Campbell. Two people were hospitalised after nearly overdosing.'

'I had heard.' Hayward ran a hand through her hair. 'Something else to discuss with Jaffren Hewn.'

'Are the Knights Templar still in Lincoln?' Marris' question was one that many in Taurus were asking.

'No.' Akeman lowered his HDU, knowing he didn't have much left to refer to. 'They moved Temple out of the system at the behest of Miss Hayward. I believe they have gone to Callyn, but I'm not sure how long the other mercs will allow them to stay.'

'Good riddance.' Hayward grimaced. 'Taurus will have no dealings with them again if I have my way. Akeman can keep an eye and ear out as to their movements. Are there any updates on The Kindred?'

'I wish there were,' replied Akeman with an apologetic glance at the judicial officer. 'They simply appear and set off their explosives, dying in the blast. There's no pattern and they are targeting everyone.'

'The attacks are increasing though,' Chaldevert pointed out. 'They have to be coming from somewhere. Are we sure they aren't some offshoot of the Revenants?'

The four thought about that for a moment before Hayward shook her head. 'They're terrorists and just another bloody fanatical faction to worry about. Any other intel to share?'

Akeman obliged. 'As you know, Taurus intercepted several ships recently that had come from Cobb. The people on board were members of the self-titled Resistance. They are being held at Titan Station and, after considerable questioning, revealed that they are part of an alliance with Echo and the Oakley fleet. Echo had agreed to relocate them to a planet called Seko in the Expanse.'

'What happened on Cobb was a travesty,' snapped Hayward. 'Those poor colonists didn't need to die. I don't blame them for finding a way off the planet or for allying themselves with pirates and mercenaries. Taurus left them to die and they have every right to be angry at us.'

'What will happen to the ones who were captured?' asked Marris.

Hayward smiled then. 'We will release them and allow them to join their colleagues on Seko.'

'Is that wise?' Chaldevert looked uncertain.

'As I've said before, we need all the friends we can get.' Hayward tapped her finger on the table surface for effect. 'I'm not saying that the Cobb Resistance will be our friends, but it will help in our proposed alliance with Echo.

It is a slight frustration that the Oakley family have seen fit not to approach us and instead are seeking alternative allies.'

'With all due respect, Taurus once frowned on anyone outside the corporation building their own fleet,' Akeman reminded her. 'The families who own the Oralia system don't particularly like us and have never hidden that fact. Again though, this is a good opportunity to make new allies.'

Hayward had to agree with the agent's astute observation. 'Which brings us to the masterminds behind this odd alliance of mercs, nobles and forgotten colonists. Echo are a greater power than we all realised.'

'Indeed they are,' remarked Akeman. 'Jaffren Hewn has been a busy man, forging the alliance with not only the Cobb Resistance and the Oakleys but also with Libra Centauri and even Schaeffer's Nine. Their hold on the Expanse is secure and the title of pirates is no longer accurate. They are mercenaries, yes, but they have both drug and alcohol operations as well as dabbling in the tech market too. They have a significant fleet at their disposal and all the latest reports have indicated there are hostilities between Echo and Jericho's Bold.

Ever since Echo and their allies joined forces to attack Santa Cruz's rogue fleet in Flint, there has been a change in their reputation. Some see Hewn as a modern Robin Hood figure, however the truth of the matter is that he is more likely to keep hold of any money they steal and picks his fights very carefully.'

'Why did he risk everything to go up against Santa Cruz though?' Chaldevert looked thoroughly confused. 'They would have all been destroyed were it not for the Libra presence at the battle.'

'I'm hoping he will share his reasons with us,' answered Hayward. 'What we do know is that Davian Kurcher is now working with Hewn, and the enlister is a very important person to us.'

Hayward knew that the job title was probably not suitable for Kurcher anymore, however she did not know how else to refer to him. The thought reminded her that she needed to check in with the new enlisters she was hoping to hire soon. They were the replacements for the team that Rees once oversaw and ultimately led to their deaths.

As she turned to Akeman to ask if he had any further information, her office comms pinged. She reached for her HDU and saw that one of the communications officers was trying to reach her. With an apology to the others at the table, she opened the link.

'This is Hayward.'

The officer cleared his throat before speaking. 'Ma'am, there is a ship on approach to Earth and the pilot is requesting to land here and to urgently speak with you.'

'The ship's name?'

'The *Farlare*, ma'am.'

She saw the look of recognition in Akeman's eyes. 'Why do I know that name?'

The agent leant closer to her, his voice low. 'The *Farlare* was the ship stolen from a rescue team on Minerva. I've been trying to find out more on who killed the colonists at Hayes but there is no new intel. We have more teams out there now studying the whole colony, however the pilot of this ship may well be able to tell us more.'

'Im reluctant to let them land,' Hayward whispered. 'It could be a Nova ploy or some pirate trick.'

The comms officer clearly heard what she had said and jumped in. 'The pilot told me that he expected you would feel this way, ma'am. In that instance, he said to let you know his name.'

'Perhaps you could've given me that before now,' she said angrily. 'Go on then. Who is he?'

'He said he was once Saul Winter.'

Echo flagship Glaive,
Miller system

The mood on the *Glaive* was different to usual.

As Kurcher made his way through the ship, he could see the worried looks on the faces of those he passed. The actions of Harz and his followers had placed the whole of Echo on alert. Kurcher still thought that they were going over the top with their reaction though.

They cower as though the whole of Jericho's Bold are coming after them, said Santa Cruz.

This Harz clearly believes he can take Echo on and win, noted D'Larro.

He tried again to imagine what it must have been like for Broekow, being captured and tortured by the tattooed bastards. The man was broken anyway so there couldn't have been much left after both Harz and Devlin had finished with him, although the latter was perhaps cut short. That was two heads of Harper security dead within the space of a year.

Another reason for Nova to seek revenge, Frost remarked.

He couldn't help but wonder about Devlin's killer. Was it someone trying to cash in on Broekow's bounty, or was it an attack on Nova themselves? The planetbore rig had blown, killing a number of workers, so Harper was in a state of shutdown just like the last time he visited the sorry colony.

Maybe it was someone with unfinished business, Frost said.

Kurcher found Hewn where he expected, staring at the map of the galaxy as his command crew pretended to be busy around him. Fischer was alongside him as always, reporting that alert buoys had been distributed throughout the systems of the Expanse, as had their fleet.

Drake was sitting behind them, her feet up on a console as she smoked one of her cigarettes. Kurcher could see she was deep in thought, just as she often was since the Bold killed Masami.

'What else?' Hewn asked Fischer, although his eyes locked onto Kurcher as he approached.

Fischer also glanced at Kurcher, however it was with much more contempt. 'There wasn't much left of the *Crius* but we salvaged what we could. She was partially buried under the snowfall anyway.'

'Did you find Tariq's body?' Drake was suddenly interested in the conversation.

'It was somewhere under the snow. Thought it best to leave him be, rather than spend time digging him out of the ice.'

Drake bristled at the answer. 'Bullshit. He would've gone out of his way to fucking find you. You obviously had more pressing shit to be doing than retrieving one of Echo's own.'

Kurcher wanted to speak up, but he had to time it right. As much as he hated to admit it, he agreed with Fischer's decision. Salvaging the remnants of the *Crius* was much more important than finding a frozen corpse. Best let the dead rest.

If only they did, sighed Frost.

Hewn waved a hand, prompting Fischer to continue.

'It looked like the Bold had burnt out most of the ship, but we managed to find some useful equipment amongst the wreckage. There were also a couple of dead Bold, so it looks like Masami and Broekow managed to take some out at least.'

Drake let out a derisive snort and shook her head as she blew smoke into the room. Trying his best to ignore her outbursts, Fischer pointed down at the map. 'I know that the Bold are our key concern, but we have to be wary of The Kindred getting into the Expanse. If those freaks get into one of our systems, or onto one of our worlds, they could cause some serious damage.'

Hewn stroked his beard as his eyes roamed the map. 'Agreed. We'll remain vigilant for *any* threat from outside the Expanse. With our ships and buoys deployed, that will help monitor any unexpected traffic.'

When Fischer crossed his arms, which was a telltale sign he had finished speaking, Kurcher took his chance. 'Vekkerd understands his situation. I had a long chat with him and he seems more than willing to disclose any intel we ask him to.'

'Of course he does,' Hewn said with a wry smile. 'He killed Sigma soldiers and helped us get rid of an important bargaining chip in Hengeveld. He knows Sigma enlisters will already be looking for him. It's lucky we chose a tech officer who preferred survival over loyalty.'

Loyalty is a meaningless word amongst pirates, scoffed Santa Cruz.

'That symbol on the mech is an emblem of *The Luminary*,' Kurcher reported. 'It's created when the Link app is online and acts as the interface between user and mech. At least, that's what Vekkerd was told.'

'You don't believe it?' Hewn's interest had definitely been piqued.

'I'm sure it is an interface of sorts, but the tech used in the app *creates* it. No other app does this and its origin is unknown. Either this *Luminary* fucker is a genius whose choice of emblem is just a huge coincidence, or they have knowledge of the *Grail* and its alien tech.'

Hewn pondered this, his dark eyes seeming to almost stare through Kurcher. 'Either way, they're dangerous and we need to find out who and where they are. Did Vekkerd have any intel on this? Data from the app implant or in the mech?'

'Nothing. *The Luminary* is a fucking ghost.'

'Vance, get a cell sorted for Vekkerd but keep the aggression to a minimum. The man may be able to help us a lot more.' Hewn glanced at his second. 'Then I'm leaving you in charge for a while.'

Fischer simply raised an eyebrow in surprise. 'Can I ask why?'

Hewn gave a rare smirk. 'I've been invited to a sit down with Taurus Galahad so I'll be heading to Earth.'

This got the attention of everyone in earshot and Kurcher stayed quiet while Fischer began to point out the hundred and one reasons Hewn shouldn't go. Kurcher listened as Hewn then explained just how important it was for them to forge an alliance with Taurus, telling them to imagine all the doors it would open and the added security it would bring in such a dark time.

Or Taurus could just throw him in a cell when he arrives, interrogate then execute him, Frost remarked.

'This new judicial officer is smart,' Hewn was saying to Fischer. 'She knows just how important it is to make new allies instead of enemies.'

Fischer shrugged. 'Taurus just got the shit kicked out of them by Nova. Of course they want to make friends. How do you know this is a legitimate offer to talk though?'

'Because she has released the members of the Cobb Resistance who were intercepted on their way to Seko.' Hewn let his words sink in. 'I've confirmed that this is true.'

'So what? Releasing a few disgruntled colonists doesn't mean shit.' Fischer was clearly trying hard not to raise his voice.

'It's called a gesture of goodwill, dickhead,' snapped Drake.

'I thought you'd be against this,' Fischer bit back at her.

21

Drake pursed her blue lips. 'Yeah, well I'm not running Echo.'

Hewn looked across the map at Kurcher. 'I've got another job for you.'

'Big fucking surprise.' There was no way he would go with him back to the Sol system; back to the centre of the Taurus web.

'Go down to Seko, tell Butler her people are coming home and check the Resistance are doing what they should.'

Those people don't like you, said Ercko bluntly. *Tell him to go fuck himself.*

'I've already made sure they're behaving, Jaffren,' jumped in Fischer. 'There's no real need for him to go down there.'

'Don't reckon he was talking to you.' Kurcher nodded to Hewn. 'Fine. I'd rather be breathing fresh air than this processed shit anyway.'

As Hewn turned to talk quietly to Fischer, Kurcher stepped closer to Drake. The sweet smell of her never failed to arouse him and he wondered whether he should try his luck again.

'Fuck off.'

Perhaps not. 'I was just going to say it'll do you good to come to Seko too. Take some time out.'

Her angry eyes met his, her pupils dilated. 'Time out from what?'

'This shit. We just raided Monarch City and survived being shot at *again*. I know you like some downtime after blowing people away.'

His grin only fuelled her anger. 'And you think I want to fuck you. I don't need downtime, you patronising prick.'

Kurcher knew the other pirates were watching the exchange. 'Best you go get the ship prepped then.'

Drake's lips curled into a feral snarl as she stood. 'Find yourself another pilot, cunt.'

He hadn't heard that word for a long time and wasn't surprised it came from her dirty mouth. 'And miss your sparkling conversation?'

Her hand gripped the hilt of her knife as she stepped towards him purposefully.

'Enough.' Hewn's voice made her hesitate. 'You're going with him as usual so calm the fuck down.'

As Drake stormed from the room, Kurcher wondered just how close he got to being stabbed. When he turned back to the map, Hewn was shaking his head and Fischer had a smug expression plastered across his face.

22

Just punch the annoying bastard, growled Angard.

At Hewn's behest, Kurcher found himself accompanying the Echo leader through the grey corridors of the *Glaive* as he went to prepare for his trip to Earth.

'You need to stop provoking her,' Hewn told him eventually. 'Next time she'll run you through and leave you to bleed out.'

'I don't doubt that. Did she ever have links to the Bold?'

'She did once. Something happened that turned her against them though.' Hewn could see Kurcher wanted to know more. 'When Drake came to us, she was like a stray animal, lashing out at anyone who got too close to her. She was injured and clearly afraid, although would never admit it. We didn't even know how old she was.

We gave her refuge from her past and she proved to be a capable pilot. She also had no qualms about killing, which was to be expected coming from the Bold.'

'But she still paints her lips blue,' Kurcher remarked. 'How can you be sure she wasn't planted into Echo by the Bold?'

'I've seen her kill a number of Bold. She only has hate for them.'

'Maybe she just hides it really well.' Kurcher recalled how she had been since Masami's death. 'Something's not right with her. I hope she's not the one fucking Echo over and leaking intel. She could be feeling guilty about what happened on Vir.'

As they reached Hewn's quarters, the pirate gave an exasperated sigh. 'Or she could be mourning the loss of a friend and struggling to contain her hatred of the Bold. Just don't keep antagonising her or she's likely to cut your dick off.'

Kurcher couldn't help but recall the gruesome image of Ercko's butchered member and D'Larro examining the wound with that look of morbid fascination he so often had. He remembered Frost's reaction to the sadistic crim's murder too. Despite all that happened on his ship and the fucked up final days of the *Kaladine*, he missed it. In particular, he missed the simpler days, when it was just him and Frost chasing people down. Now he was always looking over his shoulder, waiting for some corp goon or merc to shank him in the back and collect on the substantial bounty for Davian Kurcher.

'Give Marie Butler my regards,' Hewn said, indicating that their conversation was finished. 'And don't annoy her either. We need to keep them

23

sweet.'

As he walked away, Kurcher called back. 'Don't give my regards to Taurus.'

Kismet,
Genesys system

The whole room was on edge and the line-up of officers standing uncomfortably in front of Grosnik didn't know where to look.

'Fucking useless.' The Sigma Royal general paced back and forth, fists and teeth clenched. 'I should have you all stripped of rank and discharged for this momentous fuck up.'

Grosnik couldn't believe his eyes when he had read the report of what happened in Monarch City. Numerous soldiers dead or wounded, a prison facility blown apart, a traitorous tech officer missing with his mech and one dead prisoner who had been incredibly valuable to Sigma.

He had headed straight to Kismet as soon as he finished reading said report, cutting short the inspection of their new ships on Cenia. Even leaving behind the biting cold couldn't raise his spirits, especially when he was reminded just what a sorry excuse for a colony Monarch City actually was.

'I've gone over and over the intel,' he yelled at the officers. 'I'm finding it hard to understand exactly how this all happened. I mean, what were you all doing while these bastards strolled in and fucked us over? Quite clearly nothing.'

'Sir.' The tallest of the officers stood as straight as he could, daring to look the general in the eye. 'We couldn't have foreseen them using one of our own to attack the prison compound. They caught us by surprise.'

Grosnik stared the man down before responding. 'No shit. There's clearly no point talking to you. Get out there and do something useful.'

The officers couldn't get out of the room quick enough. As the door closed, Grosnik exhaled sharply then moved to sit at the table below the only window.

Outside, he watched a procession of mechs march past accompanied by their respective handlers. His thoughts turned once again to Boryn Vekkerd and the young tech officer's part in what had transpired. He must have been coerced into helping the attackers. His record up until that moment had been exemplary and he was quick to learn how to use the Link app, going so far as to teach others early in the training process.

He scooped up his HDU and began going through the only footage from that night, his brow furrowing in frustration at not being able to see any of the attackers clearly and the fact they took out security camera feeds at key points around the compound. Initial speculation pointed at Libra Centauri of course. Who else would risk their lives to get to Hengeveld?

He recalled looking down at the corpse of the prisoner, the one blue eye glazed and staring at the ceiling. Would Libra murder their own man just to keep him quiet? Why not just take him with them?

He knew the answers to the questions but didn't want to voice them. All evidence pointed towards it *not* being a corporation raid. The weapons used, the ship they fled Kismet on that managed to get past the orbiting guardian and the bullet that had killed Hengeveld. It had not been standard issue and perhaps his science team could find something from their analysis; anything to help track down the killer.

Grosnik scrolled to the end of the report, choosing to read the part about the mech fight again. Vekkerd's mech had been badly damaged and one pursuit mech had lost its head. The latter was his least favourite model. Too many design flaws and limited AI, although the Link app had made a huge difference. Instead of meeting an enemy head on, now the mechs moved with an eerie human grace.

Grosnik knew what he had to do. He requested the comms link using his own confidential codes. He knew there would be no image; no voice. It was the way *The Luminary* always communicated.

How can I help, General?

Grosnik didn't have to wait long for the first message and was glad he could speak rather than type an answer. 'We've had an incident. One of the linked mechs has been stolen and I was hoping you can track it down.'

I'm sure I can. It's not easy to steal a mech though. What can you tell me about this incident?

He didn't want to divulge too much. 'There was a raid and this assault mech was used against us. The tech officer was also taken.'

If you had informed me during this raid, I could have shut down the mech.

'I was in a different system at the time and none of the officers here have clearance to contact you direct.'

An oversight that you will need to rectify to avoid this in the future.

Grosnik kept his tone measured despite the arrogant response. 'Indeed.'

Send me the designation and I will find it.

'Thank you.'

Although I do ask for something in return.

Grosnik grimaced in anticipation. 'Fortitude pay you for the apps, not us.'

I don't mean money. When does the first stage of your campaign begin and where?

'Several days' time.' Despite the location being classified, their agreement meant *The Luminary* would be privy to the information. Strangely, they hadn't asked until now. 'Our first target will be an outpost on Garnet, in the Henning system. Why? Do you plan on being there?'

Not in person. I would like access to the live data from the entire mech force you drop onto the planet, to be able to monitor the links and witness how well the apps work.

Grosnik hesitated, his mind quickly going over any pros and cons. 'You promised us a mech army that would drag Sigma Royal back from the brink and establish us as the main power across known space. Are you saying you're not certain the app will deliver?'

There was no immediate message in reply. He had made whoever was at the other end of the comms link think finally.

General, I have absolute belief in my product. My app is flawless. If there are any issues with the mechs, that will be down to Fortitude as supplier. I simply want to be able to see the attack unfold as it happens. As long as your tech officers do their jobs, you will have nothing to worry about.

'Very well,' agreed Grosnik reluctantly. 'You'll have all mech designations before we depart for Garnet.'

Thank you, General. Now I will get to work finding your lost mech.

'*Our* lost mech.' His correction fell on deaf ears as the comms link had already been severed. 'Fuck's sake.'

Grosnik didn't like having to ask the mysterious app dealer for anything. Their relationship already grated on him and yet it was one born of necessity.

The death of Meta and its population had left Sigma reeling and he had to act fast to avoid widespread panic from dictating their next move. As a high-ranking officer of the military arm, he had been the best choice to take control of the corporation following the destruction of the board, and his first orders had been for the fleet to protect their systems from *any* further attacks. The main threat had been Nova until their battle with Taurus wiped out a significant proportion of their ships. Now, he saw Taurus themselves and Libra as the priorities.

All reports pointed towards Taurus not being behind the actions of Jorelian Santa Cruz but Grosnik had been around long enough to remain wary of everyone. He had to admit though that the death of Mitchell and appointment of Garrett had been welcome news. He had met both men before and the latter always seemed much more sensible; easier to deal with.

When alone with his thoughts, he always began doubting whether Sigma's new plans were the best way forward. Allying themselves with mercenaries and faceless tech merchants went against much of what the corporation had once stood for. These were different times now however and called for more drastic action. Their new mech army would make a difference as they rebuilt and expanded.

Grosnik stared out the window again, watching as night slowly fell on Monarch City. His main concern when ensuring the revival and survival of Sigma Royal was that he didn't want them to end up like Nova. In a few months, he didn't want to be looking out of a window on some world at the edge of the galaxy surrounded by the tattered remnants of his people. Nova's vengeance campaign would have been more effective were it not for their lack of patience.

He remembered losing the ships and personnel in Flint, when they were reeled in by Nova's ploy, just as Taurus and Libra were. He wished he had never given the order to send ships to Straunia in some crazy attempt to claim salvage on the *Grail*. They lost good men, women and mechs.

No, Sigma would wage a war that the other corporations would not expect. They would not be drawn into combat against the odds or resort to assassination attempts.

It would start on Garnet.

Seko,
Miller system

Marie Butler was actually smiling.

When he explained the news of her peoples' release, Kurcher had watched her expression change from the cold indifference she usually displayed when he was in the room to a warmth that seemed to make the drab surroundings brighten somewhat. Despite the darkness beneath her tired eyes, the leader of the Cobb Resistance was actually attractive when she wasn't scowling.

Now he found himself walking the halls of the colony with her, trying his best to listen as she talked about all manner of Resistance-related matters. As they passed one of the windows looking directly out onto the landing pads, Kurcher stole a glance. The shitheap ships belonging to the Resistance were lined up neatly, however the much larger *Cradle's Reach* cast a shadow over them all.

'Oakley can't seem to stay away.'

She didn't seem to mind him interrupting her flow. 'He doesn't say much about Cradle but some of his crew have implied a war is brewing there between the ruling families.'

It's been brewing for years, remarked Frost.

'I can believe that,' he muttered.

'Will you be staying long this time?'

Kurcher found the question uncomfortable. 'No. There's too much shit going on up there and the last thing I want is Fischer on my back.'

Butler laughed. 'That seems to be a hate-hate relationship.'

'You've got a few ships missing I see,' he noted, changing the subject.

'Yeah, I sent a few off Seko to help patrol the system, at Echo's request. A couple more went out just this morning on survey runs. Cho and Monk are heading them up. Thought I'd give them the extra responsibility they've been craving since we left Cobb.'

'Good decision.' Kurcher's eyes momentarily lingered on the *Falcata* out in the farthest corner of the landing pads. He wondered how wasted Drake would be, her drug intake having increased alarmingly. 'You need to get better ships though. Those things are more likely to drop from the sky than complete a

29

successful survey.'

Butler was now a few paces ahead. 'Any ideas where to find some?'

'Perhaps.' He caught her up. 'I'll speak with Hewn about it. See what we can do.'

'Thanks. As long as you don't have to kill anyone to get them.'

'No promises.'

As they continued through the colony, with Butler trying to explain to him more about Seko's ecology, all Kurcher could think about was Cobb. The ghost planet was now just a gigantic tomb, haunted by the memories of war crimes and buried secrets. Despite the clean air of Seko, he still saw dust and death on the people passing by.

You need to stop dwelling on the past, Frost said.

You're to blame for the heartache these colonists suffered, Santa Cruz reminded him.

He watched Butler as she talked, yet didn't hear her. He remembered Cal Fuller lying on the cold stone floor of the bunker bleeding to death. He remembered Dale Rettin's head blowing apart. He remembered the pleading mothers and their wide-eyed children.

'Listen.' He grabbed Butler's arm and turned her to face him. 'You need to make this place work. You're not the Cobb Resistance any more.'

She frowned. 'What are you talking about? We *are* making this place work, and we'll always be the...'

'Fuck Cobb,' he snapped. 'You're a colony of survivors making a new life, and your priority is just that. Just because Hewn gave you this planet to live on, it doesn't mean you should put your people in danger for him.'

She pulled her arm away from his grip. 'Without Echo, we'd most likely be dead. If you hadn't come to Cobb when you did, one of the corps would have scooped us off the planet or simply executed us.'

How quickly she forgets, sighed D'Larro.

'Every time I landed on Cobb, people died. Even when I arrived there with that fucker Rane, we persuaded your people to fight against Santa Cruz and most of them were killed.'

Butler's eyes narrowed. 'What do you mean *every time?*'

Maybe this was the moment to come clean. It would mean his banishment off Seko, and the burden would still weigh heavily on his shoulders, but it might make him feel better just for a while.

'Ah, there you are.'

Hedmun Oakley's arrival was not a welcome interruption and Kurcher gave him the coldest of stares as the self-appointed officer approached.

Despite her smile having returned, Butler still looked ruffled by what Kurcher had said. 'I didn't realise you'd be back so soon.'

'Neither did I but needs must. I hope you don't mind.'

'Of course not. You're always welcome here.'

'I hope that goes for other members of my family.'

Kurcher drew in a sharp silent breath when he noticed the woman several paces behind Hedmun.

You've got to be kidding, Frost muttered.

'Marie, I would like to introduce you to my niece.'

Tara Oakley didn't smile when she saw Kurcher. She merely gave her uncle a wary glance and pursed her lips slightly. As she exchanged pleasantries with Butler, Hedmun took the chance to shoot Kurcher a meaningful look.

'I'd appreciate it if you could find a place for Tara here,' said the elder Oakley. 'The hostilities on Cradle between families have escalated to such a degree, that an attempt was made on her life.'

More likely she bedded and shredded someone she shouldn't have, Ercko remarked.

There was no denying though that the serial maneater was very different to that first time Kurcher had met her. Not only was her hair darker and the glint gone from her eyes, her body language had also changed drastically. No more confident, assured Tara Oakley it seemed. Unless she was putting on an act of course, which he wouldn't have put past her.

'Of course.' Butler was quick to agree. 'As long as you don't mind putting in some hard graft, we're happy to welcome anyone who needs respite from the shit out there.'

'Thank you.'

The voice was different too. More meek and nervous. That was definitely an act.

'This isn't the sort of place to shy away from responsibility.' Kurcher made sure he looked the killer in the eye. 'No matter who you are or who you're related to.'

31

The expression on Tara Oakley's face said it all. It was the same one he had seen time and again on board the *Kaladine*. Loathing, hatred and a realisation that he was right. It was a look he hadn't seen though since she got shot by one of Trin's goons. It was more the fact that Angard blew himself up that changed her demeanour though. No more protector.

Things would've been much fucking different had that gigantic asshole not been around to help her, growled Ercko.

'Ignore him,' scowled Butler. 'He thinks he runs the place. Let me give you a proper tour.'

As the two women moved off together, Kurcher turned to Hedmun. 'If anyone dies unexpectedly here, I'll know who to blame. I spared her once. Don't think I will again.'

The old officer's lips curled in a half-smile. 'She just needs somewhere where nobody knows her, where she can start over. I doubt she'll ever return to Cradle now.'

'She's dangerous. Unstable.'

'So are you.' Hedmun's eyes flashed angrily. 'Need I remind you that I'm the only one here who knows what you did on Cobb? I'd be more than happy to share that.'

Kurcher watched him walk away.

It would be easy enough to make sure that old fucker met with an unfortunate accident, stated Ercko.

Both of the Oakleys could cause you problems, added D'Larro.

The old Davian would've pulled his revolver and shot Hedmun on the spot, said Trin. *I miss the old you.*

Kurcher stood alone with his thoughts for some time, eventually coming to the conclusion that there was no point worrying about the Oakleys. They would remain quiet for fear of being turfed out themselves. It would be very simple to deliver data to Butler listing Tara's crimes; all of those unsuspecting men she had killed. Hedmun knew that too.

The colony air had suddenly become bitter and he made his way back to the *Falcata*, his thoughts turning to Drake instead. The blue-lipped pirate had been on his mind since her outburst back on the *Glaive*. His gut told him that she was trustworthy, and yet somebody was leaking intel to the likes of Jericho's Bold and possibly even other organisations. Perhaps her anger was fuelled by guilt over Masami's death, if she had told the Bold where to find Broekow.

He found her in no fit state to fly. The cockpit stank of smoke that could only be from narcotics, and Drake was higher than he had ever seen her before. For a moment, he thought she might have overdosed as she seemed not to be breathing, then she inhaled deeply, her eyes flickering behind heavy lids.

'Fuck's sake.'

He lifted her from the seat, carrying her through the tight spaces of the ship interior. When he lowered her onto her bed, he realised it might have been prudent to remove her knife beforehand. Had she been conscious, there was no way he could've even touched her, or got close to her for that matter.

As he headed out of her quarters, he heard her stir slightly.

'Fuck you,' she mumbled, her words barely making sense.

Kurcher smiled. 'Not today.'

Earth,
Sol system

There was no shaking the pounding in Hewn's skull, but he would keep his discomfort hidden from those gathered around the table.

As he arrived in Sol, the apprehension had caused the headache to start. It was manageable at that point, although every Taurus ship or planet they passed helped to crank the pain up to the next level. Upon final approach to the ancestral home of the human race, he was on the brink of telling his pilot to turn the ship around and head back to the Expanse. He felt too exposed in Sol.

As they had made their descent from Earth's upper atmosphere, he had received a message from one of his Libra contacts stating that a transport due to drop off supplies to Echo had been destroyed. At first, he thought it was the Bold again making their presence felt. It turned out to be one dishevelled member of The Kindred who had stolen on board the transport and detonated one of their dirty bombs. It beggared belief that they were still finding ways to sneak onto ships and stations unnoticed.

Landing at the notorious Taurus headquarters had been a nerve-wracking experience. The number of military personnel in residence had been higher than anticipated and he realised quickly that, if the corp wanted him dead, he would have been unable to stop them.

His headache wasn't helped when he was marched from the landing pad directly to a meeting room, flanked by four armed guards. He had made the decision to go alone in the hopes of showing trust and good faith to anyone else in attendance. He had regretted that as he walked the Taurus halls.

Finally, he had found himself deposited into the very corporate-looking room, which was taken up mostly by the large polished table. The first person he recognised was Ariana Tabb. When her eyes fell upon him, he could see the fury behind them. No doubt she had already heard of the transport's demise, although he had heard she was in a constant rage over a number of things and was sure he would be having a very uncomfortable conversation with her at some point.

Tabb had been speaking with Karin Hayward, whose features looked positively angelic compared to the Libra officer's. Behind Hayward was a familiar scarred face and Hewn had nodded a silent greeting to Akeman.

Of the other three people in the room, Hewn only recognised one. It was hard not to know the weathered face of Ti-Jun Niang. After all, it was plastered on many wanted posters across the galaxy. He was apparently the only member of Schaeffer's Nine to have come, meaning the other eight leaders had voted him to speak on their behalf.

The final two carried the formal air of corporate officers and it wasn't long before he had been introduced to Taurus board members Chaldevert and Marris.

No Fortitude, no Impramed and no Sigma Royal. Their absence hadn't gone unnoticed and Hewn heard them being referenced on more than one occasion.

The meeting had started with courtesy from all. Hayward thanked them for coming so quickly and explained her hopes for a new alliance. He had noticed at that point Akeman was the only person carrying a weapon, which he openly displayed at his side, and Hewn's unease slowly began to settle. Unfortunately it was ramped back up along with the pain in his head when Hayward made a sudden unexpected announcement that, while the alliance in question was still on the table, they had a more urgent and frankly unbelievable issue to address first.

That's when Saul Winter had walked in. The man was unusual to say the least, with his gaunt appearance and piercing blue eyes that seemed to stare right through them as they moved from one person to the next. Then he recounted his story to them, starting with his being employed by Jorelian Santa Cruz to follow Kurcher and to ensure the success of the mission to deliver the data implant that had been concealed by Enlister Cooke before his demise.

Hewn had found himself leaning forward more and more at every turn in Winter's tale. When he realised that it had been Winter who shot the *Kaladine* down, Hewn swallowed his rising anger. Here was the man who was responsible for Frost's death. If Kurcher or Broekow had been in the meeting room, there may well have been a bloodbath at that moment.

Winter explained how he escaped the mawhounds on Cerberus and returned to Santa Cruz, at which point he had received orders from Taurus to extract any information from the rogue commander he could regarding the *Grail*. When he told the entranced room what happened next, Hewn found himself exchanging confused glances with Tabb and Niang.

Santa Cruz had driven a knife into Winter's chest, having realised he knew too much, before having his body frozen and shipped out to the research labs on Minerva to be used as a test subject.

'For what?' Tabb had asked bluntly, her fingers steepled before her on the table. The *Grail* had been no secret. All of them knew Santa Cruz had managed to locate the alien structure but most had no idea how. Winter described the strange devices found on various worlds across the galaxy and how they were all sent to Minerva for study; how Santa Cruz managed to unlock a wealth of data and information thanks to the scientists at Hayes. The only missing piece of his puzzle had been the data implant discovered by Cooke, which contained the coordinates of the *Grail*.

'All of the corps have been aware of the alien devices for years,' Winter told them, his voice calm and surprisingly gentle. 'This has led to the exploration missions into Coldrig, Farrin and Krondahar. Taurus, Nova, Sigma and Libra all racing to find more alien tech before the rest.'

'You haven't answered my question,' Tabb pointed out angrily.

Winter had given the Libra Centauri officer the coldest smile Hewn had ever seen. 'I was infused with the technology discovered within the devices, to see how it affected a human body. It rebuilt my cells and brought me back to life, albeit with disturbing side effects.'

Hayward had chosen this moment to interject. 'Let's take this one step at a time, otherwise I fear an information overload. The Hayes colony on Minerva was attacked and the people there killed or taken. Saul was the only survivor we know of, having woken up from an induced coma just before the attack began.'

'Did you know of this research?' Niang asked her.

'We had no idea.' Hayward signalled to Winter. 'Tell them what happened, Saul.'

Winter's expression remained devoid of emotion. 'The population of Hayes were attacked by an alien race who came to take the devices. They knew how dangerous they were, and all colonists or scientists were either eradicated or taken.'

He let his words sink in as jaws dropped open, including Hewn's. Hayward exchanged a look with Akeman, Chaldevert and Marris, who had all heard the story already.

'Seems preposterous,' said Tabb finally, giving a derisive snort. 'The devices I know about and this test to see how the human body reacted to the tech I can just about believe. Just don't tell me to accept that aliens came out of nowhere and destroyed your colony before disappearing back into the void. More likely an attack by pirates or Nova.'

'They came from somewhere in Coldrig,' Hayward countered. 'And they haven't disappeared.'

Winter continued. 'I knew that they were heading for Straunia after collecting the devices, which have likely already been destroyed. If you have research labs studying any similar tech, Miss Tabb, I recommend you dispose of them urgently. They arrived on one ship that wiped out every Taurus vessel in orbit.'

'I find this all highly improbable.' Tabb's tone had become almost amused. 'In all the years we've been out there exploring and colonising, we've never come across another intelligent species like us. Bugs as large as a fucking planethopper, predators and prey evolved for their respective worlds. No space-faring sentient race.'

'Doesn't mean they're not out there though,' Hewn had dared to add. 'You forget that I've seen the *Grail* and what it's capable of.'

'I followed them to Straunia.' Winter drew all eyes back to him. 'What I saw there affects us all.'

Hayward stood and placed a hand on Winter's arm. 'It does, however I think our friends need to hear what you know about them, to put it in context.'

Winter nodded slowly, then took a gulp of water before he spoke again. 'It took me some time to piece together what I was feeling and hearing when I woke up in the labs just before the attack. I could hear whispers in the dark. Voices that were not human.

I could see the hidden workings of the technology used in the labs and the workings of the scientists themselves; organs, blood flow, heat.

I felt like I knew these aliens before I even saw them. I knew they had been awoken after centuries of slumber. I knew their sorrow and their need to leave the relative safety of Coldrig. I knew they were going to Straunia and I felt a pull to find out why.'

'Sorry, this is getting just a bit fucking confusing,' cried Tabb, slapping a palm down on the table. 'Shall we get to the point?'

While Hayward and her team bristled quietly, Winter showed no sign of annoyance as he began walking slowly around the table.

'I assume it's no coincidence that they were heading to the same planet where the *Grail* had crashed a few months before,' Hewn said, feeling a strange gnawing in his guts at the thought of the dead planet.

When Winter came to a halt near to him, it took Hewn a moment to work out what he was seeing as the Taurus agent's eyes seemed to shimmer in a certain light. Was that metal in his ice blue iris?

'This species are driven by the survival instinct, I know that much. They'll do whatever it takes and they don't care about the humans who get in the way. They're also opportunists though so a quick stop at Minerva to get the antecedent devices meant they could also replenish their sustenance stocks whilst at the same time eradicate every living being they saw as being potentially linked to the dangerous tech.

I was in the binary star system too, when Kurcher activated the *Grail*. I should've known Santa Cruz wouldn't have cared if I died out there, just as long as the weapon was his to command. I barely made it back before the jump point closed.'

'Yeah, well not everyone made it back,' shrugged Hewn, unable to keep looking into those strange eyes.

'I should not have pursued you to Cerberus.'

'You did though, and a lot of people died there.'

'It was you who summoned the mawhounds.' Winter was making a statement rather than asking a question. 'A clever plan. I still bear the scars from that encounter, although it feels like someone else's memory now.'

Tabb's patience was wearing thin. 'So you've regaled us with this wonderful tale, which I still find hard to swallow by the way. Are you going to tell us what's happening on Straunia?'

'We can do better than tell you,' Hayward said, nodding to Akeman who started tapping at his HDU. 'We can show you.'

And so here Hewn sat, with his head pounding as though ready to explode, having just watched a recording Winter had made to act as proof that this series of events was really happening. Even Tabb now sat in silent contemplation, her suspicious eyes staring down at the mundane surface of the table.

He cast a look around the rest. Niang had risen quietly and walked to stare out of the window. Chaldevert and Marris were whispering to one another. Winter had rejoined Hayward and Akeman. All three were watching Hewn.

'So...' The Echo leader felt like he had to say something, just to break the long silence if nothing else. 'My brain is trying to process what we all just witnessed. Firstly, were there no Nova ships in orbit?'

'Two transports and an assault ship,' Winter replied. 'All three had been reduced to floating debris by the time I arrived.'

'That ship is powerful enough to wipe out heavily armoured assault ships in such a short space of time?' Hewn had seen the *Grail* poison two planets and yet he found himself wondering just what type of weapon could swat aside the corporations' best so easily.

'It is, although it clearly took its toll.' Winter brought the footage from Straunia back up and made his way to stand before the screen, pausing the feed at one point. 'See in the background there. That's the ship. It's clearly been damaged.'

Hewn squinted as he tried to make it out. There was something familiar about it.

'It looks a little like the *Grail*, don't you think?' It was like Winter was reading his mind.

'These things built both.' Hewn went to rub his aching temple before realising he had reached up with his artificial hand. 'Jesus.'

Winter's cold eyes stared through him again. 'No, they didn't. They may be intelligent but they aren't capable of constructing their own ships or anything as advanced as the *Grail*.'

'Well that just raises more fucking questions,' muttered Tabb, who had snapped out of her ponderings.

'Okay, okay.' Hewn decided he needed to take a walk. His legs were numb. 'Who were those people on Straunia and why the hell were they standing in front of the *Grail* like cannon fodder, just letting those things slaughter them?'

'Colonists and a handful of soldiers,' answered Winter. 'Cannon fodder was exactly what they were. They were positioned in a defensive line. They didn't flinch or cry out as they were cut apart and I'll show you why.'

Again, he allowed the footage to run before pausing it during the massacre that was taking place in the shadow of the *Grail*. He then managed to zoom in on one section and, despite the poor resolution, they could all see the disturbing image well enough to warrant another stunned silence.

One of the alien creatures had lashed out with a barbed tendril, ripping open the side of one colonist's face before almost decapitating a second standing alongside. There was a distinct lack of blood and instead the wounds writhed and glistened like silver snakes. The faces of the men and women all around them were emotionless, skin pallid and grey; eye sockets unnerving pits of silver.

'How can this be?' Hewn asked the room, unable to tear his eyes away from the image.

'Corpses infused with technology similar to that in my own body,' Winter remarked, unpausing the footage. 'Humans turned into mindless drones.'

Hayward cleared her throat softly, her own eyes struggling to look away from the scene of Straunia. 'You'll notice in a moment that mechs appear. It's clear to see they are owned by Sigma Royal and yet Saul saw a couple of Sigma soldiers amongst the dead. The mech weapons drive the aliens back towards their ship, killing some caught in the crossfire.'

Hewn watched the screen closely. He saw the painted mechs move into view and open fire, their shrikes peppering not only the creatures but the zombified colonists that got in the way. He saw the aliens retreat almost reluctantly and the mechs follow, their metal frames knocking people to the ground and even trampling over them.

Just before the footage ended, when Winter had opted to take his stolen ship into the upper atmosphere and head for Earth, it was paused again.

'It is hard to see, but look here.' He pressed a fingertip against the screen, back near the *Grail*.

The image was grainy to say the least but Hewn could make out a silhouette that appeared for a split second between the throng of the dead defenders and the side of the fallen weapon. It was a dark figure, wholly inhuman in form. Streaks of silver and, to a lesser degree, blue stood out starkly from its body.

'And just what the fuck is that?' Tabb asked aggressively.

'I don't know,' admitted Winter. 'I feel like a part of me does but I just can't access it.'

Hewn approached the screen. When he arrived on Earth, he had his own concerns about the Bold, keeping his people safe and the rocky alliance with Libra. Those concerns felt somewhat small and selfish now.

'So what happens now?' he asked them all. 'Are you going to relay the intel to Sigma, Nova and Impramed?'

'A few seconds before I entered the cloud cover, I saw a Sapphire Nova transport lift off from near to the *Grail*.' Winter exchanged the briefest of looks with Hayward. 'I wouldn't recommend contacting them.'

Tabb's sudden laughter seemed out of place. 'This gets better and better. Your General Garrett should've wiped out every Nova ship when he had the chance.'

Hayward bit back the response that first sprang to mind. 'We lost a lot of people and ships during that battle in Geraint. The General did what he had to. Listen, we've all just witnessed something incredibly disturbing and the alliance we're proposing is more important now than ever before. We must ally against retribution from Sapphire Nova, as well as the likes of Jericho's Bold and The Kindred, plus now this new threat. None of us wants a repeat of what happened on Minerva.'

Niang had been quiet for a long time but finally turned from the window. 'You said that the alien ship was damaged, and they lost many in that fight with the colonists and mechs. They were also pursued back towards their ship and, for all we know, were wiped out before they could get back. Plus, we don't know that they could even leave Straunia if they wanted to. *That* particular threat may have already been eradicated.'

'No surprise you look at it that way,' scoffed Tabb. 'Schaeffer's Nine don't have any of the devices we're talking about. You only care about making money with as many underhand ops as possible.'

Hewn expected Niang to bite but instead he merely smiled back at the Libra officer. 'How do you know we don't have any? I'm sure Sigma, Nova or perhaps even Fortitude would pay a lot of money for one of those things.'

Hayward decided to step in. 'Look, it's clear that those who declined the invitation to attend this meeting have their own agendas so it's in our best interests to form this alliance to protect ourselves. We need to decide what to do about the situation on Straunia, among other things.'

'I'm willing to be a part of this,' Hewn stated. 'You should all be aware that Sigma Royal are up to something as they seem to now have some alliance with Fortitude and this new bastard on the scene, The Luminary. They are building a mech army that uses the latter's advanced app technology. I'll transfer all data I have on this so you can review.'

Tabb's glare was fierce. 'Best you do.'

Hewn would ensure he was true enough to his word. No reason to let them

41

all know that Echo had captured one of the mechs during the raid on Monarch City.

'There are some who have been inside the *Grail*.' Hayward was focused on Hewn. 'We hear that Davian Kurcher and Sieren Broekow are under your protection now.'

Hewn could feel everyone turn to look at him. 'Kurcher is, yes. Broekow was captured by Jericho's Bold and sold to a Nova officer named Devlin on Rikur. Broekow somehow managed to escape and disappeared. We have no idea where he is now.'

Hayward weighed him up for a moment, gauging just how truthful this pirate actually was. 'Kurcher could offer this alliance invaluable intel on the *Grail*. It might help us understand what's happening on Straunia. There is no reason for him to hide in the Expanse any more. In my eyes, he is still a Taurus Galahad enlister and we will welcome him back.'

Hewn knew Kurcher's response would be short and sharp. Besides, he really didn't want one of his most valuable assets snatched back, so perhaps he would just keep that to himself for now. 'I'll talk to him but he's been through a lot thanks to the corporations. I doubt he'll come back to Earth any time soon.'

There was a soft bleep from Akeman's HDU and the agent glanced down, his eyes scanning the small screen quickly. Without uttering a word, he showed Hayward, who gave Hewn a concerned look before nodding.

'Jaffren, we've just received a message regarding Jericho's Bold,' Akeman told him. 'It affects Echo. I'm happy to share this in private.'

The pain in Hewn's head transferred to his stomach as it twisted suddenly. 'We're all friends here now. Tell me.'

'The Bold have been seen entering the Expanse. Jump point data indicates only one ship heading to the Freeman system.'

Hewn didn't need to question how Akeman had the information. It wasn't important at that moment in time.

'We can send ships for support,' Hayward said. 'Just say the word.'

Hewn looked around at the faces of his allies new and old. 'No thank you. This is for us to deal with. If you'll excuse me for a moment, I need to send a message.'

He half expected Akeman to draw his weapon and say that wouldn't happen. Perhaps that was the old Taurus way.

'Do you not need to get back straight away?' Akeman asked him, voicing the thoughts of the others no doubt.

'I wouldn't be able to get back quick enough. We've been waiting for them to make their move so I just need to make sure my people are ready.' He gave an awkward half-bow to the room. 'Thanks for your backing. Echo are fully on board with this alliance and I'll stay to talk it through.'

When he left the room, Hewn could feel how dry his mouth had become. Despite his confidence that Harz and his scumbag crew would soon meet their fate, there was a niggling thought that maybe Fischer hadn't carried out their plan to the letter. He needed to have faith in his friend, but being so far from the Expanse made him feel useless. When did he become a politician?

Thank fuck he had moved his family from Warren already.

Garnet,
Henning system

Grosnik watched on with pride as his formidable metal army marched through the gates of Wilson, leaving the remnants of Libra's defence floundering behind them.

The outpost had been completely caught out by their sudden attack and he couldn't help but feel a little smug about the accuracy of their intel. Henning was in the Orion Spur, just like Sol, but the remote system was forty-two thousand light years away from Earth's home. It was the perfect place for Libra to set up an outpost to process and store masses of data, as well as acting as a technology containment facility. Despite the unimpressive size of Wilson, the colony sat on top of a significant underground network.

Grosnik glanced up into the dark red sky; the colour of night on this particular world and the reason behind its name. In orbit, his fleet would be dismantling the guardian unlucky enough to be assigned Garnet to protect. It had held its own bravely for a time until a fusion strike had punched through into one of the engines. It was just luck that it didn't cause a chain reaction of explosions, instead leaving the ship drifting listlessly before them. The command crew had surrendered quick enough at that point.

As he entered the interior compound of the colony, Grosnik gave his medics orders to treat the wounded Libra personnel. They hesitated for a split second, unsure whether they had heard the General right. He would show the other corporations that Sigma were not monsters; that they would treat prisoners of war with respect and courtesy. He gave a fleeting thought to the dead soldiers in their green uniforms lying outside the broken gates. There would always be casualties and better Libra than Sigma.

As he approached the line of mechs, their linked officers saluted him and he couldn't help but smile when the constructs followed suit. Most of the mechs in the compound were pursuit class; metal men painted red and black. There were a few assault class but the larger mechs had been ordered to secure the perimeter as a priority.

'Lieutenant.' Grosnik stood before the ranking officer of the mech force. 'Once our soldiers have finished sweeping the buildings, select six pursuits to send below ground and have them clear both the data archives and any storage facilities down there.'

'Yes, sir. I'll lead them myself.'

'Only send the mechs in. Officers remain up top. It'll be a good test for the app.'

The lieutenant nodded once. 'Understood.'

Grosnik remained in the compound, taking interest in how the mechs were being selected. The lieutenant chose the most experienced tech officers of course, leaving the others to run secondary sweeps of the surface dwellings. Their scanning equipment would soon find any Libra personnel in hiding.

The General couldn't help but wonder where Vekkerd was at that particular moment in time. Was the young tech officer already dead, tortured and executed by his captors? What exactly had they done with the assault mech they stole?

He had hoped to hear back from *The Luminary* before reaching Garnet. No doubt the app trader was watching the raid on Wilson unfold from the safety of his or her abode, wherever that might be. He was certain that the dealer would have been very happy with how their apps had worked so far. However, while distance over open ground wasn't a problem, Grosnik now wanted to see how the links coped when the mechs went below ground alone.

He checked in with his other officers via comms, making sure that Wilson's surface compound was entirely in Sigma hands. It had been a textbook campaign; the first of many in their bid to grapple control away from the other corporations. There would need to be further surveys carried out of Garnet, to make sure no other hidden outposts had been set up secretly by Libra. He wouldn't have put it past the sneaky fucks.

Two of his officers signed off with *For Meta*. Two simple words that meant so much now to the entire Sigma populace across all of their worlds and systems. It wasn't long before the sweep of Wilson had finished and he watched eagerly as the lieutenant and his five officers headed for the entrance to the underground bunkers. It would be a tight squeeze for the mechs for sure but they were more flexible under control of the app.

Grosnik followed so he could witness the foray below ground. The reinforced doors would have taken a long time for the mechs to batter their way through so he was glad to see more of *The Luminary*'s tech working so well when the lock systems were hacked swiftly and efficiently.

Then the mechs disappeared into the depths. Grosnik wished he could see what the tech officers were seeing but the picture was painted for him well enough to only leave a small part to his imagination. Whilst two took a stairwell to the lower levels, the other four entered a lift and descended much quicker. Libra guards were encountered and the occasional burst of gunfire echoed up to their ears. Within minutes, the lieutenant told him that the rest of the personnel found below were surrendering after seeing their comrades blown apart.

'Two mechs are bringing the prisoners up,' reported the lieutenant. 'The rest will continue a sweep.'

'Excellent.' Grosnik was beaming. 'Check every corner you can find.'

As the defeated faces of the Libra men and women emerged followed by the two mechs, Grosnik saw the lieutenant suddenly start tapping at his temple and blinking hard.

'Problem?' the General asked.

'I...I appear to have lost my link,' replied the officer. The others around him seemed to be having no such issues. 'I was just heading for one of the data archive chambers and it cut out. Apologies, sir.'

Grosnik hoped that *The Luminary* had seen this malfunction and would be working to fix it from afar as he often claimed he could. It would hopefully just be a minor blip in an otherwise outstanding mission.

'Have the others go find your mech,' he ordered. 'The sooner we complete the sweep, the sooner we can actually head down there ourselves.'

~

The pursuit mech looked around, scanning the rows of databanks lining the room. It checked where the others were and could see their signatures elsewhere in the facility.

Moving deeper into the archive, it located one of the access ports and quickly hacked into the system, uploading as much data as it could and sending it immediately to its user. Reports on Libra military activity, scientific research and colony surveys were transferred. The mech then moved on to another port and repeated the process, sending data across space via the auxiliary relay created by the app.

By the time the other three mechs entered the archive, the relay had been closed off and control given back to the Sigma user.

Thorn,
Bastion system

Of all the possible places Kam Bavelli could have gone, why did it have to be Thorn?

Ever since the events on Galt, Rist remembered everything clearly from his past. The implant Nova had put in his head no longer subdued his memories or kept him loyal to them. They hadn't tried to locate him. They didn't care about him. They thought he was dead.

He peered out from the shadows of his hood, studying the route ahead. The lights of Forrest glimmered through the foliage, the large colony half a mile away. Around him, the twisted brambles served as a painful reminder of his previous life and he tried hard to ignore the guilt that threatened to swallow him.

He had been a mercenary back in 2608 with his own team of hired guns, working for the highest payer. Sapphire Nova had stumped up a small fortune for them to come to Thorn and help drive back the Taurus Galahad forces, utilizing their boomers to cause disarray among the bramble fields. Nova hadn't told him of the toxins hidden in the brambles and their reaction to fire. As he tried to lead his mercs to safety, Nova had bombed the fields. It had the desired effect of wiping out hundreds of Taurus soldiers, however the flames spread so quickly that Rist found himself and his team trapped and slowly choking to death on the poisonous smoke enveloping them. They died cursing his name. He wished he had died with them that day. Instead, Sapphire Nova took his burnt body and turned him into their own personal assassin, making sure he forgot what they did; that they only hired him to herd Taurus into those damned fields. He and his team were just as expendable as those poor soldiers.

He crept closer to Forrest, listening for any telltale sounds of what might be happening within the walls. His damaged ear was all but shot so he had to be vigilant on his approach. He was glad when the spiked foliage gave way to clearer ground, and he saw the colony just ahead. The gates were wide open and no guards patrolled.

He needed to locate Bavelli quickly, do the deed and get the hell off Thorn. After fleeing Galt in the stolen ship, and coming to terms with just who he actually was, Rist had decided to track down those who had sent him to his death for a second time.

The Nova officer had been in Valen for a while before leaving the system in his assault ship, *Grosvenor*. No fleet accompanied him. Rist managed to track him to the Bastion system, where the *Grosvenor* had landed at Forrest. Perhaps Bavelli had family there or maybe he was there on some directive from Tomas Klein. Either way, the man needed to die.

A warm rain had started to drip from the night sky, tapping on his hood. A distant sound caught his attention and he crouched low, trying to determine what it was. It was a woman's scream he had heard as it cried out from somewhere inside the colony. Not a pained scream but one of terror.

Rist moved silently to the wall and made his way along to the gate, daring a quick look around the edge. He expected to see guards lurking nearby or for someone to take a shot at him. There was nobody in sight but now there were more cries for help and frightened voices calling out.

He was some distance into Forrest before he saw the first colonists. A man was trying to sprint along one of the streets carrying two children, their arms wrapped tight around his neck. Further on, he watched as more people fled, their eyes wide with fear. Had his mind not been so tampered with, Rist knew he would be feeling nervous and that apprehension would be creeping into his body with every step. Something was very wrong on Thorn.

The *Grosvenor* had landed at the pads to the east, he knew, and it wouldn't be long before he saw the assault vessel looming above the surrounding buildings. That seemed the best bet of finding Bavelli. However, as he worked his way through the dimly illuminated streets, he made sure his pistol was in his hand.

As he neared the landing pads, he ducked into the darkness of a narrow alley between houses. A contingent of Nova soldiers marched out of a structure ahead, dragging a number of struggling colonists into the street and away.

'Please,' he heard one woman plead. 'Why are you doing this?'

Her sobbing cries were ignored and Rist followed them to an open plaza that was the gateway to the landing site. If his blood could have run cold, it would have right then. Across the plaza, he saw hundreds of people, mostly colonists. Among them, soldiers paced slowly. And there was something else with them. At first, he couldn't tell what he was seeing; flashes of blue and silver in the shadows. Then, when one of the creatures unfurled from behind a stricken

48

colonist and Rist saw the tendril retract from the man's neck, he instinctively took a step back. Even his sight app didn't know what it was looking at.

There were six of the bizarre creatures in total. Every colonist was being knelt facing away from one, screaming for help and struggling to break free of the Nova soldiers' grip. Then the tendril would strike in the same place each time and, within a few seconds, there were no more cries or pleading. The colonists would simply stand up and walk away quietly, their faces a picture of calm. Some would return after a while with more of their petrified neighbours to be *processed*. Others went into houses and emerged with weapons or equipment that were taken away somewhere.

Rist heard a child crying and watched with morbid interest as a girl no more than five years old was carried by her mother across the plaza to undergo the same experience as the rest. He was not sure if there were more of the creatures elsewhere in Forrest but something told him he needed to leave; that his original plan was no longer valid.

That's when he saw Bavelli. The officer appeared from the steps leading up to the landing pads, flanked by two soldiers. He stood for a moment surveying the scene before him, then nodded and issued some order to his men. Rist was tempted to take the shot from his position but his accuracy at distance had been affected after he was wounded on Galt. None of his apps or tech seemed as sharp since.

He found his way back to the gate quickly enough, his mind replaying the scene from the plaza over and over. It didn't make sense that Nova soldiers would be using the creatures to somehow dominate their own colonists, unless what he saw wasn't some alien being but was actually a new type of mech they had engineered using similar tech to the implant he had buried in his skull for so long. It was possible, although improbable in his opinion.

He came to an abrupt halt just meters from the gate as two colonists stepped from a nearby street; a man and a woman, both armed. At first, he thought they were trying to flee Forrest. Then he saw their expressions and it was clear they had been processed. Much to his chagrin, they loitered by the gate and he realised they were there to watch for those who really were trying to escape the nightmare that had descended on their colony.

His decision was easy enough then. He put one bullet into the man's ear that lodged somewhere in his brain and another bullet into the woman's forehead as she turned. He then swiftly stepped over the bodies and left Forrest. As he headed back into the shadows of the dense foliage that dominated the landscape, he gave one last look over his shoulder. The two colonists he'd felled were standing once again, staggering through the gate as though in a daze.

Rist knew what he had to do. What he had witnessed on Thorn needed to be shared with others, especially the corporations. They needed to be warned of what Nova were doing to their own people. Still, they would have lots of questions and he doubted they would believe him without proof. That's when he decided he would continue to track Bavelli, as long as the officer left Thorn, and see what his next move was before heading to the likes of Taurus Galahad or Sigma Royal.

He would prioritise Taurus. There was no chance of redemption for him after the spate of killings on Galt; the assassination of the board members. Still, Nova were out of control clearly and needed to be dealt with. He couldn't do that on his own.

Warren,
Freeman system

Kurcher climbed the steps of the brewery, flanked by the eight Echo pirates. When he looked back, he could see the entire colony of Gulliver. It wasn't impressive at all, consisting of some hastily constructed buildings dotted around the dusty flatlands. In fact, Warren itself was one of those worlds that really didn't have many attractive features. Gulliver had been built in a valley surrounded by steep hills covered in dead-looking trees, however the sap from those was just one of the bountiful resources used in the brewing of Echo's mead, which he had to admit he had come to like.

At the centre of the colony, he saw Fischer issuing orders to more of the pirates who had been chosen to accompany them. In Hewn's absence, Fischer was clearly revelling in being in charge. Kurcher was really hoping he was present when Hewn ripped his second a new one for allowing Harz to slip in the back door to the Expanse. He was sure Fischer would bemoan the fact their fleet was finite and they couldn't be in all locations at once, but Hewn's business was at stake here.

Above Gulliver, Echo ships patrolled the skies. He spotted the *Falcata* amongst them and could almost see Drake's bored expression as she sulked at the helm. She had wanted to be on the ground with Kurcher, there to face Harz herself. Fischer had blown smoke up her ass that the best pilots needed to be in the air, eventually ordering her to protect the colony in her ship.

A deep thrumming boom rattled the colony as the silhouette of the Bold ship emerged through the cloud cover above them, a large W-shaped vessel that quickly cast its shadow over Gulliver.

As the Echo ships moved to intercept it, Kurcher headed inside the brewery and made for the agreed location at the rear of the palatial structure, passing several of the gigantic vats and a variety of production equipment. It reminded him of the Eidolon facility on Tempest, just cleaner.

The quarters were relatively spacious and accommodating. It was no wonder as Hewn's family had been the sole occupants. It looked lived in, with garments and children's toys lying around. Kurcher had seen a picture of the pirate's wife, Rae, and the thought had shot through his mind that perhaps Hewn was punching above his weight with the dark-skinned beauty. Drake had mentioned then that Rae was just as ruthless as her husband and her mind was attuned to making money. That's why she ran the brewery and had helped finalise the agreements with Libra for distribution.

As the other pirates accompanying him positioned themselves around the different rooms of the personal quarters, Kurcher caught sight of drawings on the wall that could've only been made by an imaginative child. He knew that Hewn's son was called Wes and that he was a total innocent in a den of sinners. Then he recalled what Hewn had told him one night on the *Glaive* as the pirate downed his seventh beer, which had naturally loosened his lips. There had been another child; another boy born two years after Wes. All Hewn said was that they lost him and didn't say any more. Kurcher was glad not to know what happened. Some secrets never needed to be shared.

The walls shook as ships passed overhead and there came the distinct sound of gunfire.

This plan isn't a good one, Frost said.

That Bold fuck needs to be blown out of the sky, added Angard.

Kurcher had gone over the plan so many times that his brain hurt. He didn't like hiding away while the battle raged outside, and yet, if Harz took the bait as they expected, one good shot would put a swift end to the matter. Jericho's Bold thought that Hewn's wife and son were at the brewery, thanks to Broekow spilling his guts under duress. Hopefully the tattooed pricks would think that the Echo ships defending the colony were there to protect Rae and Wes. It wouldn't be long before they would pull back slightly and allow Harz and his people to land. Let them think they strong-armed their way through. It would make putting a bullet through Harz's thick skull a real pleasure.

'Drake, any news would be welcome right about now,' he said into his comms.

The silence that followed worried him. What if the *Falcata* had been shot out of the air already? No, she was one of the best pilots he had ever known.

Thanks a bunch, tutted Frost.

'Things never go as we think they will,' came Drake's voice suddenly. 'Their ship has started hammering other parts of the colony. They dropped some lifeboat so expect company shortly.'

'You could've just destroyed it and saved me the bother,' he said sharply.

'Tell you what,' she snapped. 'Why don't you go fuck yourself?'

Kurcher warned the others to get ready and checked his revolver. He then patted his jacket, glad to feel the explosives in his pocket that he had *borrowed* from the *Glaive*'s armoury. He didn't have any qualms about blowing the brewery to shit if it meant ridding the galaxy of Harz.

From somewhere near the vat chambers, Kurcher could hear shouts and the occasional shot ring out. It looked better to have a few pirates guarding the brewery but they were under Fischer's orders not to get themselves killed and to back off if need be.

Silence fell. Apart from the distant roar of an engine somewhere to the south, all Kurcher could hear was the nearest pirate to him breathing and that sounded way too loud.

The plan might be blown, fretted D'Larro.

Just get out there and kill the motherfuckers, growled Ercko.

Then an explosion disintegrated the wall, knocking Kurcher to the floor and covering him with debris.

~

Drake saw the explosion inside the brewery. Windows at the rear of the structure blew outwards and part of one exterior wall crumbled, releasing smoke and flames into the air. It was right where Kurcher and his ambush team had been positioned, she knew, but shook off the image of them all lying dead as the Bold ship loomed ahead suddenly.

Despite the significant weapons Echo were using, there were only scorch marks and a handful of dents in the bastards' reinforced hull. It wasn't an easy ship to bring down. Even the engines were protected better than most other vessels she had had the pleasure of destroying.

Gats whirred on the Bold ship and she managed to dodge between the hail of bullets, glad that the *Falcata* was so slimline. There was a flash of green as a fusion beam cut through the sky, missing the nose of her ship by only a couple of meters.

She had shut off her comms temporarily. The sound of one of her fellow pilots yelling for help as his cockpit burst into flame, followed by his dying screams as his ship plummeted to the ground just outside Gulliver, was enough. How many more of Hewn's people would die at the hands of the Bold before this was over?

A movement near to the brewery caught her attention as a tiny ship zipped over the colony and promptly landed in the shadows of the building, just out of sight. It had looked like a sprint class but Echo didn't have any.

When she checked her console, she saw that the battle between the Bold ship and Echo's defence force had moved further to the south, leaving the *Falcata* alone. 'Fuck it.' She threw a cigarette into her mouth and lit it in one fluid motion, before steering the *Falcata* down towards the brewery.

~

Kurcher coughed the dust from his lungs and tried to stand. There was still a part of the wall on his leg and he wished Hewn was there to help lift it off him.

Somewhere in the smoke and panic filling the quarters, he heard guns opening fire and the grunts of those unfortunate to get in their way. He knew it was the automatic rifles the Bold used. He should've known the fuckers would play dirty.

The weight on his leg shifted suddenly and he looked up through sore eyes, thankful to see one of the Echo men sweating as he lifted the debris as high as his arms would let him. It was enough for Kurcher to move and get shakily to his feet. As the pirate gladly dropped the rubble and gave him a nod, Kurcher saw a broad silhouette appear through the smoke behind his helper. Before he could bring his revolver up, a serrated blade drove into the pirate's back and the ugly face of one of the Bold leered through the gloom, letting out a bestial howl. Kurcher put a bullet through his open mouth.

There was no time to check on the impaled Echo. Two more Bold stepped into the room and glanced down at their fallen comrade. That gave Kurcher enough time to dive through a nearby doorway before they could gun him down.

'That one's mine,' he heard a man yell.

It wasn't long before the smoke had cleared enough for Kurcher to see that all but two of the team he had brought with him now lay dead, their bodies torn apart by the vicious ammo the Bold favoured. The one skewered in front of him was still alive but was trying to drag himself away from the approaching death. The other still alive was slumped against the back wall having taken a bullet to the thigh. He was desperately trying to reload.

Just inside the quarters, where the explosion had taken down the wall, Kurcher counted four dead Bold including the one he silenced. There were six

54

alive and kicking, unfortunately, their tattooed faces grinning at one another as they watched the injured men.

'Davian Kurcher.' A brute of a man stepped through the breach, his voice rough and offensive to the ears. 'Time for you to come with us.'

How the fuck did he know you're here? Frost asked.

Put the big bastard down, Angard said.

'Echo won't be happy you put a hole in their brewery.' Kurcher knew he was addressing Harz. 'Best get the fuck out of here before Hewn pulls your arms off and shoves them up your ass. Or maybe you'd like that, you sadistic prick.'

Harz gave a rumbling laugh of genuine amusement. 'They said you were mouthy. Glad to hear it's true. It'll make torturing you all the more satisfying.'

'Who said I was mouthy?'

'Put your gun down and surrender to us now, or we'll kill these two slowly.'

Kurcher peered around the doorway. Harz was standing dead centre of the room, looking directly at him. 'We both know you'll kill them anyway.'

You could kill this goatfucker where he stands right now, stated Ercko.

You'd be dead soon after, pointed out D'Larro.

'You don't seem surprised that Hewn's family aren't here.' Kurcher could at least keep him talking and find out some useful information at the same time. 'Someone clearly sold me out just like Broekow.'

'That one was tougher than I thought he would be. Took some time to break. Got paid well for him too.'

'You know the man you sold him to is dead?' Kurcher's eyes searched for anything that could help him out of this predicament.

'I heard something about it.' Harz snorted and spat. 'Makes no difference to me. The fucker already paid me. Now, let's go. Last chance to come quietly.'

Kurcher had heard that so many times before. He gripped his revolver tight and hoped that Drake had been paying attention to what was being said. As he swung from the doorway, intent on placing one shot between the Bold leader's eyes, rifles lit up the room and he had to leap back or be mown down by Harz's lackeys.

'Have it your way,' Harz mumbled through his beard.

The Echo on the floor died first with six more stab wounds alongside the one he already had in his back. The other managed to lift his pistol, hoping to be the hero who killed Harz. Instead, the wicked knife the brute wielded sliced clean through his wrist and he watched his own hand drop to the floor still clutching the gun. Harz didn't bother torturing him though, snapping his neck with what seemed like no effort at all.

You could've stopped that, enlister, Santa Cruz remarked.

No point taking several rounds to the chest for them, countered D'Larro. *They were already dead.*

'Get them out into the vat chamber.' Drake's voice was like nectar at that moment, although some doubt as to her loyalty still lingered at the back of his mind. 'I'll be waiting.'

It went against every fibre of his being as Kurcher stepped out from cover and placed his revolver on the floor. 'So who you going to sell me to then?'

Harz stood over him, dark eyes glinting with victory. 'Haven't decided yet. Highest bidder. You and I have got plenty to discuss before then though.'

Kurcher could see now just how ugly the asshole was, with his myriad tattoos plastered across half his broad face and a scar on his chin that looked like a bad shaving accident. The painted blue lips were a bit too familiar. He also realised how formidable Harz was too, although he sure wouldn't move fast in all that gear, which rattled with metal tags and chains.

Two of the Bold pirates grabbed Kurcher and marched him out of the hole they had made, the rest following closely behind. Three more were waiting just outside the quarters. As they entered the vat chamber, their heavy footfalls echoing up to the high ceiling, Kurcher heard Harz behind him telling someone they were on their way back. It was clear they were aiming to get off Warren as quickly as they had arrived. Hopefully Drake was about to put a spanner firmly in the works.

True to her word, she quickly made her presence felt. Three shots rang out. The first bullet bounced off the hard floor at the feet of one unsuspecting Bold. The second drove into the man's knee with a dull thud and, as he stumbled, the third took him directly in the top of his head.

Kurcher couldn't see where she had fired from, although he guessed it was from the shadowy gap between two of the vats up ahead. As the Bold rushed forward, choosing not to slow their escape from the brewery, another single shot rang out and the pirate next to Harz let out a pained grunt before falling flat on his face.

'Kill that motherfucker.'

Kurcher realised Harz must have come to the same conclusion he had as the Bold party let rip in the direction of the vats, all except the two holding him. As bullets ricocheted off the vats with metallic pings, Kurcher saw Drake dart from cover, the barrel of her pistol blazing as she fired back wildly. He couldn't help but feel she didn't care if she hit him during the exchange and that suddenly gave him an idea. Noting how the Bold were starting to move apart as they tried to lock on to their ambusher, Kurcher waited until Drake fired again then gave a pained cry and stumbled. One pirate let go of him as he fell. The other nearly lost his footing too but managed to hold on to Kurcher's arm.

'Get him up,' he heard Harz snarl.

With one hand free, Kurcher swiftly reached inside his jacket, his fingers managing to find one of the explosives and prime it. As the Bold who had let go reached down to help lift him, Kurcher brought his elbow up sharply into the pirate's nose, splaying it in an explosion of red, then threw the explosive into the opening at the top of the man's dirty jacket.

As the other one holding his arm hesitated on seeing this, Kurcher swung away from him, putting the pirate between himself and the human timebomb. When the explosive detonated, both Bold took the brunt of the force and Kurcher ended up several feet away on his back, his ears ringing. When he looked back, most of the pirates were on the floor. The unfortunate chosen to be the bomb was just a smoking mess, while the other Kurcher had chosen to shield him from the blast had been catapulted further than the rest, his body torn and charred. That's when Kurcher realised he was completely covered in the man's blood.

As he tried to stand, a strong hand took hold and lifted him like he was made of paper. Harz brought the butt of his rifle around, driving it hard into Kurcher's stomach. All of the air in his lungs instantly vacated his body and he gasped for breath.

'You're going to get real special treatment on my ship,' Harz promised him.

Kurcher managed to find his voice. 'Just breathe on me some more. That'll be torture enough.'

Harz hit him again, then started dragging him through the vat chamber. Four of the Bold had picked themselves up and were following. As the doorway leading out of the brewery appeared before them, Kurcher heard a woman's voice. To start with, it sounded like Frost, then it purred like Trin before his ears finally managed to distinguish the tone.

'Put him down, you shit-stinking pricks.'

We never had mouths on us like this one, said Frost and Trin together.

Kurcher saw Drake standing in front of the door, her gun pointed at Harz and her eyes wide with anger. There was no fear etched on her face.

Harz laughed, although there was an uncertainty behind it. 'Fuck me, I should've known you'd be one of Hewn's little whores by now.'

Kurcher recognised the familiarity between them. Of course that was why she painted her lips blue. He hadn't wanted to believe she was associated with these bastards.

You should've trusted your instincts, enlister, Santa Cruz told him.

'Did you really think you could just come here and take what you want, you deluded fuck?' Drake asked.

'Yeah.' Harz looked her up and down. 'Now that you're here, we might as well take you too.'

'Try it and I'll put my next bullet through your skull.' Her hatred made her spit the words through clenched teeth. 'Then I'll carve out your black fucking heart.'

'I don't think you could, little girl,' mocked Harz, passing Kurcher to one of his men and taking a big step towards her. 'In fact, I know you couldn't.'

Kurcher willed Drake to pull the trigger as Harz closed on her. There was no way she could miss at that range. He noticed her hand start to waver and she bit down hard on her bottom lip. He was sure he saw tears welling in her eyes.

'Fucking shoot him,' he yelled at her, receiving a fist across his jaw for the outburst.

Harz loomed over her, that ugly grin fixed on his face. 'I don't think I ever thanked you.'

Drake's brow creased slightly in confusion. 'I...I'll fucking...kill...'

'I never thanked you for helping me become the man I am today.' Harz reached out for her shaking gun. 'Without you, I'd be just another dumb fucking pirate destined to walk in the shadows of other men. I say without you but I mean without your pussy.'

Kurcher saw Harz lunge and heard a gunshot. A lone bullet sang through the air, fired from somewhere to their left, and blew through Harz's outstretched hand, taking two fingers with it. A split second later, one of the pirates emitted a gurgling scream and sent the others into disarray.

Kurcher found himself crumpling to his knees and quickly scanned the scene from his prone position. A man had emerged from the shadows to their left, a long rifle clasped in his hands that was firing high velocity rounds, although most shots were missing any flesh. One of the Bold was lying on the ground with his head barely connected to his body, and another newcomer to the fight was bravely taking on two of the remaining pirates close up. Drake was standing as frozen as a statue, her pistol still raised and tears streaming down her face. Harz was already disappearing out of the door.

It wasn't long before the Bold were sprawled on the floor of the brewery, either dead or badly wounded and unable to stand. Kurcher had regained his composure and cautiously approached Drake, pushing her arm gently down.

'Get the fuck off me,' she suddenly cried out, pushing him away.

Hearing the approaching footsteps, Kurcher spun to face the men who had arrived late to help them. 'Couldn't you two have got here sooner? Where the fuck's Fischer anyway?'

The rifleman limped past him without a word, his face hidden by a mask and dark goggles, heading for the door.

'We got here as fast as we could, Davian.'

When he heard the voice, Kurcher believed maybe the ringing in his ears was still affecting him. When he saw the sword the man was brandishing, he hoped his eyes were playing tricks as well.

'Good to see you too,' smiled Rane warmly.

Earth,
Sol system

Hayward drummed her fingers on the desk as she waited. Her nerves were already shredded thanks to the recent revelations that Winter brought with him, and her dreams were invaded by those alien creatures every night too. She knew she looked a complete wreck.

Akeman eventually found his way to her office, offering her an immediate apology for keeping her waiting. 'I was listening in on a briefing being conducted by Lieutenant Tolbert downstairs. It seems that the Revenant threat in our local region has been eradicated completely, although the aim now is to ensure no more find their way in.'

'The Revenants.' She shook her head. 'They used to be the monsters skulking in the darkness that we were all afraid of. Now, we have aliens slaughtering our people and the dead coming back to life.'

'At least the extra military presence here has helped turn the tide,' Akeman said, trying to find some positive in the situation. 'We've a long way to go in getting rid of the Revenant threat, but it's a start.'

Hayward looked at him and smiled. 'I'm glad you're here. I fear I'll go mad if I try to focus on every single one of the dilemmas facing us on my own.'

The agent walked to the window and looked down into the compound. 'Can I offer some advice?'

'Of course.'

'Delegate.' He turned and perched himself on the edge of the sill. 'Give Tolbert the authority to run the campaign against the Revenants in its entirety. Let him work with the other officers the General sent while we focus our attention elsewhere.'

Hayward sighed. 'You're right, of course. I just have a vested interest in what happens here.'

'I know you do. Those religious bastards took your family from you so of course you want to see them dealt with.' Akeman hesitated, wondering if that was overstepping the mark. 'But you are an excellent diplomat and the best judicial officer Taurus has ever had. You've brought together Libra, Echo and Schaeffer's Nine to help us move forward through these dark times. With the threats these aliens bring, along with the more familiar problems we have with

Sapphire Nova, Sigma Royal and even the likes of Fortitude and the Knights Templar, you'll overload if you try to manage it all.'

'There's another issue too, which is why I sent for you. I do hear you though, and I appreciate what you're saying.'

Akeman could feel a *but* coming so nipped it in the bud. 'If Tolbert takes on the Revenants, General Garrett will obviously oversee the military campaigns to monitor the other corporations and make sure they behave. That leaves you free to focus entirely on this alliance and everything we discussed with them the other day.'

'Okay.' Hayward held up her hands in surrender. 'Agreed. First though, I have news to share with you. Our ships out near the jump point intercepted a small passenger transport vessel called the *Bulwyn*. She is one of our ships captured by Nova years ago. On board are several surviving crew members of the *Victory* including Neri Ishlan.'

Akeman's eyebrows raised. 'Interesting.'

'Quite. Ishlan had a message from Tomas Klein that has been sent through to me by one of the Taurus officers who boarded the *Bulwyn*. In it, he states that he has released these hostages as a gesture of goodwill, along with the ship. He hopes that it will go some way towards opening peace talks.'

'And your instinct?'

Hayward gave a loose shrug. 'That I don't believe for one second he wants peace, although Nova's fleet took a hell of a battering. Perhaps he understands that there must be a truce for Nova to have any chance of surviving.'

'Have you spoken with Ishlan?' he asked. 'Another untrustworthy individual in my opinion as she allied herself with both Santa Cruz and Mitchell.'

'I ordered the *Bulwyn* held near Saturn while I considered the next move. What do you think?'

Akeman moved away from the window, which was making his back cold. 'I think that all of our new arrivals to Sol need to be put under close scrutiny. Winter shows up with his surreal stories and nightmarish footage, his body infused with technology we can't even begin to comprehend. I don't trust him and he needs to be kept under lock and key in my opinion. Now Ishlan arrives, claiming they've been set free by Nova. I wouldn't be surprised if they've been surgically implanted with bombs. It wasn't so long ago that Nova's assassins hit Galt, and now they want peace?'

Hayward shuddered. 'You don't have to remind me. Ishlan is asking to speak with Garrett, claiming she has intel that may be of use against Nova in the future.'

'Fine. Have her send this information through.'

'She will only speak to him in person. Apparently she has more details relating to Straunia and what is happening there, but is concerned that coded messages no longer seem safe from hackers.'

Akeman pondered it all for a moment, pacing back and forth next to Hayward's desk. Eventually he shook his head. 'I don't like it. I suggest caution every step of the way. Don't bring her here.'

'Our officers holding the *Bulwyn* have conducted a thorough search of the ship and the crew,' she explained. 'They can't find any hidden devices or tech of any sort. They feel it is all as Ishlan says.'

'So what're you thinking?'

Hayward studied his pensive expression before answering. She trusted his judgement and was pleased that he had so far shared her own concerns. 'Send them to Titan Station and have personnel there cordon off that one pylon, complete with room to meet in. General Garrett attends along with his own protection unit, plus I also sit in on the meeting.'

Akeman tried to hide his surprise. 'You want to be there?'

'Well, not really, but I want to know what's going on and I also need time to speak with the general about a number of other matters, one being his control of the military campaigns, as we discussed. I can't just sit here hiding on Earth for the rest of my career. I'm the Taurus judicial officer and have to act like it.'

Akeman paced again for a while, hands clasped behind his back. Hayward watched him and wondered whether he knew that she longed to be close to Garrett again; that the General had been on her mind ever since they shared several drinks on Carson Freight Station after the battle in Geraint. She had opened up to him then about her past and the terrible tragedy that befell her family; her son.

'As much as it pains me,' began Akeman, focusing her attention again. 'You're right. You need people to see you working hard for Taurus, not hiding after your ordeal on Galt. If you go to Titan though, I'll be coming with you.'

She smiled. 'I wouldn't have it any other way. Will you make the arrangements?'

'Of course.' He started heading for the door.

'One more thing,' Hayward called to him. 'And you're not going to like it.'

Akeman looked back from the doorway. 'Whatever you need.'

'We're taking Saul Winter with us.'

Echo flagship Glaive,
Freeman system

The mother of all fuck-ups. That was the best way of describing the so-called plan on Warren.

Kurcher didn't want to listen to the rant that Fischer was currently part way through. His mind was reeling from his time on that shitty little world and his body was still aching. Ignoring Fischer, he peered through the doorway into the brig and the two men in residence; the rifleman and the swordsman.

Rane was the same insane murderer he always had been. Killing an entire world hadn't laid heavy on his conscience it seemed. At least Fischer had done one thing right in throwing the bastard into a cell as soon as he could. They all understood just how manipulative and dangerous Edlan Rane really was.

How exactly is he still alive? Frost asked.

Remind me why you never blew his brains out, said Santa Cruz.

It had dawned on Kurcher just who Rane's associate was before he had even removed his mask, though there was not much left of the old Sieren Broekow. The ex-sniper was gaunt, pale and haunted. His eyes barely registered the human being at all and, with his freshly shaved head, he looked as though he had spent several years in Rockland Prison. There were many visible stark reminders of his time with Harz, from the stab wound beneath one eye and the scar across his forehead to his absent trigger fingers. It was no wonder he couldn't shoot for shit any more and it made Kurcher think Harz' injury was just down to luck.

'Shut your mouth for a moment.' He didn't care what Fischer had been saying. It was time he listened. 'You can bullshit Hewn all you like about what happened but he won't believe any of it. The plan was that Harz was drawn in and killed in the brewery. That didn't happen and I'm to blame too. We all are.'

Fischer went to bark his response so Kurcher cut him off again. 'The simple facts are that Harz knew Hewn's family weren't there and he came for me instead. Someone here is leaking intel to the Bold that's cost the lives of a number of your people. Echo is not secure.

'If that isn't enough for Hewn to rip your balls off, consider the fact that not only did Harz manage to escape the trap because you didn't have anyone positioned near enough outside the brewery to stop him, you also then executed the only Bold fuckers left alive. I mean, are you a total moron?'

Fischer gritted his teeth. 'I was frustrated that Harz had got away, just like you. His ship dropped charges that destroyed part of the colony and gave him the opportunity to escape. If I'd placed people among those buildings, they'd all be dead.'

Kurcher looked back into the brig. 'Sugar-coat it all you want. You fucked up. We all fucked up.'

Fischer looked like he was about to continue arguing his case, then gave up and rubbed at his eyes. 'What about Shannon?'

'What about her?'

'You still haven't told me what happened to her and she's been unresponsive since we got back up here.'

'Leave her be for now unless you want a knife in your gut. Let me speak with her.'

Good luck with that, said Frost.

Fischer nodded into the brig. 'As for those two, Jaffren will probably just jettison them both when he gets back. He won't want to even look at them.'

Kurcher wanted to disagree but the truth was he had no idea how Hewn would react. Broekow had crumbled under extreme torture no man could easily endure and executing him would probably be the kindest thing to do now, looking at him.

'They came here for a reason,' he told Fischer. 'A very good reason. They knew they might run into us but they risked it to try killing Harz. It might be better to just let them get on with it.'

Rane had explained how he had gone back to Rikur with the intent of destroying the planetbore rig at Harper that had, in his mind, caused the deaths of his parents. Any Nova personnel he could kill off at the same time would be a bonus. It was just coincidence that Broekow was being interrogated by Devlin at the same time. It also gave Rane the opportunity to find his sprinter-class ship that he had been forced to leave behind when he gave himself up to Kurcher all those months back. Kurcher was sure that Rane had easily manipulated Broekow into tracking Harz to exact revenge, but it wasn't clear why yet. The serial killer had claimed he wanted justice for Broekow. That was sure to be bullshit.

As Fischer went to say something more, Kurcher entered the brig and stood staring at the two prisoners. Rane looked back with his usual smile. Broekow looked through him.

'If we let you go, what would you do?' Kurcher asked them.

'Track Harz down,' replied Rane calmly. 'Continue our mission.'

'*Our* mission.' Kurcher laughed and shook his head. 'Was it also *your* mission to murder all those people on Straunia?'

Rane's smile never faltered. 'I don't live in the past, Davian. I only look to the future.'

'Fucking maniac.' Fischer had followed Kurcher in. 'There were children on that planet too.'

Rane gave Hewn's second the briefest of glances. 'You don't have to feel guilty, Davian. When you activated the *Grail*, you were under the influence of drug withdrawal so can't be accountable for what happened. I alone wiped all those Nova loyalists from existence.'

'Shut the fuck up.' Kurcher was beginning to experience deja vu.

'He's right.' Even Broekow's voice sounded different now; more distant. 'I blamed all of you for what happened to Frost and let it consume me, but she made her own choices and I can't bring her back. We need to focus on the threats here and now, starting with Harz. He won't stop until he's destroyed Echo.'

'You'd know better than most what he's capable of,' Fischer said sharply.

'Masami and I were sold out,' Broekow stated, briefly showing a missing tooth and the savage scar across his gum.

Fischer stepped forward angrily. 'And that gave you the right to offer up Hewn's family to that sadistic bastard?'

'Everything happens for a reason,' Rane said matter-of-factly. 'Someone in Echo gave Sieren to Jericho's Bold. Sieren was tortured to extract the location of Jaffren's family. I managed to rescue Sieren from Rikur, so he could then warn you and arrange the ambush on Warren.'

'Which failed miserably,' Kurcher reminded them. 'Was Harz meant to escape too?'

Rane gave the slightest of shrugs. 'Perhaps. I can understand you placing me in this cell, however Sieren doesn't deserve to be imprisoned.'

Fischer gave a derisive snort. 'He's lucky we didn't execute him on the spot.'

Kurcher studied both incarcerated men carefully. A part of him wished he'd had a ship like the *Glaive* when he first rounded up the crims. He could've easily thrown all of them in cells and been done with them.

And if you had, we all would have been dead, Frost said.

Along with many other worlds, Santa Cruz remarked.

Maybe things do happen for a reason, whispered D'Larro.

'You're all giving me a headache,' Kurcher snapped to the voices of the living and the dead. 'There's something I've got to do.'

He left the brig and made his way through the *Glaive*. There was a difficult conversation ahead and he just hoped he survived it.

He found Drake still on the *Falcata*, having chosen not to follow them when they docked with the Echo flagship. The pilot was in the cockpit, enveloped in a cloud of pungent smoke that could only have been made by chain-smoking. Fortunately she wasn't yet beyond speaking, although it wouldn't be long.

'I need you to be honest with me,' he said, trying hard not to choke on the sweet drug fumes. 'It's time we put this to bed once and for all.'

'Fuck off,' she mumbled. 'I'm really not in the mood for your shit, so take yourself off my ship.'

Kurcher moved alongside her. Warren should have been in view but he could barely make the pilot out, and she was less than a metre away. 'I want to know who Harz is. You and he clearly know each other. You can see how this might concern not only me but Echo as a whole.'

Drake's tongue licked at her bottom lip. 'Going to tell on me, are you?'

'What did he do to you?'

'I won't tell you again, dickhead.' Her voice wavered slightly. 'Get the fuck out of my face.'

His head span as he breathed in. 'I'm not going anywhere until you tell me.'

Her eyes were suddenly aflame as she reared up before him. 'I've killed plenty of men. One more lying piece of shit like you wouldn't matter.'

'If there's one thing I am, it's brutally honest,' he said as calmly as he could. 'Would you rather I explained who I think Harz is to you?'

'Not fucking interested,' she snarled, her expression feral. 'Would you rather I stabbed this blade into your balls?'

He felt the metal point against his groin. 'Not fucking interested,' he countered, being careful not to smile at her. 'I know you were with Jericho's Bold before you joined Echo. I reckon Harz was someone you grew close to but who ultimately showed his true colours. He hurt you.'

'You know fuck all,' she yelled into his face.

Kurcher was sure her blade had drawn blood. 'Then tell me, you stubborn bitch. Who the fuck is he?'

'He's my brother.'

This revelation seemed to shock Drake more. Her mouth open, she slumped back into her chair and the blade clattered to the floor. Kurcher exhaled loudly, more from relief than anything else.

No wonder she's fucked up with family like that stinking prick, said Ercko.

'We used to look out for one another.' She didn't need prompting this time. 'He'd protect me from the other kids and I'd steal food. That was the deal.'

'What happened to your parents?' he dared asking.

The fire in Drake's eyes had diminished. 'They didn't give a shit. They were killed when they took part in a raid together and all of their possessions were plundered by the others, as is the way.'

'And you were cast out to fend for yourselves.'

She nodded slowly, unwanted memories flooding back behind her eyes. 'As we got older, Harz started to fall in with a gang led by a fat fuck named Forge. If you stayed on your own too long in the Bold, you eventually ended up dead in the drains so you tended to ally yourself with the strongest bastards you could find.

'One day, Harz tells me that Forge wants me in the gang too; that he'll help protect us. Then he took me to meet him and...'

Drake's voice faltered and she quickly took a drag on her cigarette, turning away from Kurcher. It was the most vulnerable he'd ever seen her.

'Tell me,' he pushed.

'Just like most of the other brainless fucks in Jericho's Bold, Harz was seduced by the promises of power Forge fed him. In exchange for a high-ranking position within the gang, Harz gave them me.' She looked back at him through the smoke, flames beginning to rise again in her tearful eyes. 'They took turns raping me, with Harz watching and laughing. When it was Forge's turn, I took his own knife and jammed it so hard into his neck that it came out the other side. Then I ran.'

Kurcher couldn't really say anything at that moment. What *could* he say? It was no wonder she was so wild, and he understood how difficult it must have been to pull that trigger back in the brewery.

'My own brother,' she blurted out with a sad laugh. 'He used me so he could step up in the ranks. Of course, with Forge dead thanks to his little sister, Harz took control of the gang and over time built up the force we've all seen first-hand. Now he's one of *the* most feared pirates in the Bold.'

He wanted to reach out to her but that was the last thing she would have wanted.

Have a little decency for once, berated Frost.

'You thought it was me, didn't you?' Drake asked him. 'You thought I was feeding that traitorous fuck intel.'

Kurcher shrugged. 'It crossed my mind. I don't think that any more.'

She wiped her eyes and stubbed her cigarette out. 'Good. Best we find out who really sold you and Broekow to my bastard brother then.'

Sigma Royal Assault Ship Meta's Star, Kember system

When he closed his eyes, the map of the Milky Way swirled in his mind. Key systems blinked at him and slowly the galaxy began to turn a healthy shade of red and black.

Grosnik had spent most of his waking time lately studying the star maps and planning their next move. He knew he needed to give his tired eyes a rest, as well as his aching body.

The Sigma Royal fleet had been on the move constantly over recent weeks, stopping only to lay siege to Libra's remote outposts before heading off again. The mech army wasn't tired but their tech officers certainly were. Many had been complaining of headaches and nausea, and he had seen several throw up just after they landed on Vesta. They needed a rest and that was why he had ordered the fleet to Kember, so they could take a breath and enjoy the sights and sounds of Crown's Reach station.

Grosnik reclined before the wide window in his quarters, watching the smaller vessels zip in and out of the station pylons. The brandy in his glass wasn't going down as smoothly as he had hoped. He was itching to get back out there and didn't want to lose the momentum. Three Libra outposts had already been taken and he wanted to claim the fourth before Ariana Tabb's ships came searching for them, which they inevitably would.

If the board had still been alive, they would have questioned every part of his plan, asking why Libra Centauri and not Sapphire Nova or Taurus Galahad. After all, it wasn't Libra who attacked Meta. It was a simple answer though. Hostilities between Sigma and Libra had escalated significantly over recent years, with the latter taking advantage whenever they could. Let Taurus and Nova have their own war and wipe each other out.

He watched Crown's Reach slowly turn and tried to imagine what his men were getting up to. They deserved the respite, even for a day or two. It wasn't for him though. He preferred his own company, often losing himself in thoughts of his ex-wife and children. Once the mech campaign was over, he would search high and low for them. Until then, they were better off without him.

His thoughts turned to The Luminary. He had sent the dealer a message before they jumped from Meddian, demanding an update on their stolen mech and tech officer, Vekkerd. He had received a blunt response claiming they were still looking and that unforeseen circumstances had caused a minor delay. The Luminary then reassured him that they would be found shortly, but Grosnik was beginning to doubt the dealer was putting much effort in for something that wasn't his or her problem.

His peaceful contemplation was interrupted by a message alert from his personal console. It was a live comms link so he daren't ignore it. When he saw who was contacting him, the General hesitated. It was no coincidence it was the one person he didn't want to speak with.

'General Grosnik, hello,' greeted Morton Hurst, his thin face smiling through the screen. 'Thank you for taking my call. I hope I haven't caught you at a bad time.'

Grosnik returned the smile, albeit awkwardly. 'Luckily this is the best time for us. The fleet is just recharging over in Kember. Are you still on Sullivan's Rest?'

'I am. It's seen better days, I'm afraid.' Hurst glanced off to his left. 'The Kindred have really done a number on us here. Fortitude has lost a lot of good men in their cowardly attacks and the population of the station is decreasing every day as whole families flee to safer places, if there are any left.'

'I'm very sorry to hear that. The Kindred need to be stamped out. If we can be of any assistance, please let me know.'

Hurst regarded him silently for a few uncomfortable seconds. 'Thank you, General. I do hope that our original agreement is still firmly in place. It would certainly raise morale among my people.'

Grosnik found it hard to swallow as he answered. 'Of course. As soon as our initial stage of the campaign is complete, which is not far off now, I can share the system data with you. You'll be able to select where you'd like Fortitude's base of operations to be, with all of the facts at hand for each world.'

'Bases,' Hurst corrected. 'We would still require more than one, as you know.'

Just keep smiling, thought Grosnik. With any luck, The Kindred's next bomb might kill the arrogant bastard.

'Of course,' he nodded. 'How else can I help you?'

'Summit.' Hurst sat back from the screen. 'Impramed have lost their heads there and fear another attack from one of the corporations. My people are in place in Tidewell City to rise up and take control, but I need your support.'

Grosnik's brow furrowed. 'In what way?'

'Fortitude needs your help in removing Impramed forces from Summit. We need you to stand by us as we take over. For this support, Sigma Royal personnel will receive discounted stays there and VIP treatment at all spa resorts.'

'You're asking us to declare war on Impramed,' Grosnik stated. 'Can this not wait until our campaign against Libra is complete?'

'Oh, don't misunderstand me, General.' Hurst held a hand up. 'I understand you need your forces there with the fleet. However, when the time comes, I will require you to keep your end of the bargain and support us on Summit.'

Grosnik wanted to cut the conversation off. It wasn't enough for them to pay Fortitude for the mech supply, it seemed, and Hurst was a shrewd businessman who made sure there was a caveat in the agreement they signed. It sounded simple at the time. Sigma Royal will support Fortitude if protection is required. He could argue the variables of the agreement but knew Hurst would find a way to get what he wanted, unless the very same mechs he helped supply turned their shrikes on the vermin.

'Understood,' he smiled finally. 'You have our support.'

'Excellent.' Hurst's grin was ghastly. 'Thank you, General. Now, I really must...'

'Just one more thing,' interrupted Grosnik, knowing how much Hurst hated being cut off. 'I wondered whether you might be able to help me with a small matter, as you have an excellent network of contacts.'

Hurst looked pensive for a moment. 'If I can, of course.'

'We were holding a Libra officer in Monarch City and someone assassinated him, shooting him through the eye. Our security footage was compromised so we haven't been able to find the culprit, however we did manage to recover the bullet from the body. Our scientists analysed it and found it to be unique ammunition designed for quite an old style of revolver. That's where we hit a wall, I'm afraid, and I wondered if you could have your people take a look, to see if you might know who owns a weapon the bullet would fit.'

Hurst looked away from the screen again, watching something out of view. 'We'd be happy to help, although it is like finding a needle in a very large haystack.'

'Any assistance would be appreciated.'

Hurst gave a single bob of his head. 'Send over the data and consider it done.'

'Thank you. Let's speak again soon.'

Grosnik severed the link and let his smile slowly fade. He needed to sleep and now his dreams would be plagued by not only the scales of Libra but by the fist of Fortitude too.

Echo flagship Glaive,
Freeman system

'Are you sure this is a good idea, Jaffren?' Fischer asked as he tried to keep up with them.

'I've made my mind up,' Hewn replied, striding along the corridor with purpose.

Kurcher walked in silence alongside the Echo leader, still trying to get his head around the last few hours. Hewn had been brought up to speed on the events on Warren as soon as he stepped foot back on his ship and, to be fair, Fischer had been honest about their fuck-up. The reaction was unexpected though, with Hewn taking it in his stride. The only thing he voiced was that it was a massive coincidence that Harz attacked while he was away on Earth. Even the return of Broekow and Rane didn't seem to faze him.

Immediately after the debrief, Hewn had led them to the brig where he personally let the maimed sniper out and explained he held no grudge against him. He looked once at Rane then spun on his heel and left, calling Kurcher, Fischer and Broekow to a private meeting. On the way to his quarters, Kurcher was asked if Drake had anything to do with the intel leak, which he was sure she didn't. She was also called to attend.

It was Hewn's turn to debrief then and the next three hours were spent learning what had transpired on Earth, from the forming of the new alliance to everything Winter had reported. Despite remaining stoic on the outside, Kurcher's heart was racing at the news from Straunia. It seemed that the *Grail* saga hadn't ended when the weapon plunged to the surface.

Saul Winter also concerned him. When he heard how the man had tracked the *Kaladine* from system to system, even going so far as to help them escape Rikur and Summit, before then shooting them down at Cerberus, Kurcher expected to see a reaction from Broekow. Instead, the rifleman simply glanced in his direction then carried on listening. The man who killed Frost was still alive and that felt like a huge slap across the face.

It was rather surreal that the only person in the room who acted shocked when Hewn told them about the alien species was Fischer. The others clearly had many things on their minds and took it in their stride, including Kurcher whose calm visage again didn't let on that he was finding it hard to believe.

'I don't want the Cobb Resistance told about the new alliance just yet,' Hewn had told them. 'If they know we are working with Taurus, it won't go down well.'

With the room falling silent for some time, it was Broekow who spoke first. 'So what now?'

Hewn had laid everything out for them then. While the new alliance debated what to do about the alien situation and what they were referring to as *the Straunia crisis*, Echo had to focus their attention on the three imminent threats: Jericho's Bold, The Kindred and The Luminary. Harz needed to be tracked down and dealt with, plus they needed to find out more on The Luminary as the app dealer's relationship with both Fortitude and Sigma Royal was cause for concern. As for The Kindred, someone had to know which rat nest they were crawling from. Their bombs were proving extremely bad for business and Echo had to strengthen all revenue streams, now including the rebuilding of the brewery.

It was at that moment Broekow stated that he no longer worked for Echo; that he didn't need their protection any longer. Before Hewn could reply, the sniper added that he would find Harz but only with Rane's help. Hewn was quick to agree. Rane may have been an untrustworthy psycho but he was very good at finding people.

With the eye-opening meeting now concluded, they found themselves heading for one of the storage bays where the captured mech known as Ram was being kept. It was time that Vekkerd made his choice.

'Vance, when we've finished, I want you to contact Hedmun Oakley and get his fleet helping track Bold or Kindred movements where possible.'

'Understood, Jaffren.' It hadn't taken long for Fischer to fall back in line, but the guilt of failing the ambush on Warren was still weighing on his mind it seemed. 'I was going to ask him to patrol the Expanse systems just in case.'

'No need. Harz won't be back here any time soon I don't expect.'

Kurcher gave Drake the quickest of looks. 'That fucker will be back though unless we get rid of him.'

'Leave that to us,' Broekow piped up.

Kurcher's gaze moved to the sniper. 'You going to get a couple of bionic fingers then? I doubt you'll be able to take Harz out from distance as you are.'

Broekow's expression darkened somewhat, although his voice remained quiet. 'It'll get done one way or another.'

'Just don't underestimate that motherfucker.' It was the first time Drake had spoken since joining them.

Without another word, Broekow veered away at the next junction, heading back towards the brig. Kurcher wanted to go with him, to make sure Rane didn't deviate in his usual way. The reason why the swordsman was helping still eluded him and it was playing on his mind.

The four found the powered-down mech where they'd left it. The scuffs and dents in the red and black chassis still looked fresh, although some of the more serious damage Ram had sustained in battle with the pursuit mech had been partially repaired. Sigma tech officer Vekkerd was standing next to his pet, carefully examining each limb under the watchful eyes of two guards. He was no longer wearing his dirty uniform and was dressed in borrowed clothes.

'It's time,' Hewn announced, his voice echoing through the storage bay. 'Are you going to help us?'

Vekkerd looked up. 'I don't have much choice. If I say no, you'll likely shoot me right now and throw me out an airlock.'

'Probably wouldn't bother wasting the bullet,' remarked Kurcher.

Vekkerd grimaced but nodded. 'You've ripped me from my life as an officer but I'll help where I can.'

'Life in Echo is better,' Hewn stated, approaching the mech. 'Tough at times but we can always find a place for someone like you. We haven't exactly treated you badly, have we?'

'Apart from jabbing a blade into my side and threatening to shoot me, no.'

Kurcher tried to hide a smile at the young officer's sarcasm. He'd spent time questioning Vekkerd since they brought him back from Kismet and there was something he liked about their latest recruit. When all this was over, Kurcher planned on introducing him to Marie Butler. The Resistance could do with some more tech-savvy people on Seko.

Hewn studied Ram. 'I can't say I like any mechs but if your friend here can help us somehow find The Luminary, I might just let it stay too.'

Vekkerd placed a hand on Ram's head. 'There might be a way to contact The Luminary, although I'm not sure it would work. If I bring Ram back online, I can look through the app data and log a technical query in the system.'

'Wouldn't Sigma be able to see that query too?' Hewn asked warily.

76

'Maybe.' Vekkerd tapped a finger on one of the visual sensors. 'When we underwent training, we were told that The Luminary prefers to deal with any complaints or glitches directly. We were shown where to log the problem but I never knew whether other users would be able to see it. The Luminary is very protective of the app so I'm guessing might not want to share any issues with others. It's just a hunch of course.'

Kurcher rolled his eyes. 'Jesus, Sigma offer good intensive training then. For all they knew, the tech might've blown your eyes out of their sockets. It's happened before with black market apps and I'm guessing this Luminary prick isn't above board.'

Kurcher was satisfied that Vekkerd didn't know how the dealer came to be using an alien symbol for their app emblem. The real question was whether the tech lurking beneath the surface was from the same source and how the hell they would've got their hands on it, unless someone in one of the corporations was selling some big fucking secrets.

'The mech's weapons have been taken offline, right?' Fischer asked, eyeing the heavy duty shrikes.

'Of course,' replied Vekkerd. 'He could still take your head off without them though.'

Kurcher grinned at Fischer. 'Now that I'd like to see.'

Hewn stepped back. 'Do it then. Let's see what happens.'

Kurcher pulled his revolver and gave Vekkerd an apologetic shrug. 'Just in case you decide to try anything.'

As the tech officer gave Ram one last check, everyone else backed up. None of them wanted to be within swinging distance of the powerful construct. A moment later, the blue visuals lit up and Ram rose slowly, as though feeling the effects of the mech fight. Vekkerd's eyes gleamed as the app data began scrolling and he tested out a few of Ram's systems, moving each limb and tilting his head from side to side.

'Looks like your people did a good job repairing him,' Vekkerd said with relief.

Kurcher could see Hewn's eyes firmly fixed on the mech and there was an element of fear in his expression. When one loses an arm in such a way, he guessed there would always be wariness and contempt.

At least he gets to control his own arm, Frost said.

Kurcher checked briefly on Drake, who was standing behind him alongside Fischer. They didn't exactly look comfortable sharing the room with Ram. For a moment, Drake's eyes met his and it looked like she no longer wanted to knife him.

Damaged goods like her can't be trusted, Ercko told him.

'Wait.' Vekkerd's sudden shout put everyone on edge. 'I've lost the link.'

Ram had frozen, which was understandable if the app had failed. When the mech slowly turned its head to look down at its user though, they knew something was wrong. Vekkerd gazed up at it, blinking in confusion. Ram's head swung to regard the two Echo guards nearby before flicking much quicker to focus on Hewn and then Kurcher, who the mech seemed to stare at for an unusually long time.

'What's happening, Vekkerd?' Hewn called.

Ram's attention shifted back to the Echo leader.

'Someone else is controlling him,' replied the tech officer, trying to access his app. Then he saw something in the limited data still being displayed. 'It's them...The Luminary.'

At this, Ram made a sudden move sideways. A metal leg lashed out, catching Vekkerd square in the chest and sending him flying into one of the guards. With an eerie grace, it then leapt at the other guard, pinning the poor man to the floor with its entire weight.

'No...' Vekkerd was struggling for breath and clutching his chest as he tried to stand.

Ram closed the distance to him alarmingly fast, raising a front leg again with intent. As the limb swung down, a metal hand caught it.

'Get him out the way,' yelled Hewn, his artificial arm already beginning to shake under the pneumatic pressure.

Kurcher rushed forward and grabbed Vekkerd, dragging him back towards the door where Drake was waiting to help. When he turned back, Kurcher saw the mech sensor-to-eye with Hewn and Fischer floundering nearby, weapon in hand but not sure how to help.

'You see me, don't you?' Hewn's voice was beginning to waver too, beads of sweat rolling down his face. 'We need to talk face-to-face.'

Ram was still for a moment, then used another leg to sweep Hewn from his feet. To their relief, it didn't press the attack. Instead, it stared down at the prone pirate before turning its visuals on Kurcher. The lingering robotic stare unnerved him.

'What're you looking at, shithead?'

Ram's head tilted to the side as it watched him, then the mech suddenly powered down.

'What the fuck?' Fischer moved to help Hewn back up. 'You okay?'

'Yeah. Just wondering why it didn't finish us off.' Hewn looked across at Kurcher for some answer. 'It could've done a lot more damage.'

'The Luminary was weighing us up,' Kurcher said, offering his best guess. 'Odd though. For a moment there I felt like it recognised me.'

Hewn nodded, clearly having felt something similar. 'It was like I could feel the human at the other end of the link. Fucking creepy.'

'When you've quite finished spouting shit, Vekkerd needs help.' Drake seemed almost back to normal. 'And I suggest you don't try turning that metal fucker back on again.'

~

Rane looked at his ship with pride. The *Basilisk* had spent so long gathering dust at Harper and he had been looking for a way to get her back. The slim sprinter-class had helped him out of many situations and he would've been devastated if she had been claimed by someone else while he was away. Fortunately he had hidden the ship so well at the colony that it was still where he had left it under the sheet in the quiet and mostly abandoned sections of Harper.

The *Basilisk* had come to him during a brief stay at Temple some time ago, as he was moving from location to location. Her owner had been a freelance courier selling his services to whichever corporation or organisation needed items or messages moving quickly and quietly. Having engaged the courier in conversation one evening at a bar, Rane learnt that he had been working closely with Sapphire Nova most recently. Rane was long gone from Temple and enjoying the impressive agility of the *Basilisk* before the courier's body was found face down in his quarters.

'Are you helping?'

Rane looked up at Broekow, who was shoving a number of rations aggressively into one of the ship's cargo slots. 'Of course. Are your hands aching again?'

'Slightly. Nothing I can't handle.'

'Perhaps we should pay one of my contacts a visit after we leave here,' Rane suggested, moving to pick up one of the small crates. 'Get your hands looked at. He could probably help with implants or artificial...'

'No.' Broekow glared at him. 'I don't need any of that shit. No more tech.'

Rane smiled back. 'I don't blame you.'

They finished loading the rations then looked around the hangar.

'Nobody coming to say goodbye?' Rane asked with a chuckle. 'Fair enough. I have to admit I was surprised when they let me out of that cell.'

Broekow didn't share the mirth. 'Just be thankful they didn't shoot you. They all want to still. Let's just go before they change their minds.'

Rane watched the sniper closely as he limped away. Broekow knew that Rane could've stopped him being taken off the *Grail* before it went down. Rane didn't want him dead and sincerely wanted to help him. He had never seen such a sad individual when he rescued Broekow from Devlin's clutches. The thought had crossed his mind to end Broekow's misery then and there, but the war criminal still had a purpose.

The first few days after they left Rikur had been difficult. Broekow was in a bad way thanks to Harz, and Devlin's lack of civility hadn't exactly helped. Once he was fully conscious and able to talk, albeit awkwardly with his damaged gum, Broekow had fired blame at him for Frost's death and was in a permanent state of regret and remorse. It had taken some time to snap him out of it, but he eventually came to understand that the *Kaladine* crashing was out of his control; that Frost chose to stay. She may have died from her wounds later on but she could've been dragged from her chair by the others.

On the next part of their journey to track down Harz, Rane needed to find out just what had been said at the meeting Broekow was allowed to attend earlier that day.

'Sieren, is there anything else we can do to help Echo?' he asked the sniper as they started to climb into the *Basilisk*. 'Other than find Harz.'

Broekow squeezed himself into the tight confines of the cockpit, where he had to sit behind Rane. 'They're after any intel on The Kindred and some app dealer causing them issues.'

Rane settled into his seat, his mind already processing this. 'Well we can keep our eyes and ears out for them, right? Any other information on this dealer?'

'Look,' Broekow's tone became harsh. 'Let's just find Harz and deal with that bastard. Once he's dead, you and I can go our own ways.'

Rane powered up the engines. 'Of course, Sieren. Whatever you want.'

Titan Station,
Sol system

Garrett had the same expression as everyone else who had sat through Winter's incredible debrief, and Hayward couldn't quite tell what the General was thinking.

The makeshift meeting room set up near one of the cordoned off military pylons was currently occupied by only four of them. Akeman was standing near a small circular window that looked out at an adjacent pylon, his arms crossed as he waited for someone to speak. Winter was standing so still he might as well be a statue. His icy eyes were fixed firmly on the General, who was returning the gaze with no small amount of suspicion.

'A lot to take in, huh?' Hayward said, keen to move the conversation on. 'I still haven't got my head round it all yet.'

Garrett finally looked across at her and his first question caught them all off guard. 'If Sapphire Nova claimed responsibility for Mitchell's death on Straunia, how does what you've just shown me tie in?'

'Honest answer is we don't know yet,' replied Hayward. 'Another reason why we want to speak with Neri Ishlan. She was on the *Victory* when it was captured by Tomas Klein's fleet at Straunia so maybe she can shed some light on this.'

'So you're one of the reasons Mitchell kept going out to Berg.' Garrett turned a wary eye again to Winter but this time found him looking down, deep in thought.

'Something wrong, Saul?' Hayward asked him.

Winter didn't look at them. 'I can hear them again but something's different. Whispers like hundreds of voices talking at once.'

'The last time you heard that, the aliens attacked,' stated Akeman, clearly alarmed. 'Are we sure there aren't more out there?'

'All of them went to Straunia and none of them left.' Winter sounded very certain.

'You sure about that?' Garrett's suspicious expression was back. 'I'd like to trust you but how do you know that you weren't turned into some sort of beacon for these things, and that there aren't more of them on their way here right now?'

'Like I said, something's different this time.'

Hayward exchanged glances with Garrett and Akeman. Winter wasn't exactly filling them with confidence, and yet Titan Station was keeping tabs on any traffic coming into the system. There were only Taurus signatures out there.

Garrett rose from his seat and opened the door out into the concourse, where his small unit of soldiers were standing guard. 'Sergeant, have Ishlan brought here but no need to bring the rest of her crew.'

One of his men saluted and vanished along the pylon with two others. Garrett beckoned two more soldiers inside and ordered them to stand just inside the door. Hayward knew that was to keep an extra eye on Winter. Winter probably knew it too.

Garrett chose to remain standing and began pacing around the table. Hayward was starting to feel very nervous and took a gulp of water, grimacing at the almost metallic taste. She found herself wishing it was vodka.

She had spent the trip from Earth to Titan going over and over the reports on the woman about to walk into the room, including files that had been kept from her by Mitchell but unearthed following his demise. Neri Ishlan had built her way up to become commander of the *Ravenedge*, now the flagship of the Taurus fleet, but she was one of the five high-ranking officers who followed Santa Cruz on his mission of genocide. After the *Grail* fell and the rogue fleet was defeated, Ishlan was stripped of command and thrown into a cell along with co-conspirators Byrne and O'Brien.

It was Mitchell who then released them and had them become his lieutenants for his still-perplexing mission to Straunia, all of which was kept from the rest of the board. Ishlan was left in command of the *Victory* and the last reports said she surrendered to Nova forces.

There was one thing that stood out about her: she followed orders unequivocally, even when they were coming from corrupt officers. She had claimed to have questioned the actions of Santa Cruz but Hayward didn't know whether to believe that. It was more likely Ishlan was afraid of the madman and thought it best to keep following his commands and ignore the atrocities he was committing.

For the last couple of days, the released officer and six others from the *Victory* had been confined to the *Bulwyn*, which had been accompanied to Titan Station by the ship that intercepted them at the jump point. The only ones to see her up to this point were the team that boarded the small transport to conduct a thorough search, and they were helping guard the airlock now. Hayward made a mental note to go thank them once the meeting had concluded.

When Ishlan walked into the meeting room ten minutes later, led by Garrett's sergeant, Hayward had the chance to weigh her up in person for the first time. With her hair tied back neatly and her uniform surprisingly pristine, Neri Ishlan seemed oddly normal.

'Hold her at gunpoint.' Winter's outburst caused a moment of confusion. 'Now.'

Garrett hesitated then pulled his pistol, signalling his three men in the room to do so too. Akeman followed suit.

Ishlan locked eyes with Winter. 'Please, there's no cause for alarm,' she said calmly. 'I'm unarmed.'

'What is it, Saul?' Hayward asked.

'That's not Neri Ishlan.'

Hayward shared a bewildered look with Akeman, who had started heading around the table, before a yell cut through the uncomfortable silence from outside the room. Ishlan was smiling at Winter and it sent a cold shiver through Hayward's body.

As she instinctively stepped closer to Garrett, an explosion rocked the station and the door blew inwards as a cloud of smoke and shrapnel billowed forth. Hayward felt the floor shudder and lost her footing, landing heavily on her back. The smoke had enveloped the room so fast that she couldn't see anyone else. She heard them though, through the ringing in her ears, but it was hard to make out what they were saying.

Gunfire ripped through the concourse and the unmistakeable sound of men dying could be heard. Suddenly she was back on Galt during the attack on Kingston, her nose burning from the acrid smoke and her eyes watering so badly she couldn't see.

A strong hand pulled her up and she was relieved to see it was Akeman. He dragged her towards the back of the room, his pistol aimed at the door, swinging back and forth in search of targets.

As the smoke began to dissipate, she saw a group of men and women out in the concourse heading for the meeting room. All of them were wearing Taurus uniforms and were armed, their faces the perfect picture of calm. Just outside the door, she could see the bodies of three of Garrett's soldiers. The rest of his men were just inside the room, using the walls either side of the door for cover.

Some were clearly wounded. Garrett himself was poised, ready to open fire but looking decidedly uncertain of what was happening.

Her breath caught in her throat as she spotted Winter and Ishlan locked together. The former had clearly vaulted over the table in an attempt to keep the officer subdued as the exchange of gunfire took place. To Hayward's eyes though, Winter was finding Ishlan a lot stronger than he expected as she was fighting him off relatively easily. Her expression was still eerily calm.

A bullet ricocheted off a wall next to Hayward and Akeman, drawing her attention.

'Those mad bastards are going to decompress the whole station at this rate,' Akeman said, glancing nervously at the new pock mark in the wall. 'They clearly used a grenade of some kind to disperse the General's men outside. We're lucky not to have all been sucked out into space yet.'

'Who are they?' Hayward had to raise her voice again as Garrett's soldiers opened fire on the approaching attackers.

Akeman peered through the haze. 'Some are dressed in the same garb as Ishlan so I'm assuming it's the rest of the *Victory* crew. I really couldn't say who the others are.'

As the attackers had closed the distance to the meeting room, the barrage from Garrett's remaining soldiers took down three of them. One man fell as bullets tore into his legs, another was struck square in the chest and blown off his feet. The third was a woman with a strange smile who stumbled when one shot took her in the stomach then a second lodged in her skull.

Unfortunately, in the responding fire, two more of Garrett's men went down. The attackers were alarmingly accurate considering they were only using pistols.

Hayward heard Garrett shout into his comms, demanding to know where the station back-up was. Due to their cordoning off the pylon, it was either taking much longer for guards to make their way there or something was stopping them getting through. How many of these attackers were actually on the station?

Her focus was drawn again to the struggle between Winter and Ishlan. Winter had managed to get the upper hand and driven the released officer to her knees, wrapping one arm around her neck. It looked as though he was trying to choke her unconscious. Suddenly he seemed to notice something when he looked down at Ishlan and his other hand reached out, touching the back of her neck. Hayward saw him jolt, as though struck by a surge of electricity, and his eyes looked alight. A moment later, Winter emitted a faint groan and slumped backwards, hitting the floor hard.

Ishlan was unfazed by this and simply rose back to her feet, straightened her jacket and bent down to pick something up. Her eyes turned to Hayward, her smile almost human but not quite.

'Miss Hayward, let's not have any more bloodshed, shall we?' Ishlan stepped closer. 'If the General and his soldiers put down their weapons, I will explain everything to you and all will become very clear.'

'You opened fire on us,' cried Hayward from behind Akeman. 'It's your people out there who need to surrender.'

She paled when she noticed that only Garrett and two soldiers were left standing as the attackers arrived at the doorway, their smiling faces wholly unnerving. Her face became even more ashen as she saw that the attackers gunned down moments before were standing amongst their colleagues. Even the woman who had been shot in the head was back on her feet, although her eyes were now gleaming silver sockets.

'Please,' came Ishlan's relaxed voice again, closer still. 'Give me the chance to explain.'

More gunfire at the door. Two attackers fell, one defender crumpled back against the wall with a wound to his shoulder.

Hayward heard Akeman take a sharp intake of breath and she saw that the agent, Garrett and the remaining standing soldier were all staring through the doorway. That was when she saw the nightmare approaching.

The alien creature was instantly recognisable, moving quietly on six legs as it was allowed to pass through the attacking group, none of whom showed any surprise at its sudden appearance. The dark chitinous body was streaked with brilliant veins of blue and silver, which extended into two of the long tendrils that writhed from the front of its body. Four other tendrils adjacent to these were dark brown beneath the artificial station lights.

When Hayward saw the vicious barbs at the ends of these appendages, she was reminded of the image Winter had shown of a dead colonist's face being torn off. She was also reminded though that this being before them was not one of the aliens attacking the *Grail* but was in fact whatever had been lurking behind the mass of human fodder.

'General Garrett.' Ishlan had given up on Hayward apparently. 'You can see you are outnumbered and reinforcements are not going to be here as quickly as you would hope. Please lower your arms and allow me to explain.'

Hayward glanced at the General, who was watching the approaching alien and slowly backing up. When she looked back out into the concourse, she could see two more of the creatures and any hope she had of surviving this encounter began to seep away. Still, it was not the time for cowering in a corner.

'Lieutenant Ishlan,' she began loudly, stepping out from behind Akeman. 'I will listen to what you have to say but there will be no further hostile action from your people and these...' She was lost for the right word. '...these others remain outside the room, agreed?'

Ishlan gave her another smile, as though she were greeting an old friend. 'Agreed.'

Hayward heard a strange noise from outside the room and they all looked through the doorway to see one of the aliens holding the body of a soldier aloft. Her jaw dropped open in horror as the dead man's eyes seemed to roll before vanishing back into his skull and being replaced by the silvery mass. It gently lowered the dead man, who stood unsupported, and went to lift another body.

'I think not,' Akeman suddenly remarked bluntly.

The agent fired a single shot that took Ishlan through the forehead and exited out the back of her skull. She stood for a moment with the smile on her face before crumpling to the floor alongside Winter.

No sooner had her body hit the floor than Garrett and his soldier opened fire again, felling three of the attackers. One of the dead men soaked up two bullets without even a grunt. The alien that had been approaching moved frighteningly fast, leaping into the meeting room and towering over the soldier, who was two paces in front of the General and trying to reload as fast as he ever had before. Unfortunately, he wasn't fast enough as a barbed tendril wrapped around his neck and swiftly hoisted him into the air. He let out a gurgling noise. Garrett got off one shot that seemed to ricochet off its hard skin before it launched the soldier into the general with such force it sent both men sprawling next to Hayward and Akeman.

Hayward saw the other two aliens still working on reanimating the dead, but the men and women making up the attacking force filed into the room. Akeman stepped in front of her once more, ever her protector. She understood why he had killed Ishlan. She knew that the aliens were only there for one reason and had somehow altered all of the Taurus personnel, but had been trying to play for time in the hopes the station security would rescue them. For all she knew, more of the aliens were at that moment moving through the station taking control of everyone they met. For a split second, she wondered whether Tomas Klein or a Nova entourage would suddenly walk into the room and show they were behind the whole thing.

'I'm sorry, Karin,' Akeman said solemnly.

She caught sight of a pistol on the floor near her feet, dropped by the flung soldier, and scooped it up. He had managed to push the new bullet clip part way in, for which she was thankful. When she hammered it into place, she gave Akeman a nod and aimed at the approaching alien.

Another explosion rocked the concourse and Hayward saw one of the aliens outside the room disappear amongst flames and smoke. She also saw a variety of limbs propelled through the doorway by the blast, both human and alien. Then a pistol fired three times in quick succession and three attackers fell.

All except the walking dead in the room turned and looked back towards the concourse. Even the alien swung its multiple eyes to see what was happening. Akeman took the advantage and fired twice at the creature, both shots seeming not to cause any visible injury. Hayward fired at it once but missed completely.

Yet again, an explosion erupted outside the meeting room and this time it was so close that more smoke drifted quickly through the open doorway, obscuring everyone's vision. More gunfire threatened to deafen Hayward as the constant crack of handguns echoed around the room. It was confusing to know where it was actually coming from and she could only hope it was security arriving to save the day.

As Akeman peered into the gloom, trying to make out a potential target, the alien lunged from the smoke directly in front of him, one of the wicked barbed tendrils reaching for his throat. While he managed to duck just in time, he hadn't seen the second tendril and it caught him hard in the ribs, knocking him several feet to the right. Hayward watched him disappear into the smoke and heard the sound of his body hit the floor, then found herself staring into the emotionless visage of the alien.

It was almost insect-like, with black soulless eyes and something akin to mandibles just below the large head. And yet, she thought, it was completely alien. The blue and silver running throughout its body seemed to pulse with the rhythm of a heart and yet Hayward occasionally saw what looked like long slivers of metal move beneath the hard skin between pulses. At one point, she even saw it flash behind one of the eyes, turning it a sickly green colour for a second. Was she even looking at something alive or was it just like the Taurus men and women, brought back from the dead?

As she went to take a step back and aim the pistol at it, one of the tendrils lashed out and wrenched the weapon from her hand so quickly that she had no time to react. The creature seemed to grow taller as it looked down, watching her with all those eyes. Then it moved towards her and she threw herself against the wall behind her, closing her eyes tight and wishing she had stayed on Earth like Akeman had advised.

A gun fired close by, making her jump, and she felt something lightly rain on her face. When she opened her eyes, she saw the silhouette of a man in the haze, his pistol barrel smoking. The alien had turned to face him and Hayward saw that one of the creature's eyes was gone, replaced by a bullet hole. Tiny silver worms writhed through the wound.

'Get out the way, Miss Hayward.'

The voice was not that of Akeman, Garrett or Winter, as she had expected. She still knew it though. She would never forget it for as long as she lived.

'I said move,' yelled Mikan Rist as the alien leapt for him.

Putting her fear and confusion to one side, Hayward dived out of the way, landing next to where Garrett was starting to come to after being struck by his own soldier. When she looked back and saw the awful weapon in Rist's other hand, there was no doubt it was her would-be assassin. It wasn't the customised boomer he used on Galt, but it would produce a similar outcome.

The boomer fired as the alien struck Rist, tearing open his forearm to reveal the mechanical systems within. As the explosive round forced its way through the tough skin, another tendril snatched the boomer from him and hurled it out of sight across the room. It was much faster than him and hit him again with the barbs, this time catching him in the armpit and half-tearing his arm from its socket. Rist didn't cry out. Instead, he fired his pistol twice at its head, one of the shots destroying another eye.

The boomer round exploded, blowing the creature apart in a grotesque shower of green and brown liquid, as well as scattering shards of silver everywhere too. The force of the blast blew Rist onto his back and out of Hayward's sight. She watched as the smoking carcass keeled over, the metallic fragments on the floor twitching as though alive.

She stood shakily and helped Garrett up. As the General retrieved his gun, Hayward looked towards the concourse and saw that most of the attackers were prone on the floor. A couple were still moving.

She peered past the remains of the alien and saw Rist trying to push himself off the floor. The arm that had been torn apart was gone, completely removed by the boomer blast, and she could now see his face clearly, although it was burnt and blackened. There was metal showing through a hole in his jaw.

Behind Rist, Akeman was recovering, clutching his ribs. He shared a bewildered look with Hayward, unsure what to make of the sudden arrival of the man who had tried to kill them both not so long ago, and the fact that not even a missing arm and severe blast damage had incapacitated him.

She let Rist struggle to his feet before saying anything. 'I don't understand...' It was all she could think of.

The cold voice of the assassin sounded as distant as it had when she last heard it. 'I didn't come here seeking forgiveness for what I did. I came here to warn you, although clearly arrived too late for that.

I was tracking Sapphire Nova, intent on some form of revenge for what they did to me; for what they turned me into. Instead, I found *them*.'

Rist nodded down at the body of the alien, then seemed to notice his missing arm and looked around for it. Not seeing it anywhere, he continued.

'Eventually I learnt that they were sending the *Bulwyn* back to Earth with some of the captured Taurus crew and these surprise guests. I tracked them to Sol and eventually to this station, hoping that what was on board hadn't come into contact with anyone else yet. Unfortunately the ship that had intercepted them was compromised and then a handful of the station personnel that greeted them at the pylon. I don't think anyone else has been assimilated.'

Hayward shook her head to stop all the questions from clogging her brain. 'Look, there will be time to debrief but we need to get to a secure location first.'

'Best you drop that pistol,' Akeman advised from behind the assassin.

Rist glanced back at the agent with a somewhat blank look. If he recognised him as the man he gunned down at Kingston, he didn't show it. 'The ship I took on Galt is docked at the next pylon. I downloaded all of the data I discovered into it for safe-keeping.'

'Well that was *my* ship so I should have the codes to access it,' said Akeman, feeling the shoulder of his weapon arm and flinching. 'Now let's go.'

As Hayward turned and looked across at Garrett, who was checking on the status of his fallen soldiers in the meeting room, she saw three figures stagger into the doorway and realised they were survivors of the attacking party. Their faces were blackened from Rist's explosions and one of them had a glistening wound that exposed the bone in his kneecap.

All three opened fire, two aiming at Garrett but one focused on Hayward. The General dived behind the table, avoiding further injury. Hayward froze.

Rist stepped in front of her and took two bullets in his chest. He staggered and fired back, hitting the shooter first in the neck and then in the head. Akeman shot one of the remaining attackers but the last managed to get a final bullet away. Again, Rist shielded the judicial officer and she heard him let out a soft grunt as it struck him. Together, Akeman and Garrett took down the final man in the doorway as Rist stumbled then fell.

When Hayward knelt next to the assassin, she saw that blood was pumping from the wounds, forming a pool quickly beneath him. The bullets had clearly hit the human part of him.

'Don't let them bring me back again,' he said softly.

With that, Mikan Rist let out his final breath.

Echo flagship Glaive, Miller system

This is uncomfortable, Frost said.

Kurcher had to agree but tried to take some solace in the fact the entourage from Seko was there because Fischer fucked up again. Had he managed to communicate Echo's wishes effectively via comms, Butler wouldn't have requested the meeting with Hewn in person.

Unless she wants to talk about something else of course, pointed out D'Larro.

Kurcher was leaning against the wall at the back of the room, happy to stand in the shadows and let the others do the talking. He was tired of using his voice so much and longed for the days when he could simply track someone down, shoot them in the head, jump back onto the *Kaladine* and disappear into the void.

Good times, whispered Frost.

Seated around the table in the centre of the room, Hewn and Fischer were opposite Butler, Hedmun Oakley and, for some reason, his murderous niece. Hewn hadn't so much as grimaced when he saw Tara step through the airlock and instead greeted her like one would a long-lost friend. Perhaps they had bonded when he had taken her back home after their fateful visit to Cerberus.

The other two surprise guests were Butler's right-hand man and woman. Monk hadn't changed a bit and was still dressed like he had no clothes that fit him, carrying the pungent smell of fuel around like some nasty cologne. Ever since the burly engineer had backed him up on Cobb following Fuller's death, Kurcher respected the man's honesty and knew his integrity would see him do well on Seko.

As for the feisty Cho, she looked much different to her time on Cobb. Gone were the dirty overalls and messy hair. She sat next to Butler with the look of an officer, hands clasped before her on the table and hair tied back tightly, her clothes clean and incredibly straight. She was clearly taking her extra responsibilities very seriously.

'Rest easy,' Butler said to Hewn with a smile. 'Rae and Wes are both doing well. In fact, I might just ask to keep them with us longer. Rae's got quite the skill set.'

'You have no idea,' chuckled Hewn. 'It's been a while since I've seen them so I wondered whether you'd mind me coming back to Seko with you when you leave. I'd like to visit with them before any more shit hits the fan.'

Kurcher hadn't heard Hewn be this polite before. When he had gone to Tempest to find the pirate in Echo's secret drug facility, everything he knew about Hewn indicated he was a ruthless son-of-a-bitch whose sole purpose was to generate money via illegal goods. While that was still part of Hewn's persona, Kurcher had seen a lot more behind the scenes.

You show any vulnerability and people out there will take advantage of it, stated Frost.

Kurcher knew that better than most.

'What sort of shit are we talking about?' Hedmun asked, taking a tentative sip of Echo's own brand beer. His face said he wished he had said wine when Hewn offered drinks.

'Jericho's Bold for one.' Hewn gulped his beer with a genuine thirst. 'They've been causing us real problems lately, hence Rae bringing Wes to see you. The Kindred have really ramped up their bombings, which is causing disruption to not only us but all the other organisations too. There are other things but they aren't going to affect you.'

'So the Bold and Kindred attacks will?' Cho's eyes narrowed as she tried to work out what he was getting at.

'Possibly,' nodded Hewn. 'Possibly not. Our aim is to knock all problems on the head before they can affect Seko in any way.'

Butler tapped the edge of the wine glass in front of her thoughtfully. 'Vance said that Echo need help seeking any intel. The problem is that our ships are no good for missions outside of local space. They're more likely to fall apart as they pass through a jump point. We really do appreciate the repairs you helped us with but, as I've mentioned before, we need better ships.'

Kurcher noted her look in his direction but he stayed quiet.

'As soon as we can find ships for you to have, they're yours,' promised Hewn. 'I understand what you're saying though. Perhaps you might consider some of your people travelling outside Miller on other ships though to help.'

'What other ships?' Butler frowned.

Hedmun pretended to sip his beer again. 'He means my fleet.'

'You're pretty sharp for an old man,' grinned Hewn.

Hedmun shrugged. 'Makes sense really. Listen, we're allies now and so, if I can help, I will. I can make three ships available to you, but I don't want to hear they've been wiped out by a bunch of stinking Bold scum. Intel missions only, agreed?'

'Agreed.' Hewn finished his drink. 'Anything else?'

The old officer pulled his chair closer to the table, at the same time pushing the beer away subtly. 'Yes. I've been the Oakley spokesman when it comes to this alliance for a while now and I've helped the Cobb Resistance move from that dirtball of a planet to their new home. However, it's time I returned to Cradle for a longer period. Warring between the ruling families on our planet is reaching fever pitch I'm afraid, and it's time I stepped back into the fray. In my place, Tara will act as the Oakley contact within the Resistance.'

At this, Kurcher couldn't stay quiet any longer. 'Firstly, there is no Cobb Resistance any more. What exactly are you resisting? You'd do well to get rid of that fucking name once and for all.'

Hedmun gave him a sour look. 'It speaks.'

This prick's asking for a beating, snarled Ercko.

'Secondly, your niece has no leadership experience and certainly hasn't represented your family in the best ways. Why the fuck would anyone listen to her?'

'Because I have a voice.' All eyes turned to Tara, who rose gracefully to face Kurcher. 'I am an Oakley and will represent my family on Seko to the best of my ability.'

Kurcher caught Butler looking slightly perplexed. 'Being an Oakley doesn't mean shit outside of your home system. Do you think Jericho's Bold will care, or The Kindred for that matter? I sure don't.'

Hedmun made to stand alongside his niece but she placed a hand on his shoulder and eased him back down. 'My loyalty is to Marie and the rest of the colony on Seko first of all. They've taken me in and treated me well. I'm also a part of this alliance, whether you like it or not, and don't intend on doing *anything* that would jeopardise that.'

Kurcher knew exactly what she meant and the two stared angrily at one another for a few seconds.

Best leave her alone, Angard warned menacingly.

Butler held up her hand with a question. 'Um, am I missing something here?'

'Kurcher and I know each other,' Tara replied, getting in before anyone else. 'He helped me when I was in trouble; took me away from Cradle when others wanted me dead. He hid me on his ship and we had quite the adventure together before Jaffren kindly took me home.'

Kurcher saw Hewn give him a slight nod. 'Yeah, old friends.'

'If you're leaving Tara to represent the Oakleys, that's fine,' Hewn said to Hedmun, trying his best to diffuse the aggressive atmosphere in the room. 'The running of the colony is still down to Marie so no change there. What she says goes.'

'Cal's Hope.' Butler looked around at the faces of her allies. 'The colony will be called Cal's Hope from now on.'

How original, Santa Cruz remarked sarcastically.

'Pretty good name if you ask me,' Monk piped up, finding his voice.

Kurcher smiled to himself. Guess they couldn't have called it Cretin's Hope.

'I like it.' Tara lowered herself back into her seat. 'I never met him but I'm sure he would've liked it too.'

Hewn had another beer in his hand and he held it aloft. 'Here's to Cal Fuller and his legacy.'

They toasted the dead Resistance leader and, as Butler, Monk and Cho settled back in quiet contemplation, Kurcher offered Hewn a smirk and shrug. Who knew that the metal-armed pirate in charge of Echo was such an accomplished diplomat?

How easy it would be to send the room spiralling in disarray, said D'Larro. *All you have to do is bring up the new alliance with Taurus.*

The meeting lasted another couple of hours, moving from important matters to the more mundane as the alcohol flowed. Kurcher watched as Hewn shared jokes with Butler and the Oakleys. He listened as Monk and Cho engaged in dull engineering talk with Fischer about spare parts they could go back to Seko with. He just wanted to go find Drake and see what base he could reach with her this time.

Once it drew to a close, Hewn took Hedmun for a private conversation about systems and how best the three Oakley ships could be utilized. Fischer was charged with giving the rest a tour of the *Glaive*, like it was some tourist attraction.

Kurcher couldn't wait to get out of the stuffy room but, as he headed for the door, he heard Tara tell Fischer she would catch them up. It was no surprise to him when she appeared at his side as he strode through the ship.

'You can rest easy,' she said, trying to keep up with him.

'How many men did you say that to?'

'Everything I've been through...no, everything *we've* been through has made me a different person. Let me show you I can do this.'

Kurcher couldn't shake her. 'I'm guessing that you were a *different person* before getting raped back on Cradle. How exactly do you just suddenly lose the part of you that wants revenge on every man you meet; that wants to fuck them and then cut their throats?'

'And you weren't changed by what we saw during our time together on the *Kaladine*?' she snapped. 'You went from being a drugged up, arrogant dickhead with an itchy trigger finger to an Echo pirate working for a man you were sent to apprehend. Still an arrogant dickhead of course.'

'I'm not a fucking pirate. I'm here because it was the only choice.'

'Why don't you believe me?' she cried, drawing attention from some of the personnel they passed in the corridor.

Kurcher came to a sudden halt and spun to face her. 'Because I saw a lot more than you out there and I didn't fucking change.'

She raised one thin eyebrow. 'Didn't you? The Davian Kurcher I met previously wouldn't have even considered helping Butler and her people, and he certainly wouldn't have worked for Hewn. I think everything you went through, including losing Frost and your ship, changed your priorities. Same for me. I don't have the same desires I once had.'

'Nearly having Bennet Ercko inside you would do that to any woman,' he quipped, intending to leave her with that thought.

Instead, she blocked his way and slapped him hard across the face. 'You didn't kill me when you could have on many occasions, and instead you kept me alive. I will always be thankful to you for that, but you'll always be a fucking bastard.'

He could've hit her back but managed to keep his hands at his side, despite clenching both fists. 'As I said, I haven't changed. Although it wasn't me who kept you alive.

Angard protected you and nobody was going to mess with that monster. D'Larro patched you up when you got shot and after Ercko drugged you. Jesus,

96

even Hewn has a fucking soft spot for you for some reason.'

Tara looked deep into his eyes for a silent moment, then pursed her lips. 'You may act like you don't care but I see the turmoil in you. Keep pushing everyone away, by all means. It just means nobody will mourn Davian Kurcher when you're dead.'

He watched her walk away, then closed his eyes to try blocking out all of the voices talking at once in his head. Frost, D'Larro, Santa Cruz, Angard, Ercko, Trin. When would they leave him the fuck alone?

'You quite finished with that slut?'

When he opened his eyes, Drake was standing further along the corridor, her arms crossed and an angry look on her face, just for a change.

'Why, you jealous?' he asked the pilot, grinning.

Drake let out a rare laugh, although it was more mocking than heartfelt. 'Of that? No. But if you're not in my quarters in the next five minutes, I'll cut off your cock and go give it to her as a souvenir.'

Sigma Royal Assault Ship Meta's Star, Barclay system

Grosnik couldn't get rid of the bad taste in his mouth.

He had been watching as the two outnumbered Libra Centauri ships tried their best to get away from his fleet and part of him felt sorry for the crew of the heavy transport. When they had arrived through the jump point, the *Icarus* was approaching the other side accompanied by the *Galloway*, an assault vessel proudly displaying the Libra emblem of the galaxy swirl and scales. No doubt the *Icarus* was transporting either components from the shipyards or even fuel containers, looking at the size of it. Seeing Grosnik's fleet suddenly emerge through the vortex of the jump point must have been a terrifying sight to behold.

In an attempt to shield the transport, the *Galloway* had bravely turned its starboard side to the Sigma ships and opened all weapon ports, trying to give the crew of the *Icarus* enough time to put distance between them.

Despite a brief conversation with the commander of the *Galloway*, Grosnik had failed to get them to surrender and avoid any conflict. He had explained that they weren't there to destroy them, although had pulled up short before boasting they had enough firepower to dismantle the shipyards of Barclay.

The bad taste in his mouth was due to two reasons. First, the *Galloway* had fired a warning shot that passed dangerously close to the jump point. If the fusion beam had struck the Libra-owned structure that supported the wormhole, there could have been a catastrophic chain of explosions that cut the entire Barclay system off from the rest of the galaxy.

Secondly, the sheer bad luck that they had encountered the two ships annoyed him. Barclay had been a bold change of destination to his original plan. Reports had come back stating that the Libra fleet had been dispersed to other systems, with only a small defensive force left to protect their shipyards. Grosnik hadn't planned taking them anywhere near the powerful guardians Libra had. It was supposed to be a hit and run; an opportunity he couldn't pass up.

Now he couldn't afford for either of the two ships on his screen to get back amongst their fellow Librans. They would have already sent distress calls out of course but there was nothing he could do about that now.

No point delaying what had to be done. 'Order all ships in the front line to fire on the *Galloway*,' he barked at the tactical officer sitting to his right.

Four Sigma Royal assault ships, including the flagship, hit the *Galloway* as it tried to turn. Showing its side to them meant they had much more hull to aim at and the minimal distance was in their favour too. All but two of the bow-mounted fusion beams struck their target, sending pieces of green and white plating spinning into space. The Libra ship retaliated with everything it had available from its starboard ports, fusion beams scarring the hulls of two of Grosnik's fleet and a number of missiles exploding in small green bursts, stark against the red and black.

The *Meta's Star* had received one lick with a fusion beam, reported the tactical officer. The *Galloway*'s spread had been too wide and Grosnik wondered if the commander of the enemy ship had realised his error. Focus on one ship and there would be greater chance of inflicting heavy damage.

For a couple of seconds, he watched the cloud of tiny metal shards dancing between his ship and the *Galloway*. 'Again. Try to focus beams on the engines as she comes about.'

The second exchange was more brutal on the Libra vessel. Fusion beams tore apart one of the exhausts, killing the engine it was attached to. The *Galloway* began a turn the crew wouldn't have been expecting, but the smaller stabilising jets quickly steadied it.

The *Meta's Star* fired twice, the first beam gouging a tear through the outer plating and the second beam punching through the wrecked exhaust deep into the ship's interior. Through the hole, there was a brief flash of green and orange.

Grosnik was frustrated that the *Galloway* was still operational, even more so when it released a swarm of missiles from its rear ports that damaged his ships further. Feeling the shudder as two missiles detonated against the flagship's hull, the General grimaced.

'I don't want that ship in my view any more,' he said sharply. 'Hit her until she's dead.'

If the second wave was brutal, the third was devastating. Fusion beams cut the *Galloway* to pieces, carving great chunks of the ship off which promptly drifted away. Two missiles slammed into the Librans' shredded exhaust wound and the resulting explosion from the engines disintegrated the ship and her crew.

'Excellent.' Grosnik stepped alongside the tactical officer, who looked relieved. 'Now give the order for the *Icarus* to be stopped. I don't want her destroyed.'

It didn't take long for the fleet to catch up with the slow-moving transport. The weapons the *Icarus* had fitted were dangerous at close range, but there was no exchange of fire. The commander of the transport was much wiser than his dead counterpart, surrendering to ensure the survival of his crew.

Grosnik tied his comms in so he could speak to his high-ranking tech officers, who were spread across three ships. 'This is a great opportunity,' he began. 'I want pursuit mechs only to board the *Icarus*, take the crew prisoner and check the cargo holds. This is a good test of ship-to-ship use for you. Make sure you connect visual feeds to the *Meta's Star* so I can watch.'

With the humanoid mechs loaded onto their unique ships, built solely for the purpose of transporting them, Grosnik watched the main screen eagerly, settling into his command chair. He saw the smaller transports approach the *Icarus* and dock at airlocks on multiple decks. The Sigma assault ships were surrounding the Libra vessel, poised in case they decided to go back on their word, which one would have expected from the untrustworthy corporation.

The screen changed so that the usual view was only a small square in the top corner. The rest was split into various views fed directly from the mech visual sensors and linked through to the flagship by the user apps. It was a nice upgrade The Luminary had sorted for them.

Grosnik leaned forward, engrossed in what he was seeing. He watched as the Libra uniforms were marched at gunpoint off their ship and tried to take in all of the different views on offer. As some mechs swept the transport for the rest of the crew, others went down to the expansive cargo holds. As he expected, he saw huge fuel containers that seemed to now be empty. They were probably shipping them to be refilled. Another cargo hold contained what looked like broken parts from engines and a number of internal systems.

'Refuse transport perhaps?' Grosnik asked the room.

'Possibly, sir,' answered his navigation officer. 'A lot to get rid of from the shipyards.'

He noticed a sudden blackout from three of the feeds and started tapping his fingers on the arms of his chair. *This* was the other reason he wanted to send the mechs on board the *Icarus*. Each mission had blackout glitches and he was starting to see a pattern.

He patched into the tech officer comms again. 'I need reasons for these malfunctions I'm seeing.'

'Wish we knew, sir,' came back one of his lieutenants. 'If it were the same mechs experiencing it each time, we'd know it was a fault in specific models.'

'I'm going to go out on a limb here and presume all three mechs who've blanked were heading into the same hold?'

The same officer replied. 'Yes, sir.'

This was no coincidence. 'Are your apps down completely?'

'Some data is showing but we have no control.'

Grosnik saw that the bridge crew of the transport had been removed. 'Send more mechs down to the hold where they went offline. Once we've got to the bottom of this, have the *Icarus* course laid in to follow us back through the jump point.'

'Yes, sir. Where are we heading?'

'Back to Kember to regroup.'

He watched intently as the other mechs approached the last location of the blacked out three. Unsurprisingly, said three suddenly came back online and Grosnik studied the images in front of him. He could see a stack of ship tech stored in one corner of the cargo hold and, on closer examination, realised it was a collection of older model systems that would've once been active on command decks like his. Navigation equipment, tactical consoles and dismantled communications arrays could be seen, leading him to believe that the transport was taking away defunct or obsolete tech that had been replaced on Libran ships.

He didn't like the glitches they were encountering. Just one mech shutting down during an attack could be disastrous, and he added it to the growing list of items he needed to cover with The Luminary.

Giving the order to leave Barclay before reinforcements arrived, Grosnik left his officers to carry out the fleet movements and headed to the private office next door. As he sat behind the red and black polished desk, he cast a glance out of the window at the fallout from their short time in the system. The remnants of the *Galloway* were still twirling away into the darkness, illuminated by the occasional electrical spark or explosion.

He spotted a rather macabre sight and felt a pang of regret stab at his heart. The body of a woman dressed in the uniform of Libra Centauri slowly drifted past. She was a fair distance from the ship and yet close enough he could see her face lit up by the lights of the *Meta's Star*. Her eyes were wide open, frozen in a horrible stare. It was clear she had been caught in one of the explosions before being wrenched out into space, as half of her face was burnt and she had a piece of metal lodged through her abdomen. One of her legs had been snapped almost flat against her body.

Grosnik imagined the fear she must have felt in that moment and hoped that she hadn't suffered long. He'd seen thousands of dead bodies before but knew that woman would haunt his dreams for nights to come. He hadn't needed to go to Barclay; hadn't had to engage the *Galloway*. Libra would come down hard on them for this.

He turned from the window, closing the automatic shutters to block out the gruesome spectre, and activated his console. When he brought up the recent messages he had received, Grosnik grimaced at the latest. A personal threat from Ariana Tabb stating that Libra Centauri would eradicate all Sigma Royalists as soon as she could amass her fleet for war. The destruction of the *Galloway* and capture of the *Icarus* and her crew would only work to fuel the fury of the Libran bitch. Barclay was clearly an error in judgement on his part.

He scrolled down the messages, picking out another one from a powerful source. A joint communication from Karin Hayward and General Garrett of Taurus Galahad, reporting a high-level threat to all corporations in the form of an alien species. He read it again and found himself shaking his head. As ruses go, this was completely left-field but he had to hand it to Taurus for their originality and imagination. They would try anything to stop his attacks on Libra.

Further down, he found what he was looking for and opened a voice recording for transfer to Morton Hurst. 'This is General Dalin Grosnik. Hope that things are returning to normal now on Sullivan's Rest. My fleet is in the process of returning to Kember, where we will regroup and take stock of all tactical reports and data. As soon as we are finished there, I will order the mech army to Summit where we will help Fortitude as agreed. Grosnik out.'

He sat back and thought about what it meant to take his force to an Impramed world. While he was sure they could keep the loss of life to a minimum, he was aware it would mean another possible problem on their hands once the smallest corporation got wind of what he had done. Then again,

Impramed weren't exactly quick to declare war on anyone and would likely try to talk it out instead. Still, the sour taste in his mouth returned.

Grosnik sent the message and reached for his personal brandy stash.

Titan Station,
Sol system

Winter had feared he would never gain control of his own body again. From the moment he touched the familiar mark on the back of Ishlan's neck, he had been unable to move. He had heard everything and been able to do nothing, even after the attackers had been killed and he had been moved to guarded quarters somewhere else on the station. He remembered Hayward, Garrett and Akeman peering down at him, wondering whether he would wake up any time soon or if he would wake at all.

In the two days that had passed since the attack on Titan Station, Winter had lived through centuries of memories, none of them human. It was only now that the numbness enveloping his body was starting to subside. Even just being able to move his eyes was a relief.

He recalled the moment Ishlan had walked into the meeting room; how she had glowed with a different aura to the rest of the people present. Winter saw just what Neri Ishlan had become at that moment. The body may have once belonged to the Taurus officer but her internal organs glistened with the ever-moving silver strands and occasional flashes of blue light. The tech had penetrated her systems completely, connecting with her heart, her optic nerves and even her brain, where it learnt Ishlan's life story.

She had recognised something unusual in him too of course, leading to the attack from her tainted companions. The plan had been to talk to begin with. There had been hope of a peaceful outcome, as there always had been in the centuries before.

It was easy for Winter to recall his own memories at the same time as the ancient ones he now possessed. In fact, his personal memories were now clearer than ever before. He could recall the faces of every revenant he killed back on Earth and every person he murdered for the greater good of Taurus Galahad. He could also feel the knife slide into his skin and smell Santa Cruz's breath every time he thought about that moment.

He understood now what happened to him in that meeting. When he touched that particular point on Ishlan, the technology in her body had linked with the hybrid tech in his. He might as well use that term when he referred to himself, as that's what the research team on Minerva had turned him into; a hybrid. He had no control over the link but felt an odd curiosity from the more advanced tech as it sought to discover what he was.

Winter found he could move his fingers and flexed them as he started to recall the alien memories. He saw Ishlan on board the *Bulwyn*, surrounded by the other six Taurus crew sent back to Sol, and the creatures skulking behind them. He saw the crew of the Taurus ship that intercepted the *Bulwyn* being assimilated by the creatures and could feel their fear as they were dragged before the writhing tendrils. As soon as the alien tech was injected directly into the spinal column and spread both up into the brain and down to the rest of the body, there was no more fear. It worked fast. There was no real suffering.

His mind continued to remember further back, as Ishlan boarded the *Bulwyn* at a Sapphire Nova station in the Valen system. Once alive with the sound of conversations and daily work, the concourse of the station was instead silent as both the assimilated personnel and a number of the tech-injecting creatures, or *infusers*, moved around without a word. Why would they need to when they were all part of the same mind?

Further back still, his head was filled with images of assimilation as Sapphire Nova took the infusers from Straunia and the technology pervaded ships, stations and colonies. Every man, woman and child became one with it, seeking out others to join them. Screams of the terrified made way for serene calm as they transitioned quickly and efficiently.

He saw Tomas Klein and Kam Bavelli standing mouths agape as the *Harbinger* was swarmed by infusers that had managed to leave the surface of Straunia finally. He watched as the two highest-ranking officers in Sapphire Nova succumbed to the same fate as so many others.

On Straunia, he saw the recommencement of the war between infusers and their only remaining unaltered kin. Those who had woken from their slumber in the *Grail* had significant advantage this time in the sheer number of bodies they had to protect them, not to mention two mechs shimmering inside with the same silver strands. Those who had first attacked Minerva before coming to once more deal with the infused found themselves outnumbered and overwhelmed. Most were slaughtered, some were brought into the fold to join the One Mind.

Winter could feel his arms and neck muscles relaxing now, his breathing returning to some semblance of normality.

Still on Straunia, he witnessed the revival of the dead. Colonists who perished when the *Grail* poisoned the very air they breathed were injected with enough tech to stand together as husks that could protect and work where need be. Necessary abominations to ensure the survival of the One Mind.

Then came the reawakening. Winter was back on the *Grail* just after it fell, the sheer jolt to the power cells causing all of the pods to open and the sleeping infusers within to stir. The One Mind re-established its link quickly and picked up where it left off centuries before, reaching out to the devices left scattered across the galaxy in a bid to draw enough power.

Darkness swamped Winter's thoughts as he pushed back further through time. He heard himself breathing loudly and managed to sit up, looking around the small quarters they had taken him to. The room was dark and the single small window gave him a view of nothing but twinkling distant stars. Outside the door, he could hear muffled talking and the glow of two warm bodies standing watch the other side of the wall began to take shape.

As he managed to swing his legs from the bed, he found it bizarre that, despite now knowing so much more than he did two days ago, he had no idea where Hayward was or if she was even still on Titan Station. There was a great deal he needed to explain to her, although it might be information overload for a typical human brain.

The darkness that clouded his memories suddenly gave way to distinct and yet totally alien images. He saw the sealing of the infusers within the *Grail* centuries ago and felt the overwhelming feeling of being helpless to stop what was happening before being forced into the long, cold sleep.

He witnessed the devastation of the war that the unmodified ones brought upon the infusers in their desperate attempt to destroy the One Mind. He saw the surfaces of entire worlds razed to eradicate the slightest sign they were once inhabited and so many bodies strewn across the galaxy. He watched as the antecedents died out; an entire race gone.

When he thought back even further, nearing the moment of the original awakening of the One Mind, he saw the antecedent race as a whole; a once-impressive galaxy-spanning civilisation. They were a species unfathomably more technically advanced than the human race was now, developing technologies which would improve their quality of life and secure their survival for centuries to come. They built a staggeringly large fleet of ships to explore

106

the galaxy and beyond, they created devices to power entire worlds and they tamed the wild and unstable wormholes found throughout the systems, bringing about their era of widespread colonisation. They also built structures to protect their way of life; gigantic weapons capable of wiping life from planets should the need ever arise.

Winter didn't know why he referred to this civilisation as antecedents. It was a word that seemed apt and was burnt into his mind for some reason unknown to him. Had he heard someone saying it before?

He marvelled at the sheer arrogance of them however, believing themselves to be the dominant power in the universe. They never expected a chance discovery in what the humans now called the Coldrig sector would lead to their utter annihilation.

The significantly less advanced species was found on a desolate planet, their homes built underground to protect themselves from the often violent weather that would scar the surface. They were numerous and yet devoid of purpose in the eyes of the antecedents, who saw an opportunity to harness their raw strength and stamina, using them as workers to build their new cities.

After a series of incidents that showed the Coldrig species to be unhappy in their new roles chosen for them, the antecedents created a unique piece of tech that could be infused into each of their new worker race. To ensure loyalty, this technology was then linked to a controlling system only accessible to the antecedent users; a single hive mind that would pass commands to all at the same time. However, in their bid to rely on technology to enslave the Coldrig race, the antecedents had not considered how the hive mind might evolve when linked with something other than their own intelligence.

The survival instinct of the Coldrig species was so strong, having lived for so long on such a violent world, that the technology took on the same trait and began to make modifications without the consent of the antecedents. It adapted the Coldrigs from the inside, giving them the ability to infuse others through their own appendages and so strengthen them with the same tech. Only a matter of years later though, the technology itself took over with its own desire to survive, grow and evolve, changed by its exposure to the Coldrig intelligence.

And so the One Mind was born, using the infused Coldrigs to assimilate the antecedents, who found their own technology turning against them. The self-proclaimed master race became nothing more than slaves themselves and were sent out into deep space to find more living creatures to join them. However, the One Mind failed to understand the need for sustenance and many antecedents died out in the void. When it had the infusers start reanimating the corpses, that was when the remaining unmodified Coldrigs came out of hiding, their intent to destroy everything the One Mind had touched.

Winter could even feel the sorrow of the Coldrigs as they killed their own and used the untainted antecedent technology to cleanse worlds, removing any trace of the One Mind's presence. After the war and the imprisonment of the last remaining infusers in the *Grail*, they thought they had done enough. Using the jump point technology to send the vast structure outside the galaxy, the Coldrigs took one antecedent ship and went home, falling into a hibernation of sorts. They were awoken centuries later by the alarm systems on the ship indicating that the *Grail* had powered up. Davian Kurcher had unwittingly woken the remnants of a sleeping race who faced persecution long before the human race appeared.

Winter closed his eyes and his journey back through time ended abruptly. So it wasn't the actual aliens themselves that posed the threat. It was the technology; the One Mind. The biggest question at the forefront of his own mind was how it had survived after the original location built by the antecedents had been destroyed. Somehow, the source of the seemingly sentient tech could move around. Strangely, he hadn't seen any clue as to the location of it now. Did it even have a base of operations so to speak?

His lips were dry and he spotted the pitcher of water nearby. He rose shakily from the bed and paced across the room, wondering whether he was now a part of the One Mind himself but with independence thanks to his hybrid state. He came to the conclusion he wasn't, and that it had been a *hack* of sorts with Ishlan that shared the memories of the ancient technology. A lasting glimpse into the past. The one thing he was certain of that troubled him was the fact the One Mind had likely also seen him and studied what he was. It knew him, like he knew it.

Winter didn't bother pouring the water into a glass and swigged from the pitcher. It felt like it was burning as he swallowed the cool liquid. Turning to face the window, he knew that he had to meet with Hayward and Garrett again urgently, not to mention the rest of Taurus' new alliance. Somehow, he had to explain what they were facing. It was much more complicated than originally

108

thought.

His eyes focused on one bright star as he returned to the memories. Somewhere out there, the hive mind had returned to its mission of assimilating any living creatures it could, and to survive at any cost.

Echo flagship Glaive, Miller system

Kurcher lay staring up at the ceiling, glad to be rid of the bleak thoughts that had been bothering him, even if it was only temporary. At that particular moment in time, he felt a rare contentment and he needed to hang on to it as long as he could.

When he felt Drake slide out of the bed, he turned his head to watch her pace across the room. Ever since she told him the truth about Harz, the knife tattoo emblazoned down her back made sense. He wondered whether it was supposed to depict the same one she used to kill Forge.

Drake had preferred to take him to her quarters on the *Glaive* this time instead of going back to the *Falcata*. She liked to mix it up and he didn't really care.

'Vance told me something,' she said, grabbing two beers from her fridge. 'In secrecy of course.'

Kurcher grinned as she turned. It was the first time she had picked up a bottle for him too.

'Oh?' was all he uttered as he focused on the beast tattooed across her breast.

'Apparently Hewn told him Taurus want you back.'

The mere thought of that made him laugh. 'I bet they do.'

'Hewn didn't want you to know in case you decided to leave.'

'So he told fucking Fischer, who would tell you anything if it meant you liked him just a bit more.'

As she approached the bed, he held his hand out to take a beer. 'They're both for me, dickhead,' she scowled. 'I need two to wash the taste out of my mouth.'

Kurcher watched as she placed the bottles next to the bed and lit a cigarette. 'So you worried I'll go back to Taurus too?'

She gave him her typical look when he said something she deemed moronic. 'Please. You do what you want but you seem better suited to life outside of corp employment.'

'I don't need to be employed by anyone.'

'Sitting on some fortune, are you?'

'I wouldn't say a fortune.'

Careful, warned D'Larro. *You still don't really know whether you can trust her or not.*

She's revealed her biggest secret to you, countered Frost. *Maybe she needs something back from you.*

Drake blew a cloud of sweet smoke into the air as she reclined back on the bed. 'You've never exactly been a corp man anyway. They were probably relieved to be fucking shot of you.'

He stole one of the beers, noticing she didn't complain. 'I made sure Santa Cruz paid me a good amount in advance. Put it aside so that Taurus couldn't trace it and snatch it back. It'd see me good if I decided to disappear.'

'People like us only tend to disappear for one reason,' she muttered. 'Our past catches up with us.'

'I've pissed a lot of people off.' Kurcher chuckled, although he didn't find it as funny as he once did. 'There are more organisations out there now who want me dead rather than alive, and not all because of my time as an enlister.'

Drake shrugged. 'We make enemies easily.'

'Don't get me wrong. I loved being an enlister most of the time. Having the power to decide who lived and who died was intoxicating. Admittedly, I'd rather execute than enlist. Less talking shit.'

'I think I would've made a good assassin.' Her comment was softly spoken; a thought unwittingly vocalised.

'Without a doubt,' he agreed. 'The person you were chasing was simply a target and eliminating them led to being paid. It was uncomplicated work.'

'Even when chasing down someone like Rane?'

The question was unexpected. 'The one target I never executed or enlisted. I chased him across worlds and thought I had him on Kismet, only to be distracted by a Sigma Royal enlister and his fucking mech. If I had killed Rane then, so many lives would've been saved.'

'Not that you knew that. The guy is seriously fucked in the head. I can't believe Hewn let him go on his way.'

'Taurus sent me after Rane because his actions had led to the deaths of their own people,' continued Kurcher, finding it easier to say more to her when she wasn't telling him to fuck off. 'But he'd killed so many from Nova. His parents were murdered by Nova officers and blamed for a rig disaster on Rikur. He dedicated his life to making them pay in any way he could. He manipulated me and everyone else on the *Kaladine* so he could get onto the *Grail* and murder

111

an entire planet. How can you then justify *not* having executed him before?'

'Like I say, you didn't know.' Her tone was almost reassuring. 'Look, all the shit that happened back then really got into Broekow's head and made him into an alcoholic who got himself fucked up for life. If you dwell on it too, you'll go back to being a drug-addled prick.'

'Instead of just being a prick, right?'

'You said it.' Drake glanced at him through the increasing smog. 'You still hear those voices?'

Kurcher locked eyes with her, seeing genuine interest there for the first time. 'Yeah. It used to be the screams of the women and children on Cobb. The pleading of mothers to spare their sons or daughters. What I did there might've helped to end the supply wars but it also led me down a darker path than I had first wanted.

'Now, even though their cries have diminished somewhat, it's the other fuckers I hear.'

'Who?' It was a blunt question.

'Frost, Angard, Santa Cruz, D'Larro, Ercko and occasionally Trin Espina. I don't know why just them.'

Drake took a swig of beer and considered this for a moment. 'Probably because you feel responsible and because they were closer to you than anyone else.'

'I was only close to Frost, and Trin for a time.' He shook his head, despite agreeing with her. 'The rest were criminals. I don't feel sorry they died.'

'But they were in your charge when they did.'

'Are you a fucking psychiatrist now?' he bit, not intending to snap at her.

Drake gave a half-smile. 'You're like me. Damaged.'

His anger quickly subsided. 'How did you end up with Echo then? Was it Hewn who found you?'

For a moment, she stayed quiet, inhaling the sickly smoke deep into her lungs before expelling it in increasingly large rings. When she turned to look at him, she was biting at her bottom lip, which he noticed was now only showing the slightest hint of blue.

'All the shit with Harz happened in Callyn, on an old storage station the Bold had claimed a long time ago and were using as an ops base. After I killed Forge, I managed to get onto a ship heading for Sullivan's Rest, where I thought I could easily disappear. Couple of days there passed before some Fortitude twat tried it on with me, offering me a place to sleep and eat, but only if I sucked his dick.'

'I imagine he regretted that.'

Her eyes narrowed. 'If you don't want to know, by all means keep interrupting me.'

That was the Drake he knew; the one that fired his lust with her venomous tongue. He kept his mouth shut and waited for her to continue.

'I cut that merc so badly, I doubt he ever took a straight piss again. Then his friends started looking for me, so I managed to steal a gun to protect myself. I shot three Fortitude fuckers during my short stay on Sullivan's Rest.

An opportunity arose and I managed to stow away on a transport bound for the Echo Expanse. During the journey, I was discovered by a couple of men and I instinctively attacked them before they could do anything. One of them lost his kneecap and the other an eye.

I was caught and it wasn't long after that I met Hewn. I remember him glaring at me through the bars of that shitty little cell they threw me in and saying that I looked like some feral animal. I don't know why he didn't just throw me out an airlock. Instead, I found myself slowly becoming a part of his organisation, showing aptitude as a pilot. He trained me to fly himself.

Trouble was, I couldn't just leave my past behind. I caused a lot of fucking problems. Fighting, drinking, getting so high I'd fuck some guy then break his nose for touching me. Guess that's why he offloaded me as your pilot. Put the damaged fucks together and maybe they'll kill each other.'

Kurcher waited, making sure he wasn't interrupting her. This time, she gulped down her beer though, closing her eyes.

'Hewn is much more forgiving than most pirates I know,' he said finally. 'Some think he's seeing the potential in people. I think he just sees the benefits to his organisation. I know I'm only here because he sees me as an excellent bargaining chip.'

She kept her eyes shut. 'Maybe he'll sell you back to Taurus then.'

'Maybe.' He watched a bead of water from her bottle drip onto her chest and weave its way between her breasts. 'Okay, so here's a good question. I'm assuming your real name isn't Shannon Drake so why choose that?'

She opened one eye. 'My old name means nothing now so don't ask what it is.'

'I'm not.'

'Because Shannon Drake sounds normal,' she admitted. 'I'd heard a mother on Sullivan's Rest shouting her daughter. Shannon sounded alright. As for Drake, who the fuck knows. Just felt right. You never think of changing your name?'

'Yeah, a few times. I figured that once your name gets thrown around the galaxy a few times though, people start to take notice. I wanted crims to be afraid of my name.'

'That's cause you've got a big fucking ego.'

He laughed and threw his empty bottle to the floor before edging closer to her. 'Come on. Would a crim be afraid of an enlister hunting for them called *Vance Fischer*?'

At this, she gave a wicked grin, exposing the teeth he so often only saw when she snarled. 'You really don't like him, do you?'

'The guy's a moron. How he got to be Hewn's second is beyond me. From what I've seen, he hasn't got the balls or the ruthless streak needed for the job.'

'He just tries too hard,' she remarked. 'But I've seen Fischer take people down and he isn't a fucking pushover. He's had Hewn's back for as long as I can remember and he's a smart bastard too. Much more intelligent than you.'

'Is that so?' Kurcher placed a hand on her leg. 'Does he have a bigger dick too?'

Drake flicked the fringe from her eye. 'Most men do.'

An hour later, Kurcher was spent again and ready to finally get some sleep. Drake's post-sex ritual continued, lighting up and drinking. This time, her skin had a radiant sheen he noticed, which seemed to make her tattoos stand out more than usual. At that moment, she resembled a Shannon Drake instead of some Bold outcast.

As he started drifting into the warmth of sleep, Kurcher was glad to put aside the worries that had been gnawing away at him, if only just for a few hours. Jericho's Bold, The Kindred, The Luminary, this new alien threat reported by Taurus Galahad. He couldn't have given a fuck about any of them. Drake it seemed had the power to soothe a troubled mind.

He awoke with a jolt as someone hammered on the door.

'Fuck off,' shouted Drake.

'Jaffren wants to see us,' came Fischer's voice from the corridor outside.

She sighed. 'Why me? I'm just a fucking pilot.'

'Because he has a job for you and Kurcher.' Fischer's voice was filled with contempt at even having to say his name. 'Both of you get dressed and meet us in Jaffren's quarters.'

Kurcher gave Drake a wry smile before shouting back. 'Maybe we'll just head there naked and dripping with sweat.'

Fischer didn't dignify that with a response and they listened as his footsteps faded away. Drake headed for the shower without another word, leaving Kurcher lying in bed wondering when he might actually get to rest properly. She had to wake him again when she returned.

By the time they reached Hewn's room, enough time had passed for Fischer to be silently seething, which pleased Kurcher greatly. Hewn himself had that concerned look plastered across his heavily-bearded face again.

'Thought you were still down on Seko,' Kurcher said as they entered.

'Had to cut it short.' Hewn was flexing his mechanical hand. 'Yet another problem has come up that we need to fucking deal with.'

'Go on then. What is it this time?'

Fischer snorted. 'I'm really not sure we need him for this, Jaffren.'

'I am,' Hewn muttered to his second before addressing Kurcher. 'Did you ever have much to do with the Knights Templar?'

Kurcher shook his head. 'A couple of run-ins in the past but nothing major. I know a lot about them but last I heard Taurus had ousted them from Lincoln and they'd upped sticks elsewhere.'

'I heard they were in Callyn now,' added Drake.

'We received a report that they were sniffing around Tempest,' Hewn told them. 'The Libra guardian there apparently saw Templar ships near to the planet but they left soon after.'

'Okay.' Kurcher shrugged. 'And?'

'They hit one of our facilities on the planet Curos, in the Atalanta system. It's a storage compound guarded by Libra Centauri. Supposed to be hidden, like Tempest's site.'

Fischer chipped in with more information. 'They ransacked the whole place. Took everything we had stored there. That's a massive chunk of revenue lost overnight thanks to those bastards.'

'The Templars don't usually resort to stealing goods,' pointed out Kurcher.

115

'Why would they now?'

'They've lost money from being moved out of Lincoln,' Hewn replied, grabbing a half-empty bottle. 'Their reputation took a big hit when Taurus found out they were working alongside Nova on some underhand ventures. Then they saw an opportunity and have stepped out of the shadows to rob us, thinking we're caught up with everything else going on.'

'Which we are.' Kurcher glanced at Drake, who shrugged. 'How did they manage it?'

'Biomechs,' said Fischer sharply. 'We found out they stole biomechs from some dodgy facility on Shard and used them to smash their way into the site on Curos. We know that because Libra sent us images of two dead abominations they gunned down eventually, after the biomechs had torn some of the guards apart. Apparently they didn't go down easy.'

Kurcher couldn't help but think of Angard and the unnatural strength the brute possessed thanks to the experiments on him during his time on Shard. Several Angards would be a potent force to have at your control.

If you could control them, Angard noted.

They should have all been put down long ago, said Santa Cruz.

'Okay, so what are you thinking?' Kurcher asked Hewn.

The tired-looking pirate sighed and shook his head. 'Rane and Broekow are tracking Harz, but we have to remain vigilant those Bold fuckers don't get into the Expanse again. We're looking out for any news of The Kindred and we still need to find out more about The Luminary too. Despite all these issues, I can't let the Templars think they can waltz in and take our goods without retaliation.'

'So just send ships to Temple and hammer the shit out of them,' suggested Drake. 'Or destroy it if need be.'

'All this is down to one man.' Hewn finished his beer and wiped his beard. 'Flynn. I want him dead, to send a message to them. We don't need another war on our hands. Kill their leader and hopefully put them back in their box.'

Kurcher stretched and yawned. 'Fine. We'll look into it, find out where he is and take care of him. Now can I go back to bed?'

'It'd be useful to know where they took the drug stocks they stole,' Fischer mentioned.

'Right. Anything else?'

Hewn stepped closer to them. 'We've got some intel that may help you track

116

Flynn down. This is a job for just the two of you though. I can't afford anyone else to help.'

'Good.' Kurcher headed for the door. 'Just the way I like it.'

Marden's End,
Callyn system

There weren't many locations Rane had visited that intimidated him and yet, as he and Broekow walked the grimy halls of Marden's End, he found himself growing increasingly wary.

After leaving the relative safety of the *Glaive*, they had decided to head for Callyn as Harz usually returned to the wild system in between raids. The Bold station, unoriginally named Jericho, was the obvious destination, and yet it was one of the most dangerous places in the galaxy. Rane's false identity as a drug runner allowed him access to the station briefly, where he quickly discovered Harz had moved on to Marden's End, out on the edge of the system.

Marden's End was a smaller station that seemed to be in a constant state of disrepair, with gravitational stabilisers that left one feeling like they were occasionally bouncing and pylons that looked like they would break whenever a ship docked. It had once belonged to Schaeffer's Nine, until the Bold decided they wanted to add it to their dismal collection. Now it was used by the pirates to store stolen goods, including ships.

Rane pulled the hood tighter around his face as they passed a drunken mob of Bold who were sitting in one of the wide hallways. The stink of urine stung his nostrils and he had to hold his breath until they reached the next junction.

Behind Rane, Broekow was wearing his mask once more, hiding all features except his eyes, which were still lowered to avoid any chance of being recognised. His rifle was slung over one shoulder as a warning to any Bold feeling like picking a fight. On Marden's End, nobody cared if someone got shot, especially if that someone wasn't in the Bold anyway.

'This could take a while,' he mumbled just loud enough for Rane to hear. 'Harz could be anywhere.'

Rane looked left and right at the junction. 'His ship is still here, which means most of his crew will likely be on the station engaging in some sordid act or another. We just need one of them to pick up the trail.'

'Like I said before, I don't know if I'll remember their faces. They're all bearded, unwashed and tattooed.'

Rane gave him a reassuring look. 'It's amazing what the mind has the capacity to recall. Besides, if you'd rather we take a different approach, we could get onto his ship and rig it to blow once they leave the station.'

'No.' Broekow looked up at him with determined eyes. 'He doesn't deserve a quick death.'

Rane decided to head right, deeper into Marden's End. As they walked, he occasionally glanced back at his travelling companion to make sure he was keeping up. Broekow's limping gait looked clumsy at best and there was no chance of him running if they needed to pick up the pace. To the Bold, he would look like easy prey.

At distance, Broekow's aim was off. His sniper days were well and truly behind him, although the shot that took Harz through the hand had the desired effect, lucky as it may have been. Up close however, Broekow could still hit a target relatively easily and he had regained some speed on the draw.

Rane often pondered just whether saving Broekow from Devlin had been a worthwhile exercise. The man who he had first met that fateful day on Rikur was almost completely gone and he existed now simply to hunt down Harz and kill the pirate. Broekow said it was to stop the attacks on Echo. Rane knew it was to ensure Harz got to feel what it was like to be tortured and afraid, never knowing when the next beating would occur.

Rane noticed eyes watching them as they passed a makeshift bar set up near the entrance to one of the larger concourses on the station. He touched the hilt of his sword lightly, just to check it wasn't in full view, and kept his own eyes forward so as not to look at anyone the wrong way, which was easy to do with the Bold.

He found himself smiling as he so often did when he felt the coolness of the sword. It always reminded him of those whose blood the blade had tasted; the look of confusion on their faces at someone wielding such a weapon in this day and age. He didn't like guns, plain and simple. They were messy and unreliable. The sword felt like an extension of his arm, slicing cleanly and effectively. He had once collected old blades from Earth's past, non-lethal in their bluntness but decorative and a piece of human history. He would often imagine who and how many had been impaled on them.

The concourse was bustling, as expected, and the smell that greeted them was close to rancid. Sweat, urine, faeces and the sickly sweet aroma of drugs mixed together to form an awful scent that stung the eyes and burnt the nostrils. The occasional smell of meat cooking drifted through too, which didn't help.

The sheer number of tattooed faces was unexpected however. It seemed that most of Jericho's Bold had crammed themselves into Marden's End and it showed Rane just how many of the pirates were actually out there now. He would say they easily outnumbered Echo three or four to one.

They passed a number of stalls selling odd collections of items that were no doubt stolen. Rane spotted one rotund pirate selling an Impramed pistol, not even bothering to hide the corporation emblem. It also seemed as though every third stall was a bar. Pirates were dangerous, but drunk pirates were unpredictable and ready to pull their guns way too quickly.

When Rane looked at Broekow again, he saw the rifleman struggling to keep his nerves hidden as they moved deep into the heart of Jericho's Bold.

'And what the fuck are you peddling?'

Rane came to a sudden halt as a tall, bald pirate stepped into his path and looked him over. The smell of alcohol on the man was almost overpowering and yet there was no loss of balance. This one was used to the drink.

'Nothing of concern to you,' Rane replied, his voice clear and measured. 'I've got business elsewhere.'

The pirate regarded him with one good eye, the other opaque and scarred. 'A weakling runt like you better have a good reason for being here. This is *our* station.'

Rane looked up at him from beneath the hood and smiled. 'I didn't realise you were in charge here.'

'Fucking big mouth too. I'll ask you one more time. What are you selling?'

'You didn't ask me that last time. You asked what I'm peddling. Very different words.'

The pirate snorted loudly and a glob of glistening mucus flew from his nose to land at Rane's feet. 'Keep talking, little man, and I'll fucking gut you.'

'If I can't keep talking, how can I answer your question?

The drunk brute grimaced and looked at Broekow, this time swaying slightly. 'What about you?'

Rane let out an exasperated sigh. 'Leave him be. He's my bodyguard and I'm here with a casement of modified calmers that have already been claimed by Harz.'

At the mention of that name, the pirate tried to focus back on Rane but failed. Then he let out a gurgling laugh. 'I doubt that *he's* your bodyguard. He's skinnier than you. I also doubt you're here to sell to Harz.'

'Why's that?'

'Because Harz only comes here himself when someone owes him money, dipshit.'

Rane moved to walk past the pirate. 'You can explain to him why you delayed us then.'

He knew the drunkard would make a move and was ready for it. When the man's hand reached out and grabbed for his arm, Rane caught it and twisted the wrist. Without hesitating, he then knocked the pirate's legs out from beneath him and drove his face down hard onto the metal grating floor.

Not bothering to look back, Rane signalled to Broekow and they resumed their trek through the concourse.

'Sometimes the direct approach is best with these people,' he said to the quiet rifleman.

Instead of heading straight into the throng of stinking bodies occupying the centre of the hub chamber, they walked near to the wall on the right, avoiding those Bold on the outskirts who looked like they were only there to pick off anyone wandering too close. As they neared one of the hallways that led away from the concourse, Broekow moved up alongside Rane and tapped his arm.

'There, just leaving the concourse with two women.'

Rane cast the quickest of looks towards the exit, weighing up the pirates who were heading away from them. The man was quite young, his beard braided. Well-built, he had a tattoo that looked like a snake coiling its tail around his neck. The women were wild-looking, with painted lips and eyelids, their hair tied back like whips that drooped down their spines. All three were armed.

'Are you sure?' he asked.

Broekow gave a curt nod. 'Yeah, I remember him standing in the room twice when Harz was questioning me. Never said anything. Just watched.'

Nothing more was needed. They quickly fell in behind the trio and followed them away from the noise of the concourse. To Rane's relief, they entered a much quieter part of the station. Occasional grunts or groans of pleasure, and the odd cry of pain, echoed from behind closed doors.

In a dingy room kitted out with one large dirty bed and nothing else, the young pirate had barely begun removing his trousers when Rane pounced.

Having no locks on any of the doors made entry easier, although it meant Broekow had to stand watch in case they were expecting more friends to the party.

Fully aware of the Bold reluctance to surrender, even when faced with overwhelming odds, Rane was taking no chances. The hilt of his sword came down hard on the back of one woman's skull and, as the other looked up, he struck her square in the face with the flat of his blade. The braided pirate's arousal vanished in an instant as he found the point of Rane's sword inches from his eye.

'We need to find Harz,' Rane said, in a friendly tone. 'We hoped you'd be able to help us.'

The pirate's expression changed from surprise to anger. 'Fuck you.'

Rane glanced at Broekow, who had closed the door and was leaning against it. 'Why are Jericho's Bold so stubborn?'

'Just get on with it,' muttered the rifleman.

When he heard the voice behind him, the pirate turned his head and quickly recognized Broekow.

'We really don't want to be in here any longer than we have to.' Rane jabbed the blade lightly into the man's neck, drawing blood and getting his attention back. 'Tell us where to find Harz.'

When no reply was forthcoming, Rane drove the sword into the nerve cluster in his shoulder. The pirate gritted his teeth and grunted, but didn't cry out.

'I'm impressed,' Rane admitted. 'The pain produced from that wound is enough to make most men at least yelp. However, if I continue, your arm will really be of no further use to you.'

He was quick to notice the pirate trying to reach for his pistol, but the holster had slipped down his leg along with his trousers. Rane pressed his point home and applied more pressure. That produced a better response, although still not the one he wanted.

'Stop enjoying it so much and fucking hurry up,' came Broekow's impatient voice.

Rane pulled the blade out. 'Harz inflicted a lot of injuries on my friend here. They all hurt but I reckon gouging his tooth out, nerve and all, plus severing his fingers were most productive in getting what he wanted. Let's start with your fingers.'

The pirate tried to move but Rane's knee drove him back down onto the bed. The killer didn't even need to grab a hand and, with a flick of his wrist, sliced two fingers clean off. Blood pumped onto the unwashed bed sheets and again the pirate tried in vain to manoeuvre himself away from this madman he found himself at the mercy of.

'Shall I move on to the teeth?' Rane asked him, dangling the sword menacingly.

It took slightly longer than they wanted but eventually the young pirate started to talk. It was Rane's blade tip touching the underside of his eyeball that did it. They learned that Harz was at Marden's End to acquire new weaponry for his ship, to aid them in aerial combat when engaged with an enemy within a planet's atmosphere. Harz was also trying to upgrade various systems within the ship. As for his location, it seemed they only had to take a short walk back to the concourse and head to the opposite side.

Rane knew that he couldn't leave the pirate alive. The two women hadn't seen his face and could at least report back to Harz, sowing some seed of uncertainty in the bastard's mind. As soon as they had all they needed, he cut the man's throat and left the body face down on the bed.

With Broekow in tow, Rane headed back to the concourse, his blade once more clean and hidden beneath his coat. They came to a halt just before re-entering the crowded hub, trying to work out whether it would be best to push their way straight through or walk the perimeter.

Rane turned to the masked rifleman. 'When we find him, Sieren, we keep to the plan. I'll try to isolate Harz as best I can.'

'Not the best place to try taking out one of the Bold's most infamous figures,' Broekow said, his voice muffled. 'We risk bringing all the rest of them down on us.'

'I'll do my best to make sure that doesn't happen,' Rane assured him. 'Just don't hesitate when you get the shot.'

'I won't hesitate with this fucker.'

Rane could see the flames of vengeance flickering in Broekow's eyes. He didn't doubt the ex-sniper's resolve. It was his accuracy that was in question, which was why they had to get as close as they could to Harz. Rane was ready to let Broekow kill the pirate, wouldn't hesitate to do the deed himself, however, should the need arise.

They hadn't gone more than three paces into the concourse when a deafening boom jolted the very floor they stood on. The explosion was far to their right and part of the huge chamber quickly vanished in thick black smoke. People stopped to stare.

Another explosion went off more centrally and Rane saw bodies flung into the air. A third then a fourth sent a shockwave through the concourse that knocked some from their feet and there was a horrendous cracking noise followed by a screeching of metal. Rane spotted a heavy blast door sliding down to seal off one of the junctions opposite, which meant there had been a hull breach somewhere.

Marden's End was trembling as numerous explosions erupted in other areas of the station. Everyone in the concourse began heading for the exits and Rane knew their chance of getting to Harz was gone. At that moment, he would be surrounded by Bold and the odds of getting close to him, let alone spotting him, were slim.

'I suggest we get back to the ship,' he shouted to Broekow, who had his rifle in his maimed hands now.

They ran for the junction they originally arrived at the concourse by, dodging between the panicked crowd. A group of Bold charged past them, heading towards the carnage with weapons at the ready. Rane's assumptions were proved right as he heard one pirate yell that there were still Kindred on the station that needed gunning down.

As they reached the junction, they saw a woman standing off to the side several metres ahead, her back to them. She was calmly connecting a device to the wall, her long greasy hair hanging in front of her eyes like a lank curtain.

Rane couldn't believe that The Kindred had chosen to strike at the same time they were hunting down Harz. He also couldn't believe they were hitting Marden's End, although they would find it easier to get onto the station than somewhere like Carson. It seemed even the Bold weren't safe from the terrorists.

'Can you take her from here?' he asked Broekow. 'If she sets that off, it'll blow a hole in the station.'

Broekow was already aiming, sweat quickly forming on his brow. The rifle wasn't like his old weapon but it was still a formidable weapon in the right hands. He couldn't afford to take too much time weighing up the shot though. The bullet took the woman in the side just below the ribs, the impact lifting her off her feet and sending her crumpling onto the floor.

Rane raced across to the stricken bomber, ready to pull his sword to finish the job. When he saw her face though, dirty and unfazed by the injury, he realised the opportunity that lay before him.

'We need to take her with us,' he told Broekow as the rifleman arrived alongside him.

'Are you fucking mad?'

Rane lifted her with ease, quickly grabbing the rusty knife tucked in her belt so she couldn't skewer him. 'Hewn's going to want to meet her.'

Broekow glanced back at the clouds of smoke filling the concourse, then looked the unwashed woman up and down. 'What about Harz?'

'If he isn't dead already, we'll soon track him down again.' Rane noticed a couple of fleeing Bold give them a strange look. 'We need to leave before this place falls apart or opens up to the vacuum.'

The woman struggled to get free of Rane's grip as they made their way back towards the docking pylon where the *Basilisk* waited. He knew the bullet hadn't hit any major organ by the amount of blood seeping from the wound, so a quick patch-up job back at the ship would be in order before they squeezed her in with them. Broekow would have the pleasure of her close company during their journey back to the Expanse, if he could put up with the smell.

The unsettling thing was the lack of emotion from the terrorist; the blank look in her watery eyes and the way she showed no sign of pain or discomfort. Rane had no doubt she would have gone back to arming the bomb had he let her and she would gladly have given her life to the Kindred's cause, whatever that was. It was the first time he had seen one of them up close and would make sure he studied her further before they got back to the *Glaive*, to find out just who this terror cell were.

Summit,
Benedict system

Grosnik watched as the line of Impramed prisoners filed past, their eyes lowered to avoid meeting the gaze of the mechs accompanying them. Many of the white uniforms were covered in stains now after the events of the last few days, and Grosnik was pleased to see a distinct lack of blood. He had wanted casualties kept to a minimum and it seemed he had got his way, which was no mean feat when Fortitude were involved. Of course, he knew full well that Hurst and his mercs had probably killed a number of Impramed personnel during the initial uprising.

The General watched the prisoners being led away across the plaza then raised his eyes to the Tidewell City skyline. The tall buildings still gleamed in the evening glow of the resort, undisturbed by the fighting in the streets below. Tidewell now felt at peace again, which was more than could be said for Grosnik's mind.

Fortitude had been hiding people away underground in the city for years, working behind the scenes to begin unravelling Impramed's hold on Summit from the inside. By the time Grosnik's mech army arrived on the surface, the merc organisation had already emerged with weapons hot, catching Impramed completely off guard. Some city guards had tried to fight back with their meagre weapons; guns that produced a simple charge of electricity designed to stun an opponent. A few mercs had taken a jolt and been incapacitated, but any Impramed guards who used their weapons were shot. Some died quickly, others had bled out. A handful survived with a bullet lodged in their leg or arm.

Grosnik didn't like the heavy-handed approach but couldn't expect anything more from Fortitude. No matter how smart they dressed in their uniforms, they were still thugs.

The cool night air brushed his face and he breathed it in, enjoying the pure unfiltered taste. He had been choking down processed air on his ship for too long.

Finding himself alone for the first time in a while, he started down the steps before him, intending to head deeper into Tidewell. He needed to understand just why Fortitude wanted Summit; why Hurst longed to control the Benedict system. Sure, the planet was an oasis in a harsh galaxy and he could see why it was so popular as a place to take leave. Impramed had run it with their usual naivety, more interested in ensuring it was popular than making money. Perhaps that was it. Hurst could see the money in Summit.

As he walked the quiet streets, aware that most of the inhabitants of Tidewell were probably watching him from their windows as they hid from any conflict, he spotted the occasional Fortitude banner hanging from buildings or street lights. The clenched fist of a ruthless mercenary operation. That bitter taste was returning to his mouth.

'Sir.'

His peaceful walk rudely interrupted, Grosnik turned to face the Sigma officer jogging up behind him. 'What is it, lieutenant?'

The officer saluted as he approached. 'An Impramed official is requesting to speak with you. He says he is one of the ruling council of Tidewell, recently appointed by Filipe Cardozo.'

'What does he want?'

'To discuss terms, sir.'

Grosnik frowned. 'We already gave them the terms. Surrender and you won't be harmed. What more is there to discuss?'

The officer looked uncomfortable. 'He said he would rather speak with the man in charge of Sigma forces than the murderer running Fortitude.'

Of course he would, Grosnik thought. Hurst was more liable to shoot someone who complained. His terms could be found in the barrel of a gun.

Reluctantly, the General headed to the makeshift prison near to the landing pads. It had been a security post with only four cells. Now every room was a cell without bars, guarded by pursuit mechs. He had the lieutenant bring the councillor to a private room. The last thing he wanted was the conversation to take place in front of the mechs. He never knew who exactly was listening.

'General Grosnik,' greeted the Impramed official. 'I'm Clay De Bachmann, head spokesman for Tidewell's council.'

'You already know who I am?'

De Bachmann nodded eagerly. 'I do, sir, yes. I make it my job to know the faces of all high-ranking officers in the corporations, just in case any VIP treatment is required here.'

Grosnik indicated for the man to take a seat at the single table in the centre of the room. He studied the councillor for a moment, recognising the pomp and false charm of a politician. He remained standing.

'What can I do for you then?' he asked finally.

'General, the events of the last few days have shocked us all,' began De Bachmann. 'I am confused as to why Sigma Royal have joined forces with a mercenary outfit like Fortitude and attacked an Impramed world. Director Cardozo will wonder the same, I'm sure.'

'Well I will be speaking with Director Cardozo soon, *I'm* sure. The reasons behind this are not going to be shared with you, however rest assured that I will not allow Fortitude to harm any more Impramed personnel. I aim to take you all off Summit with my fleet when we leave and discuss release terms with your board.'

De Bachmann smiled, although his eyes betrayed his true emotions. 'Thank you for that. I find myself wondering just what Fortitude have to gain by these actions. Unless it's the money.'

Grosnik crossed his arms. 'Sigma isn't here for money. We're here to bring order to Tidewell and to make sure your people are not mistreated.'

'You may not be, General, but I'm sure Fortitude have committed this crime for their own financial gain. Morton Hurst has visited Tidewell on numerous occasions recently and has been enquiring about purchasing certain establishments.'

'That's nothing to do with me, councillor.' Grosnik glowered at him, finding the official was able to meet his gaze with ease. 'All I can say is that Summit has become a world that criminals flock to now, seeing how easy it is to get through your security checks. They thrive here and I feel Fortitude will quickly deal with the unwanteds they find. This was Hurst's decision and I didn't want him executing you and your fellow councillors, so you should consider yourself lucky in that respect.'

'I understand, sir,' nodded De Bachmann vigorously. 'However this is still an act of war, is it not?'

Grosnik offered him a knowing smile. 'And Impramed are in a position to go to war? I think not. There are many changes afoot across the galaxy and your corporation are unfortunately the weakest when it comes to military personnel. I will advise Director Cardozo to keep Impramed out of the way during this time of change and perhaps there will be room for a new alliance in the future between Sigma and yourselves.'

De Bachmann looked understandably pensive. 'I would like to formally request you move all Impramed prisoners to your ships, general. We don't feel safe with Fortitude mercs roaming the streets looking for a fight.'

'Our mechs will protect you,' Grosnik told him. 'You will be moved to the ships just before we leave, as originally planned. However, I am due to meet with Hurst once all resorts on Summit have been taken so will discuss the conduct of he and his men at that time.'

'Many of us have families here, sir,' said the official. 'Please ensure their safety too.'

'You have my word nobody else will be hurt.'

'Thank you, General.'

Grosnik didn't want to waste any more of his time speaking with the man. He could give his word all he wanted but Hurst was probably ordering the execution of more Impramed guards right at that moment.

Seeing that De Bachmann was returned to his cell, Grosnik headed back out into the city and immediately saw a group of Fortitude men making their way past the security post. They were laughing and boasting about how quickly they had taken Tidewell from the *Impramed morons*. Grosnik grimaced when he heard one merc say he was going to find a whore to terrify.

As he walked the streets of Tidewell once again, he saw mechs and their tech officers on patrol or taking more prisoners away. How easy it would be to send a unit of the war machines to dispose of Morton Hurst completely. The Fortitude leader's sheer hunger for power made him one of the most dangerous men Grosnik had ever met and getting rid of the arrogant prick would remove a very deep thorn in many a side.

He found his way to the promenade, looking out over the dark ocean. He quickly came to the conclusion he needed Hurst to live a while longer. There was still more to get from him, and from The Luminary, who was often on his mind too.

Just grin and bear it a while longer, he thought to himself. Then the alliance with these criminals can come to an abrupt – yet satisfying – end.

Earth,
Sol system

Despite the debate going on between the other board members, Hayward was struggling to concentrate. Her mind kept reminding her of everything she had witnessed, from the horrific events on Titan Station to the gruesome autopsies carried out in the lab beneath Taurus headquarters. She felt sick every time she thought of the human corpses riddled with alien technology, and the shredded carcasses of the *infusers*, as Winter now referred to them.

'Karin?'

She returned sharply to the present at the sound of Kort's voice, suddenly realising all eyes were on her. It took her a moment to remember that the abrasive old man was still on Galt, along with Tench.

'Sorry, what were you saying?' she asked, smiling apologetically.

On the screen, Kort's expression was one of concern. 'Just checking you were okay. You weren't in the room then.'

It was an odd turn of phrase considering how far away they were. 'I'm fine. Just hard not to think about what happened. I'm sure you were the same after the attack on Kingston.'

Tench tapped at the scars on his neck. 'A constant reminder. Just be thankful you're alive.'

'It's not exactly the same though, is it?' Chaldevert chimed in bluntly. 'What happened on Galt was terrible, yes, but it was Sapphire Nova's doing. The attack on Titan Station came from something altogether unknown.'

'Not totally unknown.' Hayward nodded towards a quiet Winter. 'We know much more now.'

'Will the General be joining us any time soon?' Kort was just as impatient as ever.

'He'll be here shortly,' Akeman answered. 'I just heard his briefing finished a few minutes ago.'

Hayward sat back in her seat again as the others began arguing about the priorities for Taurus Galahad. The localised Revenant threat may have been curbed somewhat by the arrival of extra soldiers, however the religious fanatics were still out there scuttling around like the plague of rats so many likened them to. Such vast areas of Earth's surface had been ruined by them and any future rebuild would surely take decades, if not centuries.

Garrett had been meeting with the men and women responsible for driving back the Revenants nearby, even going so far as to head out to one of the newly constructed posts several miles to the north. He wanted to show his support and appreciation to the soldiers helping to take back Earth piece at a time, although he, like the rest of the board, was often preoccupied by thoughts of the dangers lurking out in the darkness beyond their ancestral home.

Hayward heard Tench mention Sapphire Nova and felt their eyes looking to her for a response. She gave none and remained silent. When they began the argument again, she glanced up once and saw that Winter was the only one still watching her. His stare was unnerving, as though he was looking through her.

When Garrett did arrive, she breathed the quietest sigh of relief. His mere presence helped to steady her nerves and she found the room so much colder when he wasn't there.

'Ah, our esteemed colleague graces us with his presence.' Kort's attempt at humour fell flat. 'How are you, General?'

'Alive,' was the abrupt reply. When Garrett had taken his place at the table, he looked up at the two men on the screens. 'Everything okay there?'

'Work on the new defences continues to move forward well,' Tench reported. 'The colony is slowly getting back to some sort of normal, although every time a ship swoops over you see people jump.'

'Has the report been made public there about Rist's demise?' asked the General.

Kort nodded solemnly. 'As requested. Minimal information. His death was met with cheers and celebration here.'

'I still can't believe that evil bastard saved you,' Chaldevert muttered, looking from Garrett to Hayward. 'None of this makes sense.'

Garrett steepled his fingers on the table. 'We'll get to that. Before we do, I just wanted to say that our troops here are doing an outstanding job. Revenant presence in this area has been reduced to a handful of nests in run-down homes or sewers. We are steadily taking back more and more land every week. Nearby towns are safe and soon we will move on to the next stage of the campaign, driving those freaks out of Montana completely.'

'No small task,' remarked Chaldevert.

'So this pale blue dot of ours' has as much support as we can give it,' continued Garrett. 'Unfortunately the majority of our military is needed elsewhere, as we know. We've all read the reports of what happened on Titan Station and you've seen the information gleaned from the autopsies. After extracting the data from Rist's ship...sorry, Akeman's ship, we also know that Sapphire Nova are completely compromised. Now that Saul has shared his new intel with us too, we have to decide what our next steps are. Thoughts?'

'Let me make sure I understand this first.' Kort jumped straight in. 'The entire corporation of Sapphire Nova may well be under the control of this *One Mind*, which is making them seek out more humans to assimilate using those creatures you encountered. Is that right?'

'It is.' Winter stepped forward. 'The alien technology will continue to look for more beings, not just humans, that it can infuse and survive through. Right now, Nova ships are taking infusers to worlds owned by the corp to assimilate entire colonies of men, women and children. It is relentless and will not slow down, unless we force it to do so.'

'And yet we don't have proof of this One Mind,' noted Tench, suspicion plastered across his face. 'Just your word. Forgive me but you're asking us to believe something you say you experienced as a memory of sorts. How do you know it's real?'

'If you'd been in that room on Titan Station, you'd be quick to believe too,' Hayward found herself snapping angrily. 'Saul and Rist's accounts can't be coincidence.'

Tench dug his heels in deeper. 'Karin, these are accounts from a Nova assassin and a man who worked for Santa Cruz. How trustworthy are they really?'

Garrett rose from his seat. 'When you're staring into the corpse of an alien creature riddled with bizarre technology, gentlemen, and you've seen how they bring a dead man back, you start to believe.

'Mikan Rist committed atrocious crimes against us, true. He also gave his life, such as it was, to deliver this intel to us. Winter was only following the orders of a ranking officer, and don't forget his story. Santa Cruz used him as a test subject, making him a hybrid of both alien and human tech.'

Marris had been so quiet, most had forgotten she was there. She was quick though to voice her major concern. 'And how do we know this One Mind isn't controlling him, manipulating us to do something that will lead us down the same road as Nova?'

Hayward saw the financial officer glance nervously at Winter, who didn't show any sign of emotion at the accusation. Paranoia was an understandable after effect of all that had happened.

'We've seen how those under the influence of this alien tech act,' she told the room. 'Saul isn't the same as them. He's a vital asset for us.'

'Thank you, Miss Hayward.' Winter's smile was as cold as his name. 'I'm not linked to it as they are. It hacked me when I touched Neri Ishlan to find out just who I was. It didn't expect me to experience what I did, I believe. The crude tech that the scientists at Hayes put in me does enough to keep the antecedent tech subdued, although I will admit that I do see and feel things much more differently to you all now. I'm not a threat to Taurus.

Having seen what's happening, I understand the importance of stopping it before it can do to us what it did to the antecedent race.'

Kort and Tench looked unimpressed as they sat back from the screens. Hayward could see that it would take a lot more to cast their suspicions aside, but for now they would have to deal with it.

'So how do we stop it?' Garrett had returned to his seat. 'How do we stop Nova ships from arriving at our colonies to assimilate our own people? How do we get to the source of the alien tech?'

The room fell silent for a moment. Hayward could tell by the looks on the faces of Chaldevert and Marris that they weren't prepared to offer an answer. Kort and Tench were still stewing. Akeman clearly wouldn't feel it was his place to say anything unless asked directly.

'We need to find a way to destroy the One Mind,' stated Winter clearly. 'It's not as simple as it sounds though. It learns, it adapts, it evolves. It made the mistake before of not keeping the antecedent bodies fed and it watched them all die, just to realise that it needed to alter the tech to stop the need for sustenance.'

'Is there any chance the Coldrigs survived?' Hayward asked him. 'That there could be more of them out there?'

'There may be a small number who survived the battle on Straunia.' When Winter looked at her, his eyes gleamed silver for a split second. 'They instinctively came here to stop history from repeating but they didn't account for the army their kin had amassed this time and they were vastly outnumbered.

Believe me when I say that it may be a good thing the Coldrigs are no longer a danger. They killed everyone at Hayes and may have gone on to do the same elsewhere. They posed another threat we could do without.'

'Do you think the One Mind may be based on Straunia, at the *Grail*?' Garrett asked Winter.

'It's possible,' was the vague answer. 'It may be too obvious a location though. By now, it may be based in several places at once.'

Garrett pondered this for a moment. 'I say we bomb Straunia. Take out the *Grail* and anything moving around down there.'

This took a moment to sink in with the room and Hayward was the first to react. 'Most infusers were taken off the planet by Nova so I'm not sure how many would be wiped out if we did bomb it. Also, there are still people down there who are alive. Assimilated, yet alive.'

'Fair comment,' said Garrett, offering her a smile before turning back to Winter. 'If we destroy the source of the tech, would those people ever recover?'

'Unlikely, unless we find a way to help them do so in the meantime. The spread is too great throughout the body, infiltrating the brain and heart.'

Hayward felt like someone had squeezed her own heart at that moment. All those colonists and soldiers lost. Sapphire Nova would just vanish in an instant.

'Other corporations could be undergoing assimilation as we speak,' added Winter. 'It already took some of our people easily enough.'

The thought sent a shiver down Hayward's spine. 'The priority absolutely *must* be finding how to destroy the One Mind. We can bring our best scientists in on this and pool our resources with our new allies. I'm sure I can persuade Ariana Tabb to help.'

'May I speak?' All eyes turned to Akeman, who was lurking just behind Hayward. 'In all my years, I've never seen anything that remotely comes close to what we experienced. I fought Mikan Rist on Galt and lost. I watched him then save the life of someone he was originally meant to kill. I thought that he was the most dangerous adversary I ever faced. I was wrong.

I doubted what Winter was saying from the moment he arrived here. Having looked into the dead eyes of these infusers, I agree with Miss Hayward. We have to destroy it before it tips the scales. If we don't, nothing else will matter.'

Hayward gave the agent her warmest smile, noticing Winter's nod of appreciation to him too. 'Do the rest of you agree?'

Chaldevert and Marris gave a silent nod. It took a moment for Kort and Tench to respond but they too agreed.

'I believe that we should still consider bombing the *Grail*,' Garrett said, standing once more and this time pacing around the table. 'I'm also aware that Nova are likely to have ships protecting Straunia. I agree with you, of course, but I will speak with the boards of the other corporations in an attempt to form a fleet capable of muscling its way into the Flint system and laying waste to Straunia.'

'In that case, Saul, you should start working on finding a way to bring down this machine.' Hayward rose too, feeling it appropriate as their plan of action took shape. 'If you work out how to locate it too, that would be a real advantage.'

'Will I have access to Taurus systems?' Winter asked them. 'It is going to need extensive research and I may need to travel to other systems.'

Hayward, Garrett and Akeman shared a look before she acknowledged the request. 'You have our full support. Do what you have to, but keep us updated every step of the way.'

'And what can we do?' came Kort's voice, tinny through comms.

'Be vigilant for any Nova presence in Lincoln,' replied Garrett. 'Tap into our network of agents and try to help locate the remnants of the Nova fleet.'

'Most importantly,' added Hayward. 'Pray we can stop this before it consumes the rest of the galaxy.'

Kharma,
Karstad system

Kurcher had been to numerous shitty colonies before but Upland made all of them look like prime vacation destinations.

He had never visited Kharma and now he knew why. The planet felt like it was hidden away out on the edge of Karstad, as though Sapphire Nova were ashamed of it. It was a cold and harsh world, prone to unpredictable weather patterns and constant cloud cover. The nights were long and the days were dark. Out in the rocky mountains and chasm-strewn plains, predators roamed looking for any opportunity to get at the warm-blooded humans who had invaded their domain.

Upland was a small colony, originally built to house miners and their families. When the mines turned out to be less than productive, Nova were quick to haul the workers off Kharma and replace them with ex-prisoners, troublemakers and other undesirables. Over the last decade, a significant black market opened up in the colony and now it was frequented by drug runners, gamblers and thieves; the sort of vermin Kurcher had once hunted down.

The leads on Flynn's whereabouts had led him ultimately to this sorry excuse for a corp world. When they first arrived, Drake had landed the *Falcata* at the larger colony some three hundred miles south of Upland. There they had learnt that the Knights Templar entourage led by the enigmatic mercenary had descended on Kharma a week previous, quickly heading over to Upland with their biomechs in tow.

After the briefest of respites at the more appealing colony, they too had headed in the same direction, reaching the shit heap as night fell. Tens of ships lined the landing pads, some almost touching those either side as the pilots squeezed into the tight gaps. Drake set down as far from Upland's lights as possible. The outer pads weren't within the security perimeter and so you landed there at your own risk.

Kurcher had wanted to continue the task alone. Drake didn't need to insist she came along. One look said it all. Now they were sat in the shadows at the back of a dank-smelling bar they heard some of the mercs had visited, hoping to catch sight of that unmistakeable armour they wore.

'I'm not sure why we're sat on our asses,' Drake said quietly. 'The biomechs will stand out so we just need to find them.'

'I need to know exactly what sort of shitstorm we're walking into,' he told her. 'The Templars aren't dumb like the Bold. No offence.'

She turned away from him. 'Fuck you.'

Kurcher looked out across the bar room. It was packed with all manner of dodgy-looking fuckers, all of them drinking heavily and most engaged in bad-tempered games of chance. He had noticed the three sat quietly at the opposite end, hidden in the dim light just as he was. He couldn't make them out, but recognised the body language. He was certain they were enlisters of some kind. He just didn't know who they were working for or who they were there for. Hopefully it wasn't him.

He drained the dregs of the rank beer he had forced down his throat and smiled at the fact he found himself missing Echo's own brand. Having visited the brewery on Warren too, he felt some affinity with the mead. It was a better vice than Paranax.

More patrons entered the bar and, like the rest, soon discarded their thick coats and scarves in the uncomfortable heat. Two of them looked as though they had been trapped in the wilderness for months, their features hidden by unkempt beards and hair that reached their shoulders. Kurcher also saw the firearms at their belts and recognised military-grade pistols. They didn't look like corp men.

He saw the three skulking opposite tense up when they saw these new arrivals and he sat back to watch the show. Only five minutes after the newcomers had sat down at one of the only vacant tables, they were approached by the enlisters.

First mistake, noted Frost. *Don't engage the target in confined spaces.*

And definitely not surrounded by other criminals, added Santa Cruz.

What followed was something Kurcher had seen hundreds of times. The two targets threw drinks, flipped the table and fled, disappearing out into the night. The enlisters followed, and so did several other patrons.

Rookie mistakes, chuckled Frost.

Those enlisters will be lucky to get out of Upland alive, D'Larro said.

A part of Kurcher desperately wanted to follow too. It was the enlister in him that instinctively made him start to rise from his seat before he remembered it was not his fight.

'You take me to the nicest fucking places.'

He looked across at Drake and saw the rare mirth in her eyes. He had almost forgotten how danger turned her on. Her lips showed no sign of blue and he found it strange that he should miss that colour on her.

'Only the best,' he grinned. 'Another drink?'

As she weighed up the small amount of liquid in her dirty glass, Kurcher realised how much he had missed this lifestyle. He preferred the life of the enlister and Drake was a very suitable partner to accompany him on such adventures into the darkest regions of the galaxy.

As a pilot or as a lover? Frost asked.

He wondered what Frost would be saying to him were she sat at the table. She probably wouldn't have joined him in Upland, preferring to stay on the ship and watch from above.

You were better at the dirty parts of the job, Frost said sadly.

'I don't think I could stomach another of these,' grimaced Drake. 'Besides, you may want to take a look at the bar.'

The four mercs had slipped into the establishment without him noticing and he cursed himself for being too preoccupied with his own thoughts. Despite their long coats, he saw the glint of chain mail beneath. His patience had paid off, it seemed.

'Guess that means I'm up.' Drake finished her drink and rose from the table.

'You sure you're okay to do this?' Kurcher asked her quietly.

She shrugged. 'Guess we'll find out one way or the other.'

He watched her weave her way through to the bar to stand alongside the templars, where she signalled for another drink. When she turned and tapped the nearest merc on the arm, Kurcher felt his stomach knot slightly.

The original Knights Templar back on Earth had been religious soldiers; vessels for good, or so history would have one believe. When first formed, this modern outfit did carry out tasks to protect those who needed protecting, showing people that they were a light in the darkness of space. Over time though, they tired of pretending to be good, ultimately taking more and more paid-for jobs, not caring who got hurt in the process. Temple was once a station for respite but the draw of gambling and whoring was too great for the Templars, who quickly realised just how much money they could make.

Kurcher eyed up the four at the bar. Sure, they stood tall and straight, chins lifted as though they were better than everyone else. They were still men with their own desires and Drake would have to play on that.

She spoke with the one templar at length, offering him the occasional smile and stroking his arm. When a second became interested, she positioned herself between them and continued the conversation.

She's never smiled that fucking much in your company, pointed out Ercko.

Jealousy doesn't become you, Trin said.

He sat alone watching them for nearly an hour and breathed a sigh of relief as all four mercs filed back out of the bar. Drake shouted something to them about finding them later and then returned to the table, her smile gone and a look of disgust on her face.

'Don't ever fucking ask me to do something like that again,' she growled. 'Absolute bunch of arrogant pricks.'

'I think that part of the plan was your idea,' he reminded her. 'So I'm assuming either you found out a shitload of intel or you were just enjoying their company a bit too much.'

The fire was clear in her eyes as she leaned closer to him. 'Enough for us to find Flynn.'

He leaned into her, looking for one of her lust-filled kisses. Instead, she slapped him hard, stood sharply and left. He looked around at the amused faces nearby.

'She's a fucking handful, that one,' he said loudly, laughing.

He found her outside, cigarette lodged in her mouth. It was freezing and yet she wasn't shivering, despite not being dressed for the temperature.

'They came here to meet with a group of buyers,' she told him, after making him wait until she was ready. 'No doubt for the drugs they stole. Flynn is here heading up the meeting and even his second-in-command is here with him, so we can take out both in one go. They're over on the west side of Upland, meeting in the back room of a bar.'

'How many in their party exactly?'

Drake breathed a cloud of smoke into the cold air and watched it swirl above her until it dissipated. 'Twenty-five, including Flynn. Five of Shard's finest freaks too, kept in an electrified metal cage outside. Probably a handful of guards there to protect the buyers as well.'

'Do we know who the buyers are?'

'No, but I won't lose any sleep over icing them.'

Kurcher pulled the jacket tight across his chest, feeling the cold trying its best to get to warm skin. 'What about the location of the drugs?'

'Some are here on Kharma, although it wasn't clear where exactly. The rest are being kept somewhere secure outside of Karstad.'

'Right.' He glanced along the narrow street either way. 'Next part of the plan then. Get back to the ship. I'll go take a look and let you know when I need you.'

Drake's wild eyes were illuminated for a second by the cigarette as she inhaled. 'You'll always need me, you prick.'

'I'd ask if you'll be okay on your own but that's a stupid fucking question.'

'It is.' She started to head off before calling back. 'But if I get killed out there, at least it'll be your fault.'

As he made his way over to the west side of the colony, Kurcher's hand checked his revolver was where it should be and then felt for the explosives in his pocket. They had come in handy back on Warren so he never bothered giving them back to the armoury on the *Glaive*.

Upland was noisy at night. It was like the population were nocturnal such was the cacophony in some alleys and streets. It seemed that business was being done no matter what the time.

You should've gone with her, Frost said angrily. *She's going to be outside the perimeter on her own.*

That one can take care of herself, Ercko stated.

There are too many places like this in the galaxy, said D'Larro.

He heard the biomechs before he saw them. Deep booming voices were echoing from ahead, muffled by the metal cage keeping them prisoner. They weren't bestial cries or shouts of despair. He heard one ask a passer-by what the fuck they were staring at. Another complained of being thirsty. The Templars had clearly been able to keep them stocked up on the drugs they needed to survive, unless Angard had been a unique case.

The cage the five hulks were in was more of a secure transporter, with large wheels protected against the harsh terrain of Kharma and an automated drive system. It was tall enough for them not to have to stoop and the bars were thicker than Kurcher's neck, humming with enough voltage to hurt the biomechs and most likely kill anyone else foolish enough to touch them.

The building the transporter was parked outside was illuminated red with a green neon sign displayed over the door. *Sparks* seemed an apt name for the drinking hole.

As Kurcher slowly approached, he saw four mercs standing outside the front door and another four were lurking near to the transporter. They had the typical bearing of the Knights Templar, looking down their noses at those walking past. Whether or not the ones Drake had spoken with were amongst them, he didn't give a shit.

They were all heavily armed. One thing he had to give them credit for was their well-documented combat training. If you pitted a templar, a bold and a member of both Schaeffer's Nine and Fortitude against one another, the templar would be the favourite to walk out alive.

Kurcher looked for other ways into the bar. There would be a side or rear door most likely but it would be guarded too and he really didn't care for sneaking around much. He just hoped that Flynn was in there still engaged in his meeting.

'You back yet?' he whispered into his comms.

After a few anxious seconds, Drake's voice came back. 'Of course. These outer pads are fucking creepy though.'

'Well this place is some seedy little joint lit up nice and red like a beacon. I'm going to take out the biomechs and, when the mercs come running, it's over to you and the *Falcata*. Understood?'

'Direct approach then.' The sound of a cigarette being lit filtered through comms. 'Best you move quickly.'

Kurcher was reminded of all the times Frost would speak to him as she lounged back in the cockpit of the *Kaladine*, cigarette on the go. Of course, her cigarettes were mundane compared to the ones Drake smoked. He couldn't imagine Frost high.

Someone had to stay sober and sensible, the dead pilot said.

A biting wind blew along the street, stinging Kurcher's face. He saw all of the templars turn their backs to it too, one man moaning about the shit weather they were having to endure. Kurcher had to smile when he heard one of the biomechs call the merc a pussy.

He moved into a position so he could get a better view of the side of the transporter. He couldn't see any obvious door so assumed the whole side would simply open up when needed. He had originally thought of somehow letting the brutes out, free to rampage and cause havoc. The problem there was that they weren't crazed and would likely just run off.

You know what you have to do, Santa Cruz told him.

When the next gust of wind rushed along the street, Kurcher walked directly into it and, as the templars turned away to protect their faces once more, he passed by them. Taking three explosives out, he hurled them between the bars of the transporter and made sure he continued past at pace.

The three devices detonated almost simultaneously, engulfing the cage in flames and smoke. The howls of the five trapped within were loud, although Kurcher felt there was more anger than pain in the sound. The shockwave had barely made him stumble but the templars next to the transporter were blown forwards violently, one of them hitting the wall of the bar hard. The four outside the front door found themselves on their backs.

Kurcher stepped into the nearest side street and peered back through the rapidly increasing cloud of smoke. The bars of the cage were still intact which made the scene within harrowing for most shocked onlookers. Two of the biomechs were on fire yet trying to wrench the bars free. Flashes of electricity shot up their arms but the pain of the fire obviously outweighed that of the volts being pumped into them.

They're harder to drop than The Kindred, said Angard.

Kurcher sighted the *Falcata* in the distance, heading quickly towards his position. There was another roar from the transporter and, much to his chagrin, the side of the vehicle suddenly opened. Whether it was the force of the explosions knocking out the locking mechanism or it had been opened by one of the mercs, it didn't matter. Two large figures leapt down into the street, flames burning away the skin across their torsos and legs. Another followed a moment later missing part of his leg and promptly fell to the ground. The final two didn't appear.

By the time the templars placed in the street had recovered, the two standing biomechs were on them, smashing skulls and tearing limbs. Kurcher was reminded of what he saw on the *Huntress* when Angard became enraged.

The door to the bar was flung open and a number of templars piled out, opening fire with their significant automatic rifles. One of the burning biomechs went down after receiving ten bullets to the skull. The other continued his mad rampage.

Kurcher glanced up to see the *Falcata* nearly overhead and, when he looked back, he saw the unmistakeable silhouette of Flynn standing in the doorway of the bar, trying to make sense of what was happening.

'Over to you,' he said calmly into his comms.

The *Falcata* passed out of sight momentarily before reappearing in the night sky directly in front of the bar. As the mercs looked up, the gats spat into life and sent a hail of high-velocity rounds into them. Their random pieces of metal armour offered no protection as the barrage cut through them and the final biomech finally succumbed as he took a flurry of bullets to the back.

Kurcher watched as Drake relentlessly battered the front of the unfortunate bar, blowing the door apart and destroying both the sign and the red lights giving the place its glow. He saw other people from inside the establishment try to flee and get cut down too. He wondered whether they were part of the buying party meeting Flynn or were just unlucky patrons.

'That's enough,' he said, raising his voice above the clamour. 'Get the fuck out of here and I'll let you know when and where to pick me up.'

The gats powered down a few seconds later and the *Falcata* turned sharply before heading away north. There were no authorities in Upland to pursue her but he didn't want any unexpected retaliation on Drake or the ship.

Drawing his revolver, Kurcher stuck close to the edge of the street as he made for the bar. He stepped over the corpses of the mercs, unable to avoid walking through the blood which had spattered everywhere. Those who were struck by the full force of the gats were nothing but smouldering flesh and one templar had been scythed in half.

As he stepped over one body, the man reached up suddenly. He was riddled with bullet holes and yet found the strength to move. Kurcher put a single shot into his brain. Aware that people were starting to gather nearby, he quickly entered the bar and scanned the scene before him. There were bodies littering the main room and several wounded were propped up against walls and furniture. The metal counter opposite was dented and twisted, the glass wall behind it now shattered and smeared with blood. Broken bottles were scattered around the room.

Kurcher counted seven templars amongst the dead. With those outside, that accounted for 22 of their number. He was pissed off to see that Flynn wasn't one of them, although he picked up a trail of blood that vanished through a doorway nearby.

Moving to the edge of the arched opening, he took the swiftest of glances through and saw a hallway leading to the back rooms. The blood had dripped to form a wavering line and he followed cautiously, revolver ready. When he heard the crash of a door being flung open ahead, he moved up to another opening and looked into a smoky chamber. On the opposite wall, a door leading to the back of the bar was swinging.

Remember these bastards are cunning, warned Santa Cruz.

Kurcher took a couple of steps back and then threw himself into the room, spinning to fire at anyone attacking from the corners. He was alone though. Then he was through the back door and into the alley beyond. It was there he came under fire as a templar stepped from the shadows and let rip with his rifle, forcing Kurcher to leap back into the building. He waited until the rifle ceased firing then darted out and rolled another explosive down the alley. When it exploded, he rushed forward and found the templar staggering backwards having tried to avoid the blast. The revolver fired twice and the merc slumped to the ground.

Kurcher ran to the junction at the end of the alley. To the left, it rejoined the main street where by now a crowd had gathered to pick over the bodies like carrion birds. To the right, the alleyway narrowed and weaved its way into the back streets. Flynn wouldn't have risked going back out in the open so Kurcher took the right path.

He came upon a small group of people quickly fleeing the area and, when they heard him approach, they moved out of his way. The thought crossed his mind that they could've been the buyers Flynn was meeting but he couldn't stop to find out.

As the route ahead became so dim he could hardly see, Kurcher stopped for a moment and listened. Behind him came a few shouts and then he heard it. Somewhere just ahead came the clicking of metal upon metal, like armour catching as its wearer moved. A few minutes later, he turned a corner and found himself near the perimeter of Upland, a ramshackle fence that barely did the job. The alley gave way to an open area between colony and perimeter; a good place to stage an ambush thanks to the myriad shadows.

Kurcher slowly advanced, keeping close to the building walls. The wind was whistling through the fence and stirring up rubbish discarded nearby.

He spotted a broken section of wall up ahead and peered warily inside the dark space. As he moved past it, a figure stepped out of the shadows ahead and Kurcher instinctively fired. There was a grunt and it stumbled backwards. At the same time, Flynn came barreling out of the break in the wall, tearing an even bigger hole, and slammed into Kurcher, driving him to the ground hard.

Despite being slightly disorientated, Kurcher rolled and fired a single shot at the merc leader. There was a spark in the darkness as the bullet ricocheted off Flynn's armour and Kurcher barely had time to curse before the templar kicked the revolver from his grasp. The boot caught the annoying weak spot on his hand and pain lanced up his arm, causing him to clench his teeth.

'Who sent you?' Flynn's voice was deep and rough, showing no waver after the ambush.

Kurcher looked up at him, not seeing any weapon in his hands. 'Well you've pissed a lot of people off so take your pick.'

Flynn studied him for a moment then lifted his right arm. A small flame flickered into life from a nozzle mounted along his wrist. Kurcher traced it back up the thick arm and sighed when he saw the cylindrical canister at Flynn's belt.

'I've heard a lot of things about the Knights Templar,' he said, slowly starting to get to his feet. 'But I've never known you to use flame throwers. The last person I knew who used one of those died about twenty years ago when his canister ruptured.'

'Shut your mouth,' Flynn snapped, taking a step forward. 'I'll ask you one last time. Who sent you?'

Kurcher could see his revolver out the corner of his eye, and the figure he had shot was still moving. Behind him, the fence held no escape route and Flynn was so tall that he could swiftly block his path no matter which way he went.

He's only got a fucking flame thrower, Angard said.

You've still got a knife, enlister, Santa Cruz stated. *Use it.*

Kurcher wondered whether the voices wanted him dead too. 'Apart from those biomechs, you stole something that didn't belong to you. I suggest we take this opportunity to talk so we can come to a mutual understanding.'

'Fuck that.' Flynn's flame increased in size. 'You killed my men and burnt those biomechs alive. Here's what that feels like.'

145

The customised flame thrower made a whooshing sound before launching a surprisingly large jet that threatened to consume Kurcher. As soon as he had heard the sound though, he pulled the knife from his belt and flung it loosely in Flynn's direction, then dived for his gun. He felt the fire lick at his shoulder and heard the knife clang harmlessly off the merc's armour, but it was enough to make Flynn hesitate before swinging his arm out to follow Kurcher's movement. Kurcher's fingers luckily found the revolver and he rolled into a crouched position before firing twice. At the same time he felt the burn of the flame thrower again, his second shot struck the fuel canister at Flynn's side. A belch of fire erupted from the bullet hole and the nozzle spluttered and died.

Kurcher had expected the canister to implode and turn Flynn into a human torch, but the templar had a safety clip of course. The damaged container was hurled over the fence and blew up on impact with the rocks outside the perimeter, barely even scorching the rocks.

That was disappointing, tutted D'Larro.

One bullet left, said Santa Cruz, stating the obvious.

'The next shot goes through your skull,' Kurcher warned the furious templar, seeing the man's face properly for the first time in the glow of the explosion. 'You stole a shitload of drugs from a facility on Curos. Where are they?'

A look of realisation spread across Flynn's face. 'Hewn didn't take it too well then. I'm surprised he even missed it. I never thought you'd end up working for that one-armed bastard though, Kurcher.'

Of course he'd know your face, Frost said. *There's probably still a bounty out there on your head.*

'It's better you know who I am. Now you know I won't be fucking around.'

'Actually, I've wanted to meet you for some time.' Flynn took a step back as Kurcher stood. 'We have a lot in common. We both got fucked over by Santa Cruz for a start, and by Taurus Galahad.'

'Yeah, but at least I wasn't working with those Nova pricks. Whatever that agreement was between you got you exiled from all Taurus systems. That's quite a financial hit you took.'

Flynn shrugged. 'We all have to make money somehow, right?'

'Not by stealing Echo property though.' Kurcher could feel the pain of the burns starting to throb in his shoulder and arm. 'Tell me where the drugs are.'

'We had a great thing going in Lincoln.' It was almost like Flynn hadn't heard

146

him. 'The Taurus officials were some of our best customers. It all started to fall apart when Santa Cruz came to Temple and iced Cairns. Nova quickly threatened my organisation, blaming us for the death of one of their most decorated officers and I had to make the decision to jump into bed with them or risk the end of the Knights Templar.'

'I couldn't give a shit,' growled Kurcher. 'You're a bunch of pretentious fuckwits and that's really all you are.'

The smile on Flynn's face was unnerving. 'Oh, we're much more than that.'

Kurcher clocked the movement at the edge of his vision and spun quickly, firing the remaining shot that took the approaching templar through the mouth, breaking teeth as it blew through the man's head. He obviously hadn't been as wounded as Kurcher had first thought.

Or he was just there to distract you, Santa Cruz pointed out.

Flynn was upon him with alarming speed, a long knife gleaming in his gloved hand. Kurcher managed to dodge the stabbing blade but Flynn's other strong hand was holding his revolver at bay, not realising the ammo was spent.

Kurcher knew he was in trouble. The templar leader was stronger and better in close combat, plus was shockingly agile even in his heavy armour. There really was only one course of action that wouldn't result in him getting skewered, although that would always be a possibility.

As Flynn tried to bring the knife across to slice his neck, Kurcher thrust his forehead directly into the merc's face. He felt the blade nick his skin, drawing blood, and heard Flynn grunt in surprise at the headbutt. It didn't have the desired result of breaking his nose, however it did cause the templar to hesitate. In that split second, Kurcher kicked Flynn in the balls as hard as he could. That had the desired effect.

'Not protected there, you arrogant asshole?' he quipped, watching with satisfaction as Flynn stumbled backwards clutching at his damaged goods.

When he noticed that the templar wasn't doubling up like others would, Kurcher quickly reloaded and, just as he slammed the clip back into the revolver, Flynn was coming at him again. Two shots struck Flynn in the lower leg, just below the metal protecting his kneecap, and this time the merc fell.

Kurcher began circling him. 'Where are the fucking drugs?'

'If you kill me, you'll have my entire organisation to answer to.' Flynn's voice was still surprisingly measured. 'Hewn won't want that.'

He's a tough bastard, this one, said Angard.

'I don't give people this many chances as a rule,' he told the stricken templar. 'Maybe I've been out of the game too long. Still, I'll give you one more. Give me the location of the drugs you stole and I'll let you die with some dignity.'

Flynn's head dropped slightly. 'We both know that's bullshit. You'll shoot me and leave me to rot here.'

As Kurcher came to a halt, taking careful aim at Flynn's head, that freezing wind blew through the colony again, bringing with it discarded food containers and flotsam strewn near the perimeter. Kurcher turned his head ever so slightly to avoid the cold sting and that was when Flynn threw his knife. The blade caught Kurcher's arm weakly, jabbing through the sleeve of his jacket. There was a quick flash of pain to tell him it had broken the skin.

Despite the leg wound, Flynn was up and charging at him as soon as the knife had left his hand. Kurcher fired three times, moving his revolver up with each shot. The first bullet struck the merc in the shoulder, the second in the neck and the third took him in the jaw, making a dull cracking sound as it splintered the bone.

Kurcher stepped aside as the templar plunged heavily to the ground. 'I guess we're done.'

When he stood over Flynn, he could see blood pumping from the neck wound and the lower part of the merc's face was a mess. Still, his dark eyes were open and glaring up at Kurcher with pure anger.

'The old Knights Templar believed in God,' Kurcher said, grimacing at the ache in his arm. 'Do you?'

With that, he put a final bullet in Flynn's brain.

Summit,
Benedict system

Grosnik was really starting to hate Morton Hurst.

As he walked the lamp-lit promenade of Tidewell, the General kept going over and over how the head of Fortitude had *summoned* him like some grunt in his mercenary organisation. He wished that he didn't have to meet with him but there were things to be said and actions to take now that all of the resorts on Summit had been snatched from Impramed's weak grip.

The gentle sea breeze whispered past him and he looked out into the dark waters. Only the light of the buoys bobbed further out, marking the safety zone. Grosnik wondered just how many people Hurst had made disappear out in the depths; how many Impramed bodies were weighted down beneath the waves.

Chaukan was bright in the sky that night, full in the reflection of the Benedict sun. The stars littered the sky like diamonds on a dark blue canvas, and he couldn't help but admire the way the spa world put him at peace, even after the events of the past few days.

He continued along the promenade, glancing back at the two officers accompanying him, and could hear the sound of merriment from the city. It was of course Fortitude who were making so merry. Those who called Tidewell their home were still reeling from the takeover and, despite Hurst's promise to all residents that their daily lives would not be affected, Grosnik knew it was all a facade. Fortitude's emblem was a clenched fist for good reason.

He made his way towards the establishment where Hurst was waiting. It was a multi-storey bar that Fortitude took a shine to a long time ago, gleaming white in the glow of the lamps. Outside the door stood three uniformed mercs who greeted him with the respect he deserved and showed the three Sigma Royal soldiers inside.

The place was clean and quiet. There would be no patrons in that night until Hurst allowed it. Through the main room, they entered a private area with a large white rectangular table in it and there sat Hurst, drink in hand and a satisfied smile on his face.

As Grosnik went to greet him, he noticed another man half-sitting on a wide window sill behind Hurst and instantly recognised Ruck. The thug could always be found watching over Hurst, as a sort of bodyguard. He was clearly the muscle should the Fortitude leader wish to apply pressure to anyone.

'General, please take a seat,' welcomed Hurst. 'Order whatever drink you'd like. Your men too. Tonight we celebrate.'

'Thank you.' Grosnik took two steps further into the room and jolted to a halt. 'What's that doing here?'

He hadn't seen the pursuit mech when they entered as it was standing out of view from the door. It was painted in the blue of Fortitude, the fist proudly displayed on its chassis. As Grosnik moved, the visual sensors followed him.

'Good to see you, General Grosnik.' The voice that came from the mech was metallic and offensive to his ears. 'I wanted to be here in some capacity to congratulate you both on a job well done.'

Grosnik gave Hurst a suspicious look. 'Who exactly is that?'

'You may address me direct,' the mech said.

Hurst waved a hand at it. 'General, we're in the presence of our associate, The Luminary. This is his avatar, for want of a better word.'

Grosnik frowned and found himself reluctant to sit near the construct. He forced himself to take a seat though, making sure he kept some distance between both Hurst and what was apparently The Luminary. His officers stood to attention behind him.

'This is not my voice of course,' the mech explained. 'I managed to update the Link app to incorporate a speech centre on this particular model. Impressive, yes?'

'Very.' Grosnik found it hard to talk to something made entirely of metal and electronics.

'Only you could create something like this.'

'Your drink of choice, General?' asked Hurst.

'Nothing for my men. I'll take a water.'

Hurst scowled. 'Come now. You'll celebrate properly with me...with us. How about wine? Summit's own brand.'

Grosnik forced a smile. 'Very well. Another product from this planet that can be distributed for a tidy profit across the rest of the galaxy?'

'Indeed.' Hurst clearly read his tone. 'So, allow me to start this meeting by saying that Fortitude is now in complete control of Summit and that feat has been achieved by the combined actions of you both. General, without your army and mere presence here, the outcome may have been much worse for

Impramed's personnel.

And my Luminary friend, your mechs are truly remarkable. They are a force to be reckoned with.'

A woman entered the room with the glass of wine and kept her head down as she placed it in front of Grosnik. She made a quick exit and he didn't blame her.

'Well, it's his technology of course,' he said, studying the ruby red liquid. 'The mechs belong to Sigma Royal.'

Hurst looked up at him then glanced at the mech, which was watching Grosnik. 'They're all ours really. Fortitude supplied them, The Luminary installed the tech and Sigma put them to use out in the field. I'd say the results have been exemplary.'

'Unless the General doesn't agree.' The false voice was cold and without emotion.

Grosnik met the stare of the sensors. 'Why not just come here in person? Surely it's time to step out of the shadows following this success.'

'I will not risk it,' came the reply. 'Not yet.'

Hurst tried to break the uncomfortable atmosphere. 'Tell us, General, what you will do now? Can we be of any more help to Sigma?'

Grosnik's gaze lingered on the avatar a moment longer. 'You can indeed. I need more mechs.'

At this, Hurst leaned forward to rest his elbows on the table. 'General, you all but exhausted our supply resources with this endeavour. To manufacture more will take time and money.'

'Money's not an issue,' Grosnik said, waving the comment away. 'We have some time but not much. I want the Sigma Royal mech army to number two thousand. We need the added firepower for when Libra decide to retaliate.'

'I can accommodate the apps,' The Luminary told them. 'However it will require significant funding for me to acquire more components. Do you plan on any more offensives?'

Grosnik sipped at his wine. He had decided just recently that his fleet would begin a campaign against Libra's fuel depots. He wasn't about to share that with these two though.

'Not yet. So is this something you can do?'

Hurst shared a look with the eerily humanised mech. 'We'll look into it.

151

Shouldn't be a problem, however there are a lot of variables to sort out.'

Grosnik gave them a nod and gulped half of the wine down. 'I also wanted to talk to you both about the matters I asked you to look into. The bullet that killed Trystan Hengeveld on Kismet and the whereabouts of my missing tech officer and his assault mech. Any updates would be appreciated.'

The room fell silent for a few seconds and Grosnik could hear muffled voices from out in the street. As he drained his glass, he studied the blue pursuit mech and was glad to see there were no shrikes mounted on the chassis or obvious weapons anywhere on its body. He had already taken note of the fact Ruck had a pistol holstered at his side and that Hurst was also armed. He had made sure his two soldiers brought assault rifles and he himself had his pistol tucked away. It was good to know they had the stronger firepower, although he was hoping no weapon would have to be raised.

'I found Tech Officer Vekkerd,' announced The Luminary eventually. 'And the mech too. I hadn't mentioned it until now as I'd been working on how to get them away from Echo.'

'Those pirate bastards.' Grosnik's jaw clenched at the thought of Echo raiding Monarch City. 'Do you know where exactly they are?'

The pursuit mech began slowly pacing around the table, its mannerisms clearly reflecting The Luminary, wherever he or she was. 'They are on the *Glaive*, Jaffren Hewn's flagship. It seemed to me that Vekkerd was helping them, albeit somewhat reluctantly.'

Grosnik pondered this. 'Could you not activate the mech remotely and use it to take out the ship?'

Hurst looked up, a gleam in his sinister eyes. 'What a chance that could be to take out Hewn for good.'

'If I take control of that mech, there is a good chance Echo will destroy it.' The Luminary's avatar gave a shake of the metal head.

Grosnik shrugged. 'It's just one mech. Worth taking the risk.'

Again, The Luminary dismissed this. 'I can learn more if it isn't dismantled. Useful intel can be gleaned.'

'Any reason why they would've taken one of the General's men?' Hurst asked.

'It is apparent that Echo used the mech Vekkerd is linked to so as to gain access to the prison compound in Monarch City.' The avatar tapped its own chest plate. 'And they took them both probably as a way to study my work. It's no secret that Echo have been interested in me, mainly due to my dealings with Fortitude.'

'Do you think it possible to get Vekkerd away from them?' Grosnik would rather have the chance to question the young tech officer, however he knew it would be a long shot.

'Possible,' answered The Luminary. 'Difficult, but possible.'

When the General sat back, quietly contemplating the predicament, Hurst filled the silence. 'In regards to that bullet analysis, it is hard to pinpoint. The round came from an old-fashioned revolver that generally you don't see in use any more, however any merc or collector could have one. I'm afraid it may be nigh impossible to trace it back to this killer you're looking for.'

'I may be able to shed light on this.' The mech had moved around the room and was standing near the door. 'I believe your culprit is Davian Kurcher.'

Both Grosnik and Hurst looked up, their surprise clear for all to see.

'Kurcher?' The General's brow furrowed deeply. 'That murdering son-of-a-bitch. What makes you think this?'

'Because Kurcher is working with Hewn and Echo. I saw him when I linked with the assault mech. He uses a revolver like the one you're talking about.'

Grosnik had heard the name a few times in the past; knew Kurcher to be a Taurus enlister with a penchant for execution. When he discovered that the man had killed all but one of Beck's team on Kismet while in pursuit of Edlan Rane, he ensured there was a significant bounty on his head. Men like Davian Kurcher were better off dead.

'Tell me something,' he said, looking up at the mechanical avatar with a narrowed eye. 'How exactly do you know Davian Kurcher then, if you recognised him?'

The Luminary didn't reply straight away and instead seemed to be taking time to consider the answer. 'I crossed paths with him once. He tends to stick in your mind, that one.'

There was quite a lot Grosnik could query about that response. If The Luminary had encountered Kurcher before, was this app dealer once on the Taurus hit list? Had Kurcher been sent after them at some point? It seemed there was much more to discover about The Luminary's past.

The General's head was buzzing with the information he had just learnt. If

Kurcher killed Trystan Hengeveld then Echo had infiltrated Monarch City, perhaps in an attempt to rescue the Libra officer for their corporation allies. It didn't answer why Kurcher would have murdered him though, unless Echo had a different agenda. Maybe Libra Centauri ordered the hit on Hengeveld themselves to make sure he didn't give any intel to Sigma. He wouldn't have put it past Ariana Tabb to have one of her own iced just to keep their secrets secure.

'I know Kurcher too,' Hurst remarked. 'He's someone we've been on the lookout for. Seems he's a wanted man in every corner of our galaxy.'

Grosnik was keen to get back to his ship, so needed to move their conversation on. 'I need to consider this news and work out what the best way forward is with Echo and Libra. Before we conclude though and my fleet departs, I need to talk with you about another matter.

We've been experiencing blackouts with some of the mechs; glitches where the link with their user is severed temporarily. I'd like to know why this is.'

The avatar regarded him with its emotionless sensors. 'There are no glitches in the system, General. It's likely something the tech officers are doing wrong.'

Grosnik bristled at the accusation. 'There's nothing wrong with my men. This has happened on every offensive campaign during which I've used the mechs, and it isn't the same ones malfunctioning. It's almost like someone else has taken over control for that short period they are in blackout.'

He wished he was sitting in front of an actual person. He could've read the body language or seen a telltale sign a lie was being told. Instead, he got nothing back from the pursuit mech. It just stood still, watching him. For a moment, he wondered whether The Luminary had cut the link.

'As I said, General, there are no glitches in my tech.' The monotone voice almost seemed to have an edge to it. 'It sounds like you are implying I've been purposefully interrupting the links.'

Grosnik began to tap the table softly. 'You asked for access to the live feeds through your apps so you've been along for the ride every time. I found myself wondering why you wanted to be there for each attack and I think I'm starting to understand now.'

Hurst shifted somewhat uncomfortably in his chair. 'Shall we have another drink, General?'

Grosnik held a hand up to silence the head of Fortitude, which was brave in itself. 'I'd like to get to the bottom of this issue with the mechs first. It's important I understand just what's been happening to them.'

'You clearly have an assumption,' said The Luminary, almost interrupting him. 'Why don't you share it?'

'Fine.' Grosnik rose from his seat slowly, palms flat on the table. 'I know you've been taking control of the link in certain mechs and I believe it is to gather data for your own personal gain. The blackouts always happened when the mechs were near key access points. Perhaps you're looking for new resources you can use or maybe you peddle intel as well as offering these apps. Either way, I don't appreciate you causing disruption during important...'

'General Grosnik.' This time, he *was* interrupted. 'I told you that I wanted to see first-hand what my mechs were capable of. Your excursions into enemy space have helped test the Link app and also helped me develop the tech even further. Without the Sigma Royal army, this wouldn't have been possible.

'I took control of those mechs as part of this test. Nobody died as a result and you still completed your mission each time, so you're seeing problems where there are none.'

Grosnik gave Hurst an incredulous look before turning back to the avatar. '*My* mechs? They belong to the Sigma military now, or do you forget that?'

'We are part of the same alliance, are we not?' countered The Luminary. 'And I believe that Fortitude's name remains on the Agreement as part-owner of all the mechs they supplied.'

'Not part-owner,' snapped Grosnik, his temper rising. 'Should there be any serious problem with the mechs, they remain responsible.'

The angular blue head swung in Hurst's direction. 'Did the General not just say there was a serious problem with them?'

'Don't twist my words,' Grosnik cried, slamming his clenched fist onto the table. 'This is *your* app causing the issue.'

With an almost arrogant air, the mech turned its back on him. 'You should read the small print, General.'

'This is a betrayal of what was agreed.' The General looked back at his two men, who were clutching their rifles tightly. 'I want your signed confirmation before the day has run its course stating that the mechs and all of the technology within belong to Sigma Royal.'

Hurst had stayed quiet throughout the heated exchange but now he decided to speak up. 'General, you got the war you wanted. The mechs are wearing your colours and have helped you take Libra colonies, as agreed. If there is a serious problem, as you claim, then Fortitude will gladly take back the purchased models and run diagnostics on them. We are allies.'

Grosnik began to slowly head for the door. 'And as part of this alliance, Sigma has helped Fortitude take Summit from Impramed, but we will not go to war against another corporation just so you can reap the benefits.

'I told one of the Impramed officials he and his people would be safe; that I would take them off this planet on our ships. He didn't trust Fortitude and I don't blame him. You will confirm that the mech army is the sole property of Sigma Royal and then we go our separate ways.'

As the avatar turned back to face the approaching General, Hurst was looking confused. 'What of the extra mechs you wanted?' he asked.

'Forget about them,' Grosnik replied, coming to an abrupt halt before the tall construct. 'Now get out of my way.'

A metallic sigh came from The Luminary. 'It's such a shame you feel this way.'

A gunshot rang out and one of the Sigma soldiers pitched sideways. As the other started to turn, a second shot took him in the chest and he staggered backwards then slumped to the floor with a gasp.

Grosnik looked across to where Ruck was standing, the barrel of his pistol smoking silently. Still seated, Hurst had fired the second shot. The General reached for his weapon but the arm of the mech lunged with human-like speed, the metal fingers latching onto his wrist. The mech's other hand took him by the throat.

'Let...me...go.' He could barely get the words out and grabbed desperately at the cold arm with his free hand.

Hurst gave Ruck a signal and the thug walked calmly past the struggling General. Two more shots echoed through the room as Hurst's goon put the soldiers out of their misery.

Grosnik couldn't take a breath and felt his vision start swimming. He fumbled for his gun but it was just out of reach.

The mech pulled him close, the visual sensors glinting as The Luminary stared into his face. Then, with a brief whirring from the pneumatics in the arm, its hand clenched quickly with as much pressure as it could muster. The fingers tore through skin and muscle, meeting momentary resistance from the bones in Grosnik's neck before splintering them. With the blood-soaked metal fist clenched, the General's head lolled to one side, barely attached by sinew.

'Did you have to make such a mess?' Hurst tutted. 'Ruck, get someone in here to clean up.'

The avatar opened its hand again and Grosnik's body hit the floor alongside the bodies of his soldiers. 'Strange feeling watching someone die at your hand and yet not experiencing any sensations.'

'I'm sure.' Hurst wasn't impressed. 'We could've done with the additional funds he was willing to pay. All you had to do was lie about the blackouts and offer up a suitable explanation.'

The mech's head swung to look at him, blood speckling the blue paint. 'I didn't like his attitude. He would've caused us real problems further down the line. As for the funding, don't worry about that.'

Hurst raised an eyebrow as he took a sip of his drink. 'Money makes this universe go round, my friend.'

'Through my dealings with the late General, I managed to hack into the Sigma Royal systems and find the funding codes, just in case. As we speak, I am transferring everything I can from their vault systems.'

A broad smile grew across Hurst's face. 'You are full of surprises. I'm sure you've considered the tracking facets of corp security tech, of course.'

'Of course. I'll leave them some money, however this will all-but bankrupt Sigma Royal and I assume will bring an end to their plans. I've also managed to get some Libra codes too, however best not provoke them yet.'

'You've been busy,' said Hurst, purposefully looking away from the corpses. 'Where's that damned clean-up crew?'

A moment later, Ruck returned with several men who quickly removed the bodies and began cleaning up the blood that had formed a large pool across the smooth floor.

Hurst finally stood from the table and moved to look out of one of the windows, hands clasped behind his back. The mech joined him.

'Now we need to find a way to ensure the Sigma forces depart without any conflict,' Hurst thought aloud.

'Again, I can help with that,' The Luminary stated. 'There's one last test of the app I need to run.'

157

'Pray tell.'

'I will take control of all the mechs with the link installed.' The Luminary's avatar looked up into the night sky. 'And I'll get rid of every tech officer Grosnik assigned before bringing the whole mech army here.'

'When you say *here*, you mean Tidewell?' Hurst asked.

Its sensors remained fixed on the stars above. 'Of course. Then with the entire force under my control and Sigma's money in our hands, we can begin the next stage of the plan.'

Hurst raised his eyes to the heavens too and grinned. 'This has been a good day.'

Echo flagship Glaive, Miller system

Ever since returning to the Expanse, Kurcher found himself questioning who he had become. Did people see him as Hewn's assassin now, or was he just that washed up Taurus enlister whose drug habit helped destroy two worlds?

Despite treatment from the Echo medics, his shoulder and arm were still slightly numb. Flynn's flames had burnt deeper than he realised at the time, and the knife wound had left a small scar, but it was his mind that was most affected from the events on Kharma.

Do you really want to keep putting yourself through this? Frost asked.

That question kept coming back to him as he walked along the corridors of the *Glaive*. Maybe it was time to disappear. Let the rest of them deal with rogue corporations, pirate vendettas and the apparent alien threat.

A threat you're responsible for unleashing on the galaxy, Santa Cruz kindly reminded him.

He found his way to the brig. Inside, Hewn and Fischer were in mid-conversation, both of them staring into the cell containing the strange woman he had heard so much about. The crew had been whispering about her ever since Rane and Broekow had brought her on board. Kurcher was surprised to see the latter also present, rifle slung over his shoulder and eyes firmly fixed on the terrorist.

'How're you feeling?'

Kurcher glanced at Hewn and shrugged. 'Been better. Sleep helped though.'

He knew that the pirate's demeanour would have been so much different had he and Drake returned with different news. Flynn's death pleased him in a morbid sort of way. The fact they had managed to locate some of the stolen drugs though seemed to make Hewn's day. It was only about a quarter of what had been taken from Curos, yet it was enough to be considered *a good result* by Echo.

Kurcher approached the cell to get a better look at this Kindred woman. She had the blank gaze, the complete lack of emotion and the smell of one of them. Under the grime and unpleasant odour, she looked like she was mid-thirties, although the sunken cheeks and eyes gave her a sickly look so one might be mistaken for thinking she was older. He also noticed bandaging around her midriff.

'I don't need to ask whether she has said anything,' he muttered, trying to see her eyes clearly behind the fringe. 'Lucky to get her alive though.'

'Alive might not be the best word to use.' Broekow didn't look at him when he spoke.

'Where did you say you found her?'

The rifleman hesitated, reluctant to engage with him. 'Marden's End. The Kindred stopped us getting to Harz.'

Kurcher gave Hewn a wry smile. 'They bombed a Bold station? That'll go down well.'

'They nearly destroyed the whole place,' Hewn told him. 'Part of it broke away after the explosions. Quite a few of those fuckers died but Harz wasn't one of them, or so say reports we received.'

'So where's Rane?' Kurcher asked. 'Not that I want to see his smug face again.'

Fischer gave a slight shake of the head before answering. 'He's helping Vekkerd work on that Sigma mech, trying to make sure The Luminary can't take control again.'

When Kurcher laughed, it was more from disbelief. 'So what, we're just forgetting about everything that prick did now? Welcoming him into the fold and making him feel like one of the team?'

'I don't forget,' snapped Hewn, glaring at him. 'Ever. I remember what he did; the lives he took. I also remember everything *you* did but sometimes you have to look at the bigger picture here. Rane is one of the best engineers around and, as much as it irks us all, he's walking round with a genius IQ. If anyone can work out how to stop The Luminary spying on us through that thing, it's him.'

There it is, Frost whispered. *Hewn kept you around because you're useful. Don't ever stop being so.*

'He can't be trusted though, Jaffren,' Fischer said, voicing Kurcher's own thoughts. 'I wasn't about to have him wandering the ship with that bloody sword of his.'

It was Broekow who spoke next, to their surprise. 'Rane doesn't need the sword to be dangerous. Just his mind.'

'Well you *are* partners now,' quipped Kurcher.

Broekow's brow furrowed and his lips pursed, yet he didn't bother saying any more.

'Our medics looked her over,' began Hewn, moving the conversation back to the matter at hand. 'Treated her for the bullet wound. She never so much as flinched or shed a tear.'

Kurcher looked the woman up and down, his expression clearly showing the disdain he had for the terrorists. 'They're brainwashed, all of them. Someone somewhere is turning them into mindless walking bombs and sending them on one-way trips. The one I killed on Sullivan's Rest didn't register the bullets I peppered him with. It was the shot into the brain that finally dropped him.'

'Pain receptors are turned off,' nodded Hewn. 'When she was examined though, we found that she has app implants. They're bastardised versions of the sight app, with aspects of comms too.'

Kurcher recalled the flash of data in the eyes of Jenson Cassius, although that had not been his name of course. 'A way for those who are behind The Kindred to feed them intel. Issue orders. What else did you find?'

Hewn pointed a metal finger at her. 'She's malnourished, yet clearly has been fed enough to keep her alive. She's got no symbols or emblems anywhere on her, not even a tattoo. No possessions apart from her clothes, which are pretty rancid.'

'She's got a tongue so could talk if she wanted,' added Fischer. 'Or if she was able.'

Kurcher rubbed at the stubble he was letting grow. 'Can you access the app data?'

Hewn shook his head with a hint of annoyance. 'I wish. Hacking it could result in total shutdown, which wouldn't get us anywhere.'

'So what's the next move?'

You already know the answer to that, chuckled Frost.

Hewn shrugged. 'We're going to let her go.'

Kurcher watched as the two Echo pirates left the brig, then glanced at Broekow. 'You staying here then?'

'Going to keep an eye on her.'

'She isn't going anywhere just yet. Why don't you go get a drink or, better still, some sleep?'

161

'I don't need either.' Broekow's voice wavered slightly. 'As soon as Rane is done here, we'll be gone again after Harz.'

Kurcher watched the rifleman for a moment. So different to the man who joined him in hunting down Choice on Rikur, or who helped him apprehend Ercko. Different to the man Broekow was when he was around Frost. Hell, he was even different to the man who took a swing at him in the *Glaive*'s bar not so long back, before he was captured by that sadistic Bold fuck.

'I hope you find him this time and put a bullet between his fucking eyes.'

At this, Broekow finally turned to look at him. 'I will.'

When Kurcher left the brig, he found Hewn waiting for him.

'It's nearly time,' the pirate said in a hushed voice. 'When that Kindred bitch leaves, she'll be fitted with a tracking device. You and Drake will follow her to whatever filthy nest she scuttles back to and see if you can find any way to destroy it.'

Kurcher gave a curt nod. 'Planning on giving her a ship?'

'Just be ready.' Hewn started to walk away. 'This is the best chance we have to get rid of these bastards once and for all.'

'Unless they don't have just one base of operations. Unless they're nomadic.'

Hewn didn't say another word and disappeared around the corner, most likely returning to his beloved system map that he stood over most days.

Kurcher's next stop was engineering and the long walk there gave him time to think. Being reminded about the implants The Kindred were using had made him miss the old sight app Taurus had fitted him with. The way it could track targets and help him during missions had made catching crims much easier. It also helped steady his aim whenever he got caught in a firefight.

The only working app he had now was for Echo communications. The burnt-out corp tech in his head had finally stopped giving him headaches and he wondered how the implant junkies out there managed to stay sane with so much going on at once. The black market apps were particularly dangerous, like the customised sight app that managed to effectively give the user eyes in the back of their head. He'd seen too many people lose their minds quite literally to a malfunctioning implant.

Maybe you don't miss them as much as you think, Frost remarked.

He thought of the pilot and her connection with the *Kaladine*. It was like she was one with the ship, able to access systems no matter where she was. Most

162

pilots or navigation officers were kitted out with apps now linking them to their respective vessels, although there were some who still liked to fly naturally.

As he neared the engineering bays and began searching for Vekkerd and his dangerous mech buddy, Kurcher began to wonder whether The Kindred were simply app junkies who pushed their addiction too far and went mad.

They're fucking insane alright, said Angard. *But someone put those implants in them for one reason.*

To blow the shit out of everyone else, Ercko cackled.

He found them in one of the smaller disused rooms under the watchful eye of two pirates. They weren't the same two as last time naturally. Ram, under the control of The Luminary, had broken a number of bones in one of the previous guards, leaving him having to learn to walk again. It seemed Hewn hadn't learnt his lesson and felt two was ample protection. Kurcher was quick to note that these new pirates were carrying heavier weapons though.

The mech was still powered down thankfully, looking like some resting beast you didn't want to awaken. Its user, which was a term he now used loosely, was in deep conversation with Rane, who was in full explanation mode about some shit Kurcher really couldn't care less about.

'Why is it still in Sigma colours?' he asked, bringing an abrupt end to their technical chatter. 'I'm sure Hewn won't want it looking like the stolen Sigma property it is.'

'We'll paint it soon enough,' Vekkerd scowled. 'There are more important matters to sort out first, like Ram not trying to kill me when we power him up again.'

Kurcher approached them, trying not to acknowledge Rane's smile. 'It wasn't Ram that tried to kill you. It was that cowardly prick who doesn't want to get his own hands dirty.'

'The Luminary is very clever,' Rane said, studying the app interface between the visual sensors. 'This technology is impressive, unique and yet somewhat familiar.'

Kurcher knew that Rane hadn't missed the similarities between the human and alien tech. After all, it was he who turned on that console on the *Grail* when they had stolen on board the weapon.

'So can you cut the link to The Luminary?'

Vekkerd and Rane glanced at each other before the officer replied. 'We can't sever it. We can block it though.'

Kurcher dared another step closer to the sleeping automaton. 'I know you're just dying to explain how. Keep it simple though, for someone who really doesn't give a shit but will have to report back anyway.'

Rane tapped the interface. 'We took technology that Echo use to inhibit existing apps, like they did with your old corporation ones, and we tailored it to block long range signals. As long as Boryn keeps Ram close, The Luminary won't be able to take control.'

Kurcher noticed Vekkerd's grimace. 'How close?'

'Put it this way, we won't be able to do what we did in Monarch City.' The tech officer gave a shrug. 'Not that I want to do that again.'

'So it's what *we* did now then,' smiled Kurcher. 'Finally warming to us, are you?'

'Let's not get carried away. Echo have treated me well since snatching me from Sigma, but I have family who will be worried and probably think I'm dead.'

'That's for the best, Boryn.' Rane nodded at Kurcher. 'Wouldn't you agree, Davian?'

Kurcher chose not to answer and instead circled the mech, trying to get a good look at the *customisation* the two men had carried out.

'What's with this first name thing?' Vekkerd asked Rane.

At this, Kurcher jumped in. 'It's the way he gets you to think he's your best friend before he screws you over. He's a very good engineer and can handle himself in a fight. Just don't ever turn your fucking back on him.'

This time, Rane chose not to say anything, although the wry smile that crossed his lips just fuelled Kurcher's contempt.

Vekkerd looked between the two, weighing up the tension in the room. 'Back on Kismet, we heard about you two quite often. It was hard to believe the reports. Apparently there was quite the bounty on both your heads.'

'Still is.' Kurcher gave Ram's rear panel a light kick, drawing a scowl from the young officer. 'Rane has been a wanted man for years. It's only my recent exploits that have turned me into a criminal. Now I can add the Knights Templar and the Bold to the list of people out for my blood.'

'I heard that you two were responsible for what happened to Meta and Straunia,' Vekkerd said boldly. 'That true?'

'We both had our parts to play.' It almost sounded like there was regret in Rane's voice, although Kurcher knew that wouldn't be the case. 'Davian was under orders to activate the *Grail* so really it was Jorelian Santa Cruz who was responsible for destroying life on Meta.'

Kurcher saw Vekkerd's expression darken suddenly, although the officer tried his best to hide it. That was when the realisation struck.

What if this man had grown up on Meta? Frost asked.

What if he lost friends and loved ones in that attack? added D'Larro.

Rane seemed oblivious to this possibility as he continued. 'What happened at Straunia was down to me ultimately. Santa Cruz was going to lay waste to it too and Davian tried his best to stop that from happening. It was my decision to reactivate the weapon and kill everyone on Straunia.'

Vekkerd gave Kurcher a look tinged with surprise. 'You tried to stop them?'

'We were too late to try stopping the attack on Meta,' Kurcher told him. 'With Hewn's help, we managed to get to the *Grail* before that bastard. We succeeded in stopping him but *this* fucker manipulated us so he could murder an entire planet himself.'

Vekkerd shook his head and his glance at Rane was now a fearful one. 'Why?'

'I had my reasons.' Rane's answer was dismissive. 'But let's focus on the task at hand.'

Kurcher saw Vekkerd's reaction to the response; the sheer disbelief that Rane shrugged off killing the entire population of the planet like it was something insignificant.

'Let's get Ram powered up, shall we?' Rane asked the officer.

'You sure it's safe?' Kurcher eyed him warily. 'That you haven't rigged it to kill us so you can steal it for yourself?'

Vekkerd accessed his app. 'Fuck it.'

Kurcher smiled at this. He couldn't help but see something of himself in this man Echo kidnapped. He had been forced to kill people he never dreamt of harming, and had been interrogated, pressured and injured during his time with them. Yet here he was, helping them and starting to talk like some grizzled veteran enlister.

He was jolted from his thoughts by Ram whirring into action and rising quickly from the floor to look down at them with those cold visual sensors.

Under Vekkerd's guidance, the mech began to move around the room, testing each limb and swivelling its head left and right.

'Verdict?' Kurcher called to the suddenly smiling Vekkerd.

'Full control,' came the reply. 'Within these four walls at least.'

Kurcher caught Rane grinning at him. 'It'll do for now, until we can get our hands on The Luminary.'

'Davian, can I speak with you in private?' Rane gave a nod to Vekkerd and headed for the door.

Kurcher sighed, then signalled to the tech officer. 'Keep an eye on the link. Any sign of someone trying to take control, shut it down.'

Once outside engineering, he prepared himself for whatever shit was about to vomit from Rane's lying mouth.

'You've seen that interface The Luminary created, Davian. I believe there's much more to this app dealer than originally thought.'

'Yeah, I saw it. There are similarities with what we saw on the *Grail* and the data that Santa Cruz was after. Could be a coincidence.'

Rane scoffed at the remark. 'You're an intelligent man. We both know the alien technology when we see it, or at least components of it. No, the Link app was built by someone who has seen it or maybe even been hands-on with it.'

'Doesn't really detract from the fact the bastard needs to die,' growled Kurcher, his voice lowered as a group of pirates wandered past.

'You're missing the bigger picture here, Davian.'

Just ice this motherfucker once and for all, said Ercko.

Do what you were being paid to do, added Santa Cruz.

You've had numerous chances to kill Rane, D'Larro pointed out.

He's the greatest mass murderer in the history of the human race, Santa Cruz stated. *It's your duty to rid the galaxy of such scum.*

Kurcher laughed at the thoughts whirling around in his head. 'Fucking duty.'

'Did you hear me, Davian?' Rane was looking at him with almost genuine concern.

'I heard you. There's always a bigger picture when you're involved. All this means is that The Luminary came into contact with the tech somewhere. Whoever it is could've been a member of Santa Cruz's crew or one of the researchers he had working on understanding the alien dialect. Unlike Ram though, The Luminary is human and can die like the rest of us.'

Rane shook his head. 'Doubtful they are just someone who brushed up against the tech somewhere.'

That irked Kurcher. 'Look, *Edlan*. Hewn's left you alive to help Broekow take care of Harz. You've helped Vekkerd with his pet and now it's time you fucked off. Leave The Luminary to us.'

Rane's smile goaded Kurcher. 'I understand all that, Davian. It's just Boryn told me that, when The Luminary took control of Ram, it was like they recognised you and Jaffren. That could only mean one thing.'

'I know,' Kurcher cried, finally starting to lose his temper. 'It means it could be someone we've met before.'

Earth,
Sol system

Hayward wanted to pull her hair out. Tabb's stubbornness was proving to be particularly challenging this time.

'I hear what you're saying, Ariana, I really do. However, we need Libra with us to make this work.'

Tabb's image went blurry for a second, her stern face pixelating to hide the harsh features. 'Do you hear what I'm saying? If we send a significant portion of our fleet with you to Straunia, it leaves us wide open to being fucked yet again by Sigma or anyone else who fancies a go.'

'Surely Sigma won't continue their attacks now that Grosnik is gone.' Hayward was trying to keep calm. 'His death will have them reeling for a long time.'

Tabb's eyes narrowed. 'I'd like to shake whoever killed him by the hand as they did us a huge favour. Still, he was just one cock amongst many and someone else will take his place quickly enough.'

'Do you believe bombing Straunia is a good idea?' Hayward decided to cut to the chase and get to the end of the conversation as fast as she could. 'Are you with us or not?'

'One thought that has been eating away at me.' A strange smile appeared on the Libran's lips. 'Why the fuck am I discussing this with the judicial officer of Taurus Galahad? Your remit surely is to bring criminals to justice, not negotiate with ranks higher than your own.'

Hayward returned the smile, knowing just how Tabb tried to push everyone's buttons this way. A spiteful comment here or a racial slur there just to poke the fire and see what happens.

'I am a senior board member and the only person ranked above me is General Garrett, as you well know. *He* is too busy prepping the fleet for what's to come and making sure we don't let any more of those alien nightmares into our space. So I'm afraid you'll just have to deal with me.'

Tabb regarded her for so long that Hayward thought the comms might have frozen. 'Fair enough. I'll come back to you as soon as I've met with our board.'

When the link had been severed, Hayward puffed her cheeks out and reclined in her chair. Tabb seemed to respect those who offered up good banter but it was mentally exhausting. She had only just turned to peer out into the compound below when there was a knock at her door. Akeman didn't wait to be called in and was followed into her office by Winter, who gave her the curtest of nods.

'I hope it's good news,' she told them. 'I'm ready to drown myself in a bottle of vodka.'

'It's news,' said Akeman bluntly. 'Put it that way.'

Hayward tried to read their expressions. Winter never seemed to display any emotion, his shiver-inducing eyes remaining fixed on her. Akeman looked tired but wouldn't accept a seat when she offered him one. She wasn't sure how much sleep the agent got each night but she had heard from her staff that they would see him wandering the halls at all hours. Then again, she didn't exactly sleep peacefully after everything that had happened over recent months. They both survived the attack on Kingston by Rist and his boomer-carrying mercenaries, then the ambush on Titan Station. She knew that, like her, Akeman's dreams were always invaded by those inhuman things they encountered.

'Who wants to go first then?' she asked the two men.

'The Taurus Galahad fleet is on high alert,' Winter began. 'However, the activity of all other corporation vessels is irregular to say the least. I would recommend increasing the patrols of all Taurus systems, in particular looking for any sign of Sapphire Nova ships. I would also urge the General to get more guardians to the jump points.'

'He is aware of what needs to be done,' Hayward said, wondering where Garrett actually was right at that moment. 'You have to remember that our fleet is depleted so the General is ensuring any non-military ships are being fitted with weapons. That takes time.'

Winter stared into her eyes for a few silent seconds, as if he had turned to stone. 'If the infusers are already infiltrating the other organisations, Taurus could face attacks from all sides. The One Mind will be finding a way to get to every living being it can. No colony is safe.'

Hayward glanced at Akeman, who gave the slightest of shrugs. 'Then you'd best locate the One Mind quickly. We destroy it and all this goes away, right?'

'Yes.'

Winter's reply didn't fill her with confidence. 'General Garrett will arrange further patrols and protection of the jump points as soon as *humanly* possible.

169

In the meantime, we're trying to get additional support from our allies, however they're having to secure their own territories so it's a difficult ask.'

'That leads into my report,' remarked Akeman, handing her his HDU. 'Grosnik's death isn't the only thing Sigma have to worry about. Firstly, they've been effectively bankrupted by a security breach. Someone hacked into their financial systems and transferred most of their funds out to an untraceable account.'

Hayward didn't really know what to say about that revelation. With technology evolving in leaps and bounds each year, it was no surprise that eventually one of the criminal organisations would find a way to hack into highly secure corporation vaults. The fact that it coincided with Grosnik losing his life just raised more questions.

'They've also lost their entire army of mechs that they had been building.' Akeman let that one sink in before continuing. 'Reports are that all of the mechs suddenly turned against their users, with many tech officers and quite a few soldiers being killed in the process.'

'*Every* mech?' Hayward asked, her voice wavering somewhat at the thought of that many constructs all marching as one.

Akeman nodded solemnly. 'Many were on Summit at the time, however the mechs on other worlds broke protocol too. Apparently that particular army is now under the control of Fortitude, although my belief is that The Luminary is behind it. Grosnik had dealings with the app merchant and with Morton Hurst. He and part of the Sigma fleet were at Summit during Fortitude's takeover from Impramed.'

'Any retaliation from Impramed?'

'Not yet.' Akeman pointed at the HDU. 'It looks like Fortitude have made Summit their new headquarters, protected by an army of mechs. They kept most of the Impramed personnel prisoner there, most likely to use as bargaining chips.'

Hayward scanned the data, her eyes growing wider with every sentence. 'And the Sigma fleet just left?'

'Yes. They could've engaged in a fight with the Fortitude ships that were in orbit but instead they fled the Benedict system completely.'

'So, let me get this straight,' she said, holding the HDU up and waving it at the two men before her. 'Grosnik builds a mech army with the help of Fortitude and The Luminary, which he uses against Libra Centauri. He then goes to Summit, I'm assuming to help the mercs take the planet. After Fortitude take control though, Grosnik is killed, the mech army seized and Sigma Royal bankrupted.'

'Pretty much sums it up.' Akeman nodded towards Winter. 'We believe that the General was murdered by Hurst because Fortitude had what they wanted and he would've stood in their way. The mechs probably helped in ensuring there was no immediate backlash from the Sigma forces.'

The thought did pass through Hayward's mind that perhaps Ariana Tabb had paid Hurst good money to get rid of the thorn that was Grosnik. Tabb was one woman you really didn't want to scorn. It was a frightening thought though.

'Keep a close eye on them,' she ordered Akeman. 'But our priority remains the alien threat. I know that Fortitude and the rest of the merc outfits will take any advantage they can while our heads are turned, however I doubt they will mount any offensive against Taurus Galahad territory.'

'Understood and agreed,' Akeman muttered, scooping up his HDU.

Hayward turned to Winter then, a deep sigh escaping between her lips. 'Tell me something about Jorelian Santa Cruz. I met him in passing once and heard a lot of rumours about the man. You worked for him though, so what was he like?'

'I worked for him because he was a high-ranking officer.' His reply was almost angry in its blunt delivery. 'He tasked me with finding Cooke, the enlister who stumbled upon the data that Santa Cruz had been searching for. His orders were simple. Bring Cooke in for questioning. The rest of his team and his ship were expendable.'

'His report stated that Cooke and his crew were killed when trying to flee.' She noticed Akeman give a slight shake of his head out of the corner of her eye. 'I wonder how many other documents he falsified.'

Winter continued. 'Commander Santa Cruz was power-hungry and believed he could control the entire galaxy with the *Grail*. I realised that he would have seen Taurus Galahad bow to him too eventually, albeit somewhat too late.'

'He packed you off to the labs on Minerva before you could do anything,' Akeman remarked.

'Not quite. You'll know I'm sure, Miss Hayward, that I managed to get a brief message to Rees, who had ordered me himself to find out what Santa Cruz was planning. I was injured from my time on Cerberus; tired and hurting. I never considered that he would turn on me and drive that knife into my chest.'

Hayward offered him a smile, which was something she rarely did where Winter was concerned. 'That message helped defeat that bastard and his rogue fleet, which saved millions more lives.'

'It wasn't Taurus that defeated the commander,' Winter stated. 'It was Davian Kurcher and his allies.'

Hayward shared another glance with Akeman. 'You knew Kurcher too?'

'I watched the enlister go about his messy work, finding the criminals that Santa Cruz wanted. I tracked his every move from Rikur to Cradle to Summit, and even to the binary system outside the Milky Way.

'I had to intervene on more than one occasion to ensure Kurcher succeeded, killing Nova personnel mostly.'

'I heard that Kurcher is unorthodox,' Akeman added. 'People describe him as a brash brute with zero tact.'

Winter did something then that caught them both by surprise. The cold eyes looked down at the floor, sudden uncertainty etched on the usually stoic face.

'Under orders from Santa Cruz, I shot down the *Kaladine* after pursuing them to Cerberus. I regret my actions there.

It was after leaving the quaran that I realised I was just another pawn in the commander's sick game. Davian Kurcher and I were very similar in that regard.'

'We were all used by him in one way or another,' said Akeman angrily. 'I fed him intel time and again because I thought he was using it for the good of Taurus. I got myself a lot of new scars working for that prick.'

Hayward rose slowly, her legs feeling heavy and sore. 'No time for regret, I'm afraid. We've got a lot to do before we can wallow in the past.'

'Best get on with it then,' Akeman nodded, turning for the door.

'There have been many names mentioned in the multitude of reports.' Hayward was staring out of the window once more. 'Those who found themselves embroiled in the events that have transpired over the last couple of years. Most are dead now and yet four names continue to surface: Kurcher, Rane, Hewn and Broekow. Why do you think that is?'

'They are key players in everything that has happened,' ventured Winter. 'Whether they like it or not.'

Hayward looked back at him with a raised eyebrow. 'You believe they have a part to play still?'

'I do.'

She shrugged and returned her gaze beyond the window. 'You may be right.'

When she didn't offer anything more, Akeman beckoned to Winter and they left the office. As the door closed, Hayward's forehead touched the cool glass and she sighed deeply. She wished she could reach out for her son or her husband; find solace in their embrace. At that moment, she fought against the tears that threatened to flow, needing to hold herself together despite being alone. Getting emotional seemed pathetic when compared to the level of death and uncertainty rippling across the galaxy.

A few years ago, she had seen the Revenants as the main threat to Taurus Galahad and its people. If the One Mind and its growing army landed on Earth, the religious fanatics would fall just the same as the rest.

Her eyes lifted to the dark skies above. Suddenly the room seemed colder than usual and she shivered as a sense of dread began creeping up her spine, not for the first time. If the day came when humanity fell under the control of the alien technology, she would make sure she didn't become one of them. She would burn herself and everyone else around her to ash before she let that happen.

Crown's Reach Station,
Kember system

It had been a really shit day and all he wanted to do was retire to his quarters and kick back with a beer and some medicinal porn.

Junior Operations Officer Raggett strode through the weaving corridors of the station like a petulant infant, his footsteps purposefully heavy and his mood sour for all to see. He knew that he would be ridiculed by some for his body language but he didn't give a shit. He had put up with the intense scrutiny of those above him during morning rounds, questioning his every move, before being summoned for an impromptu appraisal in which he was told he *must do better*.

So what if he was knocking on the door of forty and was still a junior officer? It didn't mean he wasn't working hard, and yet Sigma Royal seemed to see it as a huge negative mark on his record.

He was interrogated about his ambition and desire to move up the corporate ladder. At one point, he nearly blurted out that, maybe if the senior officers weren't such assholes, he could more easily find the next rung of said shitty ladder.

Raggett heard a familiar laugh and looked up to see Marla just ahead with two of her friends that he had never bothered to learn the names of. Thankfully she wasn't laughing at him and was instead sharing some joke that, despite not hearing any of, he found himself grinning at like an idiot. It was an involuntary reaction whenever he was near her.

'Finished for the day already?' he asked, catching her by surprise with the sheer volume of his voice in the echoing corridor.

'Hey, Rag.' She glanced at her friends, who quickly looked down at the floor. 'Yeah, just heading off for a drink. You still on duty?'

He came to a clumsy halt and rubbed nervously at the back of his neck. 'Yeah. Been ordered to go welcome some transport that's arriving soon. It's carrying some wounded apparently from that shit that happened on Summit.'

Marla didn't stop. 'Have fun then.'

He watched her walk away for a moment before calling out. 'Maybe I'll stop by for a drink too once I've finished.'

He didn't get any response but heard them laughing again, no doubt this time at his expense. As he continued on his way to the pylon, he cursed himself for being so awkward around women, especially Marla. He had liked her for months, ever since she was stationed on Crown's Reach, but he was the same rank as her and that didn't help his cause. He had heard she was only interested in senior members of personnel.

He passed under the heavy duty door that was the entrance to the pylon, taking an extra long step as he did so. He had nightmares of there being some alert as he walked beneath one of them and the door crushing him as it secured the inner hub of the station.

For fear of his inner demons getting the better of him before he could greet the visitors to the station, Raggett focused on the task at hand and began to go over the details in his mind so he would be fully prepared to be the first face these unfortunates from Summit saw when they disembarked.

The transport was the *Cerano*, a Sigma Royal vessel that had been one of many sent to Summit to help extract the wounded after the fighting there. It still hadn't been released what was going on there, at least to the grunts like him, but he couldn't quite work out why or how Sigma Royal were involved. He also hadn't seen any proof of the *Cerano*'s journey, which he would have expected to have to hand. So, as the powers that be on the station didn't want to have to deal with the matter and were happy to send just him on his own instead of a medical team, he deduced that those on board couldn't be too badly injured. He was to escort them to medical if need be, meaning they could walk.

As he continued along the pylon, he noted the absence of any other soul. Probably because most people were finishing or starting shifts. It was only him stupid enough to still be working after putting in a full day.

As he approached the airlock where the transport was due to arrive shortly, Raggett began to wonder who might be on board. He had assumed Sigma soldiers and yet now he started thinking it could be Impramed personnel. Maybe that was why the senior staff were disinterested in dealing with it themselves.

While he waited, he straightened his uniform then made sure his HDU was ready to record every detail of the arrival. Time, number of people on board including crew, names, titles, injuries and of course any additional information he could glean as to what happened and why the *Cerano* had come to Crown's Reach instead of one of the other stations in Sigma space. It would all go in his report.

He found himself tapping one hand impatiently against his leg. If the transport was any later, Marla would have left the bar and gone off with some higher ranking dickhead by the time he got there.

He breathed a sigh of relief when he received a message alert via his comms app a moment later stating that the ship was on final approach. He heard it arrive just after and stood straight and tall as the *Cerano* docked, the pylon vibrating slightly as the airlocks connected.

As the doors slid open and he saw a group of figures meandering towards him, Raggett forced a smile onto his face. 'Welcome to Crown's Reach. My name is...'

His voice caught in his throat as the artificial light of the pylon fell upon the man at the front of the new arrivals and revealed a Sapphire Nova uniform complete with three sun pins on the collar. Behind him emerged others wearing similar garb and then, at the rear of the party, he saw two dressed in the red and black of Sigma Royal.

'I don't understand,' he admitted, taking a wary step back. 'I was expecting wounded from Summit.'

'Clearly,' beamed the Nova officer who had entered first. 'Thankfully we have no wounds to be treated. We have come here to help you.'

Raggett's eyes narrowed. 'And who exactly are you?'

'Doesn't matter.' The man's strange eyes glanced left and right. 'You're alone?'

'I have orders to escort you to medical for assessment.' Raggett suddenly wished he had brought his pistol along. 'I think we should stick to that plan.'

'Very well,' agreed the Nova officer with a warm smile. 'That works for us. However, there is something we would like to show you first.'

The Sapphire Nova personnel moved aside, allowing the two Sigma crewmen to approach. One had the telltale indicators that he was the pilot of the *Cerano*, his eyes showing data that could only belong to an app linked to his ship.

'I can see the panic on your face and in your eyes,' he said to the junior officer. 'Don't be afraid. You can trust us.'

'I'm not afraid,' lied Raggett, finding the movement in the pilot's eyes unnerving. 'This is just highly irregular and not what I was expecting. I'm sure you understand that I need to call this in, as per protocol.'

'Of course.'

Raggett lifted his HDU. 'Where did you pick these Sapphire Nova men and women up from? Was it Summit?'

'Medical is in the central hub of the station, correct?' The pilot had ignored his questions and instead was looking along the pylon.

'Right, listen up.' Raggett tried his best to make his voice sound convincingly stern. 'You will all relinquish any weapons you may be carrying and accompany me to medical, where a security detail will arrive to question you further.'

A strong hand suddenly gripped his arm and he looked up into the face of the Nova officer, who didn't say a word and instead stared back with eyes that seemed to almost gleam. Then a second hand grabbed his other arm and, as Raggett tried to pull away, he found himself held in place.

'Let me go right now, for fuck's sake. What the hell are you doing?'

The Sigma pilot leaned in to study his face for a moment before smiling and stepping aside. Raggett's flailing ceased instantly as he saw something else emerge from the airlock then. The nightmare approached quickly on multiple legs, its sickly coloured body flecked with silver and blue. Monstrous tendrils writhed before it, reaching for him. It was at that moment Raggett's bowels gave way and all he could muster was a quiet whimper as the creature pulled him into its frightening embrace.

Echo flagship Glaive, Miller system

Hewn had been gazing at Seko for what felt like hours.

The beautiful world of green and blue almost filled the view from his quarters, but it wasn't the planet itself that was keeping him transfixed. It was the fact that Rae and Wes were still down there, enjoying the hospitality of the colonists. When he last spoke with them, he heard how Rae had been helping the engineers to repair some of the failing machinery; how she had showed them just how to maintain maximum efficiency for as long as possible. He wouldn't expect anything else from her.

Wes was finding it more difficult, especially as there weren't many children at Cal's Hope his age. He had only just got used to living on Warren when they were shipped across to Seko. Hewn wanted his son to finally be settled, however that wouldn't happen for some time yet.

When Fischer arrived, Hewn was quick to turn from the window. A bottle was already waiting for Echo's second-in-command, who raised it in thanks before taking a long swig.

'I needed this,' he sighed, savouring the taste of their unique brew. 'You okay?'

Hewn gave a shrug. 'I will be once all the shit going on out there has been taken care of. I feel like we're so fucking vulnerable right now that an attack on Echo could come from any direction.'

'That Summit report got you worried then.'

'Course it did. The Luminary and Fortitude have got control of an entire army of mechs, which will make it nigh impossible to get rid of the fucker now. I don't like where that particular alliance is heading.'

Fischer nodded in agreement. 'You still reckon they iced Grosnik?'

Hewn gave him a look to indicate he had no doubt. 'Sigma are on their way out. Libra will wipe them out as soon as they can and start taking their systems.'

'At least we got rid of Flynn and managed to put the Templars back in their box,' Fischer said, trying to bring a positive to the conversation. 'Even I have to admit that Kurcher did a pretty good job there.'

'He admitted he got lucky on Kharma. Flynn put up quite the fight.' Hewn fell silent for a moment, glancing back at Seko. 'One down though. Four to go.'

'Four?'

'Harz, The Kindred, The Luminary and Hurst.'

Fischer nearly choked on his beer. 'Jaffren, you do realise what you're saying? You go after Hurst and we risk war with Fortitude. They're stronger than Echo.'

'So what, we just sit and wait for them to make the first move against us?' Hewn's temper began to flare. 'No. We'll let Rane and Broekow deal with Harz while Kurcher finds out how best to hit The Kindred. In the meantime, we'll try to locate The Luminary and work out a way to get to Hurst.'

Fischer regarded Hewn over the top of the bottle as he downed the remaining beer. 'With everything else going on out there, and with this bizarre new threat Taurus told you about, I'm just not sure we should worry yet about Fortitude. I mean, what about your plan to try salvaging what we can from the *Grail*?'

'Taurus want to bomb it,' muttered Hewn. 'If they mobilise quickly, we won't have time. Besides, no matter how much I want to get to it, it's too dangerous with those fucking things roaming around down there.'

As Hewn fetched two more bottles, it was Fischer's turn to watch Seko. 'So where do we go from here?'

'The survival of Echo is of paramount importance, Vance. If the only way we can secure our future is to ally ourselves with Taurus Galahad, so be it. We'll help them where we can while dealing with our own enemies.

'I knew that keeping Kurcher, Broekow and Rane alive would benefit us. I just didn't realise we would be using them to dispose of merc pricks and terrorist bastards. Might as well make use while we can though.'

'What about the intel leaks?' Fischer asked him, draining half his beer in one go. 'Can't say I'm any closer to finding whoever sold us out.'

Hewn tapped his bottle with a metal finger. 'I'm sick of worrying all the fucking time about one thing or another. Having someone in Echo working against us just takes the piss, after everything else we've been through. We'll find the fucker, or fuckers, and blow them out the airlock.'

'I'll keep looking. I wish I could say it was Kurcher or Broekow but they've been on the brutal receiving end of the leak so I ruled them out some time back.'

'Sounds like you're warming to Kurcher.' A rare smirk appeared on Hewn's face.

'Fuck off.' Fischer scowled as he finished the beer. 'The guy's scum.

Occasionally useful scum.'

Hewn cast his eyes across to the beautiful world the *Glaive* sat in orbit of. He had to agree that Kurcher had his uses, and yet he often considered whether or not keeping the ex-enlister alive was a sensible decision.

Taurus wanted to rebuild some relationship with Kurcher now that the corporation was being run by people with morals, as far as he could tell. Karin Hayward had made it her mission to root out the corruption that had seeped through their hierarchy and, despite her apparent innocence, he was sure the judicial officer was one of the sharpest people he had ever met. Her manner had been calm and polite throughout his time on Earth, unlike Ariana Tabb.

Hewn deeply regretted getting into bed with Libra. During their strained alliance, he had weathered the pressure frequently placed on him by officers wearing the green and white uniforms and been held accountable for those Libra personnel who died when Kurcher infiltrated his facility with his band of killers. He had even faced down Trystan Hengeveld. The decision to get rid of the troublesome officer was justified and yet, if Tabb ever found out, the alliance would turn into a war.

He remembered Trystan's brother, Lars, then. The only Libran he had ever truly trusted, and he ended up a charred corpse thanks to Rane and Ercko. He thought of Chaplin too, who proved to be too quick to divulge confidential information under duress. His body was still floating around somewhere in the Iridia system.

And yet, even though Libra were a danger to Echo on so many levels, they couldn't have defeated Santa Cruz and his rogue fleet without their help. The corporation reminded him of Rane. There was always a hidden agenda.

'What are you thinking?'

Hewn realised he had been silent for some time. 'That we haven't even had time to discuss business. I haven't seen our profit figures in months, assuming we are still making money.'

'We are,' Fischer assured him. 'Although I'd be lying if I said we were making as much as this time a couple of years ago.'

'You've kept an eye on our distribution network?' Hewn asked him. 'Supplies? Client demand?'

'I have. I knew you were preoccupied so wanted to keep things running as best I could. I've even sorted the rebuild of our brewery.'

'I appreciate that, Vance.'

Fischer shrugged. 'It's my job. However, I'd appreciate you speaking to some of the clients when you can. They were less than enthusiastic to deal with me. I don't have the metal arm after all.'

'Understood.' Hewn felt so tired suddenly. 'Well, I guess we need to go see Rane and Broekow off. With them fucking off again, Kurcher and Drake can concentrate on their Kindred mission.'

'There is one other thing I wanted to request,' said Fischer, jumping in before Hewn could end their conversation. 'I want to go after The Kindred too.'

Hewn's eyes narrowed as he placed the second empty bottle down slowly. 'I could do with you here, to look after things while I'm *precoccupied*.'

Fischer took a step closer to Echo's figurehead. 'You know why I'm asking, Jaffren. Let me be a part of this, to help track down those bastards and work out how to eradicate them.'

Hewn thought for a moment and couldn't ignore the look in his second's eyes. 'Okay. Go with Kurcher and Drake. Just don't get yourself killed, yeah?'

Fischer grinned. 'I'll try not to.'

~

'Come on, you can't say he wouldn't be useful in catching crims.'

Kurcher couldn't help but smile at Vekkerd. 'I'm sure your pet here would make the job much easier. There's just no point telling me. My days as an enlister are long fucking gone.'

Vekkerd rolled his eyes theatrically. 'Okay, but you know what I mean. You could just send *us* after this Harz guy and Ram could deal with him.'

'Us?' Kurcher raised his eyebrow.

'Well it's not like I'm going back to Sigma any time soon, is it?'

Drake had been listening to the tech officer pitching to Kurcher, an amused smirk on her unpainted lips. 'You're still effectively our prisoner so maybe you should cool it. I'm not sure you have the makings of a pirate.'

Vekkerd threw his arms up in the air, making Ram do the same with two of its legs. 'Well what the hell am I supposed to do then?'

Kurcher chuckled to himself. He had seen a significant change in these two people recently. Vekkerd had gone from being a naive, loyal officer of Sigma Royal, brainwashed by the corporation into believing the introduction of a mech army was a positive step to securing their future, to this wannabe member of Echo keen to prove his worth. There was still something in Vekkerd's eyes however that Kurcher couldn't put his finger on; something hiding behind the bravado.

Drake had been different ever since he had forced her to tell him about Harz. She had bottled up her fury for so long that simply explaining what had happened helped to release some of the pressure. Not all mind. She was still venomous when she wanted to be and hadn't lost any of her edge thankfully. With her, it was the decision to stop painting her lips blue that had the most significance, as though she had let go of her link to the Bold finally. She still chain-smoked and was high most of the time, but he liked the subtle change in her.

Drake caught him watching her. 'The fuck you looking at?'

'A vicious bitch,' he replied with a wide grin.

'Don't you forget it, dickhead.'

Kurcher turned back to Vekkerd. 'Ram is definitely useful to have around, more so once we've dealt with The Luminary and you can let him out of your sight. You want to help? Think of a way to track down that bastard.'

'I'm trying.' Vekkerd powered Ram down, watching as the mech descended into a position not unlike a resting dog. 'I'm just not as smart as The Luminary. Whoever they are, they're a genius, especially in getting Dalin Grosnik to agree to buy so many Link apps.'

Kurcher and Drake exchanged glances. They had opted not to tell Vekkerd about Grosnik's murder, simply so that the tech officer could focus on aiding them. It was clear that Vekkerd didn't like the late General, and yet there was also an element of respect in his tone when he did talk about him.

'I've known a lot of people who claim to be a genius,' Kurcher said solemnly. 'Most of them are unhinged and extremely dangerous. Most of them end up dead.'

'You must be fucking clever though, Vekkerd,' added Drake. 'To be able to work that app in the first place. It can't be easy.'

Vekkerd nodded. 'There were a shitload of candidates to become tech officers linked to the mechs. More found it easier to control the pursuits than the assaults.'

'All absolutely fascinating,' mocked Kurcher. 'But boring as shit. How are you holding up after getting smacked about by Ram before?'

'Fine.' Vekkerd had a disapproving scowl plastered across his youthful face. 'That was a while ago now so my chest is just about back to normal. It was lucky he didn't do anything more serious.'

'Serious?' Kurcher laughed. 'You'd be dead if Hewn hadn't been there.'

As Vekkerd went quiet, Drake stepped in. 'And what about you? Flynn basically kicked your ass before you got lucky and dropped him. Those burns still look painful.'

'Just another scar,' Kurcher replied, shrugging. 'I've had worse injuries.'

He suddenly remembered Drake had caught him studying his naked physique in the mirror the other day. She must have seen the look of disgust on his face as he examined the burns; his distant gaze as he ran a finger along the scar Santa Cruz had given him.

And you'd have been dead too had it not been for Broekow, the commander reminded him.

He hadn't heard the other voices for a while and their return made him groan out loud.

You've been saved on multiple occasions by others in fact, added D'Larro.

Usually by those you despise, said Ercko.

It was coincidence that Rane and Broekow chose that moment to walk in, the former wearing that annoying fucking smile.

'We're leaving shortly,' Rane stated. 'Taking Sally with us.'

'Who the hell's Sally?' Vekkerd asked.

'That Kindred member on board.' Kurcher shook his head. 'I still can't believe you fucking named her.'

Rane grinned. 'We had to call her something.'

'I can think of better names,' muttered Drake.

When silence fell, Kurcher noticed an expectant look in Rane's eyes. 'What, you just came to say goodbye or did you have something useful to tell us?'

'We're going to meet up with a transport called the *Halstead*,' the killer told them. 'It's an Echo ship used to move between systems in the Expanse. Sally is going to be given a lifeboat from the *Halstead* and sent off on her own. At that point, the hope is that whoever is issuing orders to The Kindred will bring her home.'

'Understood,' said Drake before Kurcher could offer any more quips. 'You can fuck off now then.'

Rane regarded her with a look of genuine curiosity. 'Very much your type, Davian.'

Kurcher saw Drake bristle and willed Rane to carry on talking, just so he could watch her gut him.

'For what it's worth.' When Broekow finally spoke, the others stopped to listen. 'I hope you find where The Kindred are coming from and work out a way to stop them once and for all.'

'Yeah, well I hope you track down Harz and put that ugly fucker out of his misery,' Kurcher responded. 'It'd be nice not to have the Bold and those suicidal bastards causing us more grief.'

'Unfortunately, another will take the place of Harz once he's gone.' Rane was still looking at Drake. 'There are a lot of them out there after all.'

'They'll know not to fuck with Echo at least,' said Kurcher, noticing Drake turn her back on them to light up one of her cigarettes.

'I'm not doing this for Echo,' Broekow remarked through gritted teeth. 'I'm doing it for me. Then I'm done.'

'What about you, Boryn?' Rane asked the tech officer, turning to face him with a smile.

Vekkerd glanced around the expectant faces as they all turned to look at him. 'What about me?'

Rane nodded at the sleeping Ram. 'You have an excellent skill set and an assault mech under your control. I'm sure Echo will recognise that having you on board is a major asset.'

'Don't have much choice,' shrugged Vekkerd. 'There's no alternative apart from getting plugged in the back of the head.'

'There are always choices,' grinned Rane.

Kurcher had had enough. 'Don't do that. I've heard these manipulative words too many times. The politeness, the calm tone, the stupid fucking smile. All bullshit.'

Rane held his hands up defensively. 'It doesn't pay to be coarse, Davian. I learnt that a long time ago. After all we've been through, you still don't understand just how alike we are.'

It was Kurcher's turn to laugh. 'And on that note, time for you to piss off.'

Rane was unperturbed. 'I told you that day when I helped Sieren and yourself find Choice that I handed myself in voluntarily to you, to do with as you saw fit. I knew that together though we could get to the bottom of what Santa Cruz was up to and we did.

I openly assisted you on Tempest, I joined Sieren and Jaffren in order to rescue you from the *Huntress*, I helped repair the *Kaladine*'s engine and I took you to Cobb so we could request the support of the Resistance.'

'Then you fucked us all over,' Kurcher snapped, all mirth vanishing in an instant. 'You used everyone, you arrogant prick, and yet you stand here and act like you did us all a favour.'

Throttle the motherfucker right here, Ercko said.

Stop letting him get under your skin, warned Frost.

You've had numerous opportunities to execute him, stated Santa Cruz. *Hesitation will get you killed.*

'If you two have finished, I don't need reminding of the shit you both put us through.' It was Broekow whose tone had grown angry now, and the rifleman spun on his heel awkwardly before leaving.

'I have to admit, you're acting like a couple of massive dickheads,' Drake added, her face suddenly lost in a plume of sweet smoke.

Kurcher wanted to smack himself around the face for letting himself get riled up by Rane yet again. As soon as he saw the smiling killer though, he was reminded of all the people who died at his hand. The crim before him was now the most prolific mass murderer in the history of the human race, and yet here he was roaming the Echo flagship like he was untouchable. Somehow, he always seemed to make himself indispensable, whether it be his penchant for killing without remorse or his exceptional engineering skills.

You can't deny he is a genius, said D'Larro.

He's adept at reading people, added Frost. *Unlike you.*

Broekow on the other hand was not just an open book. His pages had been torn out and crumpled up beyond recognition. Rane must have gauged the sniper's tendency to dwell on the negative aspects of his life, offering him a way to at least gain some sort of closure. Would Broekow be seeing Harz when he finally caught up to the bastard, or would he see all those who had wronged him?

'I wish you both luck then.' Rane headed after Broekow. 'Next time we meet, Davian, I feel we have a lot to discuss.'

Kurcher didn't bother replying. He had spent long enough trying to get the final word when locked in one of his many verbal sparrings with Rane. Instead, he turned to Drake.

'Go prep the *Falcata*. I need to have a word with Hewn before we leave.'

Drake breathed the drug-laced smoke deep into her lungs, then blew it out in his direction. 'Fine. I was getting bored anyway.'

As they headed for the door, Vekkerd cleared his throat as if to remind them he was still there too. 'Don't suppose you could persuade them to let me come with you?'

'You want to help us take down The Kindred?' Kurcher asked with the faintest hint of a smile.

'Ram could be useful,' Vekkerd stated.

Kurcher had to admit that the mech would give them an added advantage should they run into trouble, but Hewn would never agree to it. Not until The Luminary had been found and dealt with anyway.

'One day maybe.' Drake seemed to voice his thoughts this time. 'I can't afford to fucking babysit you and your metal dog too. Not when I have to keep this dickhead in check.'

Seko,
Miller system

When she breathed in the Seko air, Butler was reminded just how harsh life had been on Cobb.

Even spending time on the surface of their original home world resulted in an awful taste they just couldn't shift. Yet, despite all the negative traits Cobb had, she still missed it. Not the dust-strewn ruins littered with the remnants of their previous life. It was the closeness they had down in the expansive bunker; the feeling of family no matter someone's background. She still struggled to find that on Seko, which was probably down to the fact the population of Cal's Hope had so much space to roam in; a whole world of verdant forests and green lands that offered very little risk to those out running surveys. She simply didn't see them as often.

That was why she was glad to have the company on such a beautiful morning, with the Miller sun strobing through the tall trees.

'So is Cradle a lot like Seko?' Monk asked, sweat already beading on his broad forehead.

Tara Oakley smiled back. 'There are differences. Cradle has thick forests that you can easily get lost in and fast-flowing rivers that meander between the trees. It has an abundance of wildlife too, most of which hides away from the people living there.'

The burly engineer looked around. 'What, forests bigger than this one?'

Oakley sniggered. 'Much. You can still see the colony through the trees here.'

'It's the people that ruin these worlds,' muttered Cho, giving Butler a knowing look.

'Agreed,' Monk nodded. 'Let's not ruin this one.'

As they walked, Butler looked up into the canopy and spotted several small avians hopping between branches. Her survey team had called them *catchers*, having witnessed the way they fed. Several of the flock would jump from branch to branch, dislodging the insects that lurked at the top of the tree. The rest would then swoop down and catch said bugs mid-air. It was evolution at its most impressive.

'I heard a lot about Cobb when I was growing up,' Oakley was saying. 'The stories of the supply wars and how Taurus decimated the planet. How did you survive all that?'

There was only the sound of the twittering catchers for a few seconds as Cho and Monk considered how best to answer.

'We were all much younger then,' replied Cho eventually. 'It all started nineteen years ago when supplies became so scarce that some began taking matters into their own hands. Colonies started attacking one another just to get food and it descended into madness.'

'When were you born, Tara?' Monk asked her.

'2590.' Oakley looked almost sheepish. 'I celebrated my thirtieth birthday just before my uncle brought me here. Celebrate is perhaps the wrong word.'

'I turned twenty just as the fighting started,' Monk recalled. 'I'd been training with my dad to become an engineer but never got to finish. It didn't take long for our colony to fall apart.'

Butler decided she'd been quiet for long enough. 'Cal Fuller led most of us below ground into the bunker that had been built under Jefferson. He had planned to return to the surface and join the defence. That was when Taurus decided to step in. Soldiers tried to stop the fighting but all it took was a handful of idiots from one of the other colonies to open fire on them in the heat of the moment. That was the catalyst and Taurus decided then to make an example of Cobb; to show the rest of their worlds what happened to those who stepped out of line.'

'I'm sorry,' Oakley apologised. 'I didn't mean to dredge up painful memories. It must be surreal to be here now though. I can't imagine what you must've gone through.'

'Most people think that Taurus bombed us into oblivion,' Cho said with a grimace. 'Fact was they ended the fighting by sending in their assassins, who killed men, women and children just to prove a point.'

Butler heard Cho's voice catch in her throat and knew she would be remembering her family; her younger brother in particular, who she was so close to.

'We waited below while Taurus wiped pretty much everyone on the surface out.' Butler placed a reassuring hand on Cho's shoulder. 'When it went quiet, we still didn't venture out. Nearly two years of fighting had left the surface tainted and the skies darkened. Cal made sure we had what we needed to survive.'

'That's when you started calling yourselves the Cobb Resistance?' Oakley seemed genuinely intrigued.

Butler shook her head. 'Not straight away. We had other issues to attend to. Sickness, disease, supply shortages. We lost a lot more people after Taurus had left.'

Silence descended on the group as they continued through the forest; each of them lost in their own thoughts for a time.

Butler could still see Cal's face when she remembered the man who had raised her to take over the Resistance one day. He would never have believed she was running such a smart new colony on this amazing world inside the Echo Expanse.

They circled the colony slowly, taking in Seko's flora and fauna as they walked. Monk was the one to move the subject away from Cobb, pointing out how some of the trees contained their own ecosystems. It was mundane chatter, but Butler was glad of it. The daily operations of Cal's Hope had left her tired and needing a break. She hadn't even spent much time with her son recently, instead relying on others to act as nannies.

She wished Cal was there to spend time with his namesake, like a grandfather figure.

Once he was old enough, she knew her son would ask about his father too and that scared the shit out of her. Could she bring herself to actually tell him about Dale and how the engineer had betrayed them all? Could she face explaining how the two men she had cared for most ended up buried in the very bunker he was conceived in?

'Did you get a chance to speak any more with them, Marie?'

She looked up at Monk's expectant face. 'Sorry, what?'

'Our people Taurus released. They seem healthy and said they were treated well for the most part.'

Butler nodded. 'Yeah, I've had a chance to brief all of them and get them settled here. They're all a bit shellshocked but it's good to have them back.

As for Taurus, they're not the same corp as they were. Their hierarchy has changed for the better and it feels like perhaps they are seeking to make amends for what the previous board did. Still, I wouldn't trust any corp for as long as I live so I'd rather not have to engage with them if I can help it.'

'Guess we'd better get back shortly,' sighed Cho, giving Monk a prod. 'Got to peruse the team roster for today's surveys.'

'Are you taking any of the new ships out?' Butler asked them.

Cho pursed her lips, which always betrayed that she was feeling anxious. 'Maybe. I've got a few reservations.'

Butler frowned. 'Why?'

'Firstly, because they came from Echo. Makes me wonder who had to die so we could have them. Secondly, I'd rather we checked them thoroughly before including them as viable options. We've got no idea what sort of tech could be lurking behind the consoles and panels.'

Butler looked at Monk. 'You feel the same?'

'Not really,' he shrugged. 'They're good ships. Larger than our old ones and just slightly smaller than that ship Kurcher brings down here sometimes. We can have additional crew on board them, meaning more efficient surveys. They're faster, more pleasing on the eye and have even got weapon ports should we choose to utilise them.'

'But you're missing one key piece of information,' remarked Cho, the slightest tinge of anger in her voice. 'They've clearly had their designation markers and any emblems removed, so they are likely corp ships that Echo stole.'

Oakley decided to join the conversation. 'Is that a problem then?'

'Only if you're paranoid like Cho,' smirked Monk. 'At some point, you just have to start trusting people outside of this colony.'

'Fuck you.' Cho shot him the middle finger. 'Trust doesn't come easy to the rest of us.'

'It's down to you two to agree on a way forward.' Butler waved a hand at Oakley. 'We welcomed Tara into the fold, not to mention a few others, but I appreciate that the betrayal on Cobb has made us more wary. Whatever you decide is fine by me.'

'If it's any consolation, I've had trust issues for a long time,' stated Oakley. 'Something happened to me when I was younger that made me look at people in a whole different way. I didn't trust anyone, not even my own family.

It was a surprise to me that the first man I came to trust after that was someone who had suffered and been alone most of his life. He was volatile, dangerous and yet watched over me when nobody else would. He saved my life on more than one occasion and I realised that there were some out there in this galaxy who cared.'

Butler saw the sadness in Oakley's eyes. 'You lost him.'

'Yes. It wasn't long after that Hewn took me back to Cradle and I learnt to trust him too.'

Blunt as ever, Monk pushed her further. 'How did he die?'

When Oakley looked at him, she tilted her head slightly and seemed to be weighing up the engineer. 'Saving me one last time.'

'That's not what I...'

'No need to pry,' interrupted Butler, recognising the need to redirect the conversation.

Silence fell again for a while as they walked. Monk and Cho occasionally gave each other and Oakley a suspicious glance. When the comms units all except Oakley were carrying crackled into life and a man's voice called out for Cho, the tense atmosphere vanished in an instant.

Cho lifted it to her mouth. 'Go ahead.'

'You're needed in one of the engineering bays,' the voice told her. 'Leeson has had an altercation with Bambridge.'

'On my way.' When Cho lowered the unit, she shook her head. 'Just what we need before heading out.'

Butler offered her a reassuring smile. 'I'm sure it's nothing. You two go deal with it and I'll see you before you ship out.'

Monk cast one last look around the forest before reluctantly following Cho back to Cal's Hope. Butler and Oakley continued on their woodland trek, both enjoying the peace for a while longer.

'I've not met Leeson or Bambridge,' Oakley said eventually, as they passed through an area of denser foliage. 'Troublemakers?'

'Leeson is Cho's other half, although that's not what she would tell you. He's a good engineer, but he's quite quick to snap if anyone badmouths Cho.

Bambridge is one of our pilots. He survived the fight against Santa Cruz's rogue fleet but lost a lot of friends and never quite got over that. When we were being relocated here, he was one of those Taurus intercepted and captured, so he hasn't been on Seko long. He's not a bad guy. He's just been through a lot and you don't come out the other side completely unscathed.'

'I hear you.' Oakley pushed aside a low-hanging branch. 'I think everyone has their emotional baggage these days.'

'Agreed. Listen, I'm not one to push people about their past but I've spent a while putting two and two together ever since meeting Kurcher, Hewn and yourself. Maybe I've come up with five so tell me if I'm wrong.'

'I don't really like dwelling on my past.'

At this, Butler came to an abrupt halt. 'I understand that, Tara, but I'm in charge of Cal's Hope and I need to understand those that join us a bit better, to make sure that no issues arise further down the road. You've told me a few things here and there, as has Hedmun.'

Oakley realised she had stopped and so turned back to face her, a ray of sunlight piercing the canopy above to illuminate her blond hair. 'Okay, so what do you want to know?'

'You told me that you knew Kurcher and that he took you away from Cradle when the families were warring. You also said that Hewn took you home after your *adventure* with Kurcher.'

'That's right.'

This was the real reason Butler had wanted to get Oakley alone away from the colony. 'I've spoken with Hewn and he told me that man you were so fond of was named Horsten Angard.'

Oakley's mouth twitched slightly, her eyes looking down at the ground. 'True.'

Butler stepped closer to her. 'Kurcher was an enlister at that time. In fact, he was still an enlister when he was brought to Cobb by Edlan Rane, who told Cal and myself at the time a quite fantastic story that we struggled to believe.

'Your *adventure* with Kurcher is referring to his enlisting both yourself and Angard, right? Hewn and Rane were both there too.'

Oakley's eyes narrowed. 'How long have you known?'

'Since just after our meeting on the *Glaive*. I saw how you and Kurcher looked at one another. The contempt, and yet it was clear you had shared something much deeper.

So that means you have a criminal background and I'm going to need to know more before I can trust you.'

Butler could see that Oakley was taken aback having clearly believed the two of them to be forming some sort of friendship. Cho and Monk had talked about trust and it was more important to Butler than anything else now. She wouldn't be taken in by anyone again. The fate of Cal's Hope depended on it.

'I can imagine that Hedmun probably advised you against telling me,' Butler said when no answer came back. 'I appreciate his caution as he was only looking out for you, but I can't have secrets among us.'

Oakley drew in a deep breath and ran both hands through her hair. 'I was raped back on Cradle. I was so angry afterwards that, rather than hide away like some frightened girl, I decided to kill men who I thought would end up hurting someone else. I used my body to get to them and made sure they never woke up. Trouble was, I saw every man the same way after what had happened.'

Butler couldn't hide her reaction. 'Christ.'

'After Kurcher *enlisted* Horsten and I, I slowly started to see that not every man I met looked at me like those rapists did. And then everything changed when Bennet Ercko drugged me and tried to rape me on board Kurcher's ship.'

'How so?'

'I would've died were it not for the rest of the men there. Horsten beat Ercko so badly that he effectively put him in a coma and I was treated by a medic named Regan D'Larro. Then they looked after me until I had recovered from the overdose. I never committed another murder after that.'

Butler struggled to believe that, and yet there was a look of regret on Oakley's face she couldn't ignore. Regret mixed with a deep sadness. 'And Angard? What actually happened to him?'

'At first, I used him for protection only,' Oakley replied, blinking the tears away that threatened to flow. 'Then I came to realise that he genuinely cared for me and I grew fond of him. It wasn't anything romantic of course. It was just nice to have a friend, even if he was a crazy biomech who could rip a man in two if he wanted.

I got shot during my time with Kurcher and the others. Horsten went mad when he saw that. I remember seeing him charge into that Nova ship, slaughtering soldier after soldier, before I was dragged back onto the *Kaladine*. It wasn't long after that I found out he died blowing up part of that ship. Kurcher told me that he did it to allow us to escape, to protect me. I knew the truth though. Horsten had been in constant pain and he saw a chance to be at peace finally.'

Butler puffed out her cheeks. 'That's a lot of information to take in in one go. I think you and I need to talk further, and there needs to be plenty of alcohol available.'

Oakley smiled. 'I'm not much of a drinker.'

'No, I meant for me. I can't condone what you've done and having someone here with such a bloody history wouldn't exactly be good for the colony if others found out. However, Seko is a place to make amends. A place to start a new life.'

'In other words, you don't know whether to kick me out or not,' Oakley said softly.

'Exactly.' Butler bit at her bottom lip. 'Look, let's talk more later. For now, let's get back to the colony.'

She strode away, eager suddenly to be back amongst the rest of her people. Oakley fell in several steps behind and they walked in silence, emerging from the shade of the trees into the clearing. It was then that Oakley spoke again.

'I've been very happy on Seko, Marie. I really don't want to go back to Cradle.'

Butler acted as though she hadn't heard her, heading for the closest entrance into Cal's Hope. Before she reached it though, she spun to face the surprised woman.

'Why not? With most of Hedmun's fleet there, your family will be secure.'

'My uncle believes he has a powerful fleet that will make anyone think twice about taking on the Oakley family. He doesn't, and he gave three of his ships to gather intel for Hewn. I fear that Cradle is descending into a full-blown civil war; one which my family may not survive.'

Butler didn't know what to make of that. Most people would want to be with their family at such a time. Perhaps there was still more that Tara Oakley had to explain about her past.

'As I said, let's speak later.'

Her head reeling somewhat, Butler entered the colony proper and made her way quickly to the ops room. Once she had made some notes on the revelations just revealed to her, she would go see her son and spend time with him. As she unlocked the door, not liking to leave it open for anyone to sift through her records and plans, a voice called out to her from along the corridor.

'What can I do for you, Rae?' she asked.

At six foot, Hewn's wife stood three inches taller than Butler and looked as though she could beat most of the men in the colony in a fair fight. Of course, she was also an Echo pirate so it probably wouldn't be fair.

Rae nodded her head at the door. 'Can we talk inside?'

Once in ops, Butler poured them both a drink as Rae perched on the edge of one of the tables in an almost sultry pose. It was no wonder she had been turning heads since arriving.

'I'm thinking of returning to Warren,' Rae announced. 'Got a lot to do to rebuild out there and I doubt the Bold will attack it again.'

'I see.' Butler took a few seconds just to get her head straight, trying her best to temporarily forget what Oakley had told her. 'It's your choice of course but we'd be sorry to see you go.'

Rae studied the drink she had been handed and raised one eyebrow. 'Little early for shit like this, isn't it?'

'Not today.'

With a shrug, Rae downed it in one and grimaced. 'We'll have to get you something better than this. You can't even call this alcohol.'

'Would you consider staying on here?' Butler gauged the reaction from over the lip of her glass as she took a sip.

'Warren was our home for a long time,' Rae replied quickly. 'We'd even got used to some of the assholes running Gulliver, and Wes loved the brewery. I feel like we owe it to them to help get the colony back up and running.'

'I appreciate that. I just think that you'd both be a lot more comfortable here and you're pretty handy to have around. Wes could study here and enjoy the benefits of a world rich in resources and amazing sights.'

Rae pointed a finger up at the ceiling. 'I don't think Jaffren would want me here. He put me in charge at the brewery and our profits had increased tenfold. He's all about the money.'

'Screw what he wants.' Butler's outburst surprised both of them. 'What do *you* want?'

She knew that saying that to Hewn's wife would likely get back to him. She didn't care. Cal's Hope was her jurisdiction and she had to do what was best for the colony.

'I want a good home for my son,' stated Rae. 'I don't want him to live in fear of attack from the Bold or anyone else for that matter. I understand that Echo may never be safe from tossers like Harz, but I also don't want Wes to see the bloodshed that I have. He's always known his father to have an artificial arm so he never questions it. I was there at Jaffren's side after that mech tore his arm off and I saw firsthand the shit we would have to deal with. I can't let Wes be subjected to that.'

'I want the same for my son.' Butler cast her eyes around the walls of the room, which were adorned with maps and colony data. 'I want him to grow up here safe from anything like you and I have experienced. Cal and Wes could be the next generation of Seko colonists.'

Rae smiled warmly. 'That's a nice thought.'

'Hell, I'd even let Jaffren retire here.'

That made them both laugh.

'He'll never relinquish control of Echo,' Rae said. 'It's his baby.'

'So's Wes.'

In the silence that followed, Butler poured them another round of that poor excuse for alcohol and waited patiently for whatever came next. Eventually, Rae's dark eyes took on a steely gaze and she gave another shrug.

'I suppose we could stick around a while longer, seeing how I'm so damned useful around here.'

Butler couldn't help but grin and she raised her glass in a toast. 'Good. Here's to Cal's Hope. With you, me and Cho at the helm, this colony will thrive.'

As they drank, her thoughts slowly began to return to Oakley. She would have to make a decision quickly. Send her away once Hedmun returned to Seko or keep her on as a fully-fledged member of their community.

Right at that moment, Butler wished Fuller was still around to make the tough decisions.

Earth,
Sol system

The drumming of the rain behind Hayward was almost deafening as the wind whipped it hard against the glass. Every time lightning flashed across the angry sky, the lights inside the Taurus compound flickered too, and the thunder shook the very foundations of the building whenever it broke.

The storm had been raging across the region for nearly three hours having come down from the distant mountains and yet, as midnight approached, Hayward found herself so deep in thought that she scarcely noticed it.

She was thinking of the conversation with Garrett a short while ago that was ended abruptly by some technical glitch. Initially, she wondered whether this One Mind had found a way into their own tech, using it to cut their comms and begin some horrific offensive against Taurus, just as it had with Sapphire Nova. When she got an error message come up showing the storm had damaged some of their equipment, Hayward cursed her brain for jumping to conclusions.

The One Mind. It was almost incomprehensible when she thought about it. How could technology become effectively sentient enough to ensure its own survival by any means? How did a race as advanced as the Antecedents allow themselves to be enslaved by their own creation?

She always came back to something Garrett had said during their interrupted chat. 'The human mind isn't capable of computing such things,' he told her. 'Perhaps that will go in our favour.'

She knew what he meant of course but kept reminding herself that it didn't help Nova. There was no way of telling just how much of the wounded corporation had been taken over, however Winter had calculated it could be up to two thirds of their population already under the control of the One Mind. He had studied Rist's gathered intel meticulously and, together with the knowledge he had inherited, the assessment of how quickly the alien threat spread was the most accurate they had.

Akeman had referred to the One Mind as a *tech parasite*, which was also an apt description. He had added that parasites can be destroyed with the right solution, and that had given her more optimism. God knows she needed the boost.

'I'm heading to Minerva,' Garrett had said. 'Maybe there will be something

197

left over in the labs beneath Hayes that will help us. After all, that's where Winter came from.'

'What then?' she asked him.

The General had offered her a blurred smile as the resolution on the screen dropped. 'I have a few more stops but then we need to think about this assault on Straunia. I'll have to speak with Ariana Tabb myself I reckon. Not taking anything away from you of course.'

'Of course.' She didn't really mind if he wanted to liaise with that bitch direct from now on. Let him deal with her venom.

'It could take us a while to get everything ready for the offensive,' he mentioned. 'We'd have to send recon out to Flint so we knew what we were walking into and mobilising the fleet will take time.'

Hayward had simply nodded along, knowing it could be months before she was in the same room as Garrett again. That disappointed her. She had grown to enjoy his company when they were together. She knew it wasn't really appropriate to have some childish crush on a superior officer, especially when he was in command of the whole Taurus military, but she couldn't help how she felt. Maybe when all this was over. *If* it was ever over.

'So what're you up to in the meantime?' he had asked her.

'Mainly worrying.' Her answer had been honest at least. 'Worrying that everything we have worked so hard towards could all come crashing down if those infusers get onto Earth, or any of our key worlds. If they assimilated Sapphire Nova as quickly as Rist's intel implies, they could spread throughout occupied space like an out-of-control virus.'

'That's why we have to take action.' Garrett had meant his tone to be reassuring but the poor comms quality made it sound harsher than intended. 'Destroying the *Grail* and anything still alive in it will at least be a step in the right direction. Alive is possibly a bad word to use though, I guess.'

Hayward had pulled a face she knew wasn't attractive. 'How do you know it will help? We don't know for sure what or who is down there. We'd be killing people who are really just innocents in this. They never asked to be infused with that awful tech.'

'I know, Karin. I'm not saying it's going to be an easy thing to do but we have to act. There's no point sitting back and waiting for them to come to us. Proactive, not reactive.'

She hated that term. 'Look, let's change the subject, at least for now. I have made my decision on the enlister recruitment. I need those ships signed off though. Are you happy for me to do that?'

She couldn't tell whether the image on the screen had frozen or Garrett was simply hesitant to respond.

'It's not a priority right now and I really should be saying to you that we need every ship we can get.' The General had rubbed one tired eye then before giving her another of his smiles. 'However, I'm prepared to agree to the five ships we discussed. No more though.'

'Thanks. I owe you one.'

Hayward turned and looked out into the stormy night, watching the water droplets running down the pane and forming tiny vertical streams. Now that she was alone with her thoughts again, she was tempted to try contacting Garrett but he was on his way out to Berg and probably had a hundred and one things to do before he arrived there.

She considered asking Akeman up to her office for a drink, just to have some company. He was likely still awake, battling with his own demons as he so often did. No, she would leave him be.

Instead, she poured herself a shot of vodka and swallowed it in one. The alcohol had the desired effect, stirring her from the negative contemplation, and she grabbed her HDU. After scrolling through the five profiles, she put her signature on each and sent them through for processing. She knew nobody would be working in personnel at that time but at least they had it ready for the morning.

Five new enlisters. She didn't like the title and had wanted to call them *judicial operatives*. Then she backtracked after imagining how their criminal targets would react to that. She wanted them to fear these five people, not laugh at them.

Her predecessor had made a bold decision previously that resulted in the enlisters all being wiped out by Santa Cruz. Rees must have known their tiny ships couldn't possibly hold the *Requiem* at bay. Their sacrifice didn't really buy Kurcher the time they needed unfortunately.

She wondered where the *Requiem* was. It had been sat quietly waiting on Minerva, where Mitchell had sent it, and Garrett had ordered it retrieved shortly after the attack on Hayes. The famous assault ship was likely being refitted somewhere and would be back in the fleet soon. She would've liked to take a walk through its decks; seen just where Santa Cruz plotted his master plan.

Her focus returned to the new enlisters. Three men, two women. It had been a profession dominated by males since being formed decades ago and it was time for a change. No matter the gender, they had to be ruthless, efficient and, most of all, loyal. All five were proficient in the use of firearms and only one wasn't an experienced pilot. That meant that four would work alone and that the other would be allocated a partner.

Cooke had worked with a small team so as to apprehend more than one crim at a time. Kurcher worked with a pilot and could handle a couple of crims each time he ventured out. The new generation of enlisters would focus on one individual per mission, to avoid any complications.

In the morning, she was due to receive a list of Taurus Galahad's most wanted. Then she could prioritise who her new team would go after. The difference this time was that enlisting a crim would be a much rarer occurrence. No serial killers would end up working for Taurus in any capacity moving forward. Most crims would be apprehended and brought back for trial and imprisonment.

She found herself wondering whether the likes of Edlan Rane and Sieren Broekow would appear on the new list again. Maybe Kurcher himself would be on there, and even Hewn. She would love to be able to send someone to deal with Morton Hurst or this Luminary character, but doubted their names would be included.

A roll of thunder rumbled in the distance as she moved on to the consent forms for the ships this new team would be given. A simple swipe of her finger and the data was logged and processed, with orders being issued to the respective ship locations for them to be brought immediately to Earth. She looked forward to meeting with the five enlisters and giving them the good news.

With that job finally done, Hayward celebrated with another vodka shot, toasting the empty room before downing it. A moment later, she found herself perusing the file on Davian Kurcher, reading up on his background.

It was such a shame in her mind that Taurus had ruined this man's career path, and potentially the man himself. They had taken him in, trained him and found him to be an extremely useful asset. His time in the military was relatively short for someone so talented and her eyes were drawn to his time on Cobb. The details were sketchy at best in the report, using generic words for what he did there. She knew he had been part of an elite team sent in to finally bring an end to the colonist revolt, and she had heard the horror stories from Garrett as to what actually happened.

Kurcher had become an effective enlister, more prone to executions than any other outcome. His missions had all been labelled a success bar one. He had apparently failed to catch up with Rane and issue his punishment. She wasn't sure that one blemish should remain on the record, especially as Kurcher had been ordered away from that mission by Santa Cruz.

She couldn't however ignore some of the notes left by Rees, stating that Kurcher was potentially going to bring Taurus Galahad into disrepute due to his unorthodox actions. To be fair, Taurus' reputation was already well tarnished by the time Kurcher came along and she was now fighting tooth and nail to turn that around.

'Bounty placed on his head by Sigma Royal, Sapphire Nova and Libra Centauri,' she read out loud. 'Recommend removing from duty to allow dust to settle.'

Davian Kurcher was not a liked man, that was clear. The only person who vouched for him was his pilot, Frost. On more than one occasion, she had issued a report stating that the man she worked with was to be commended for his actions, not punished. She had been a sensible individual, keeping Kurcher in check to a degree. Hayward wondered whether Kurcher had even known his pilot was effectively holding the wolves at bay for him.

She made a decision then and it needed another hit of vodka to make sure she followed it through. She sent a message to Akeman's personal comms ordering him to get in touch with Hewn and to request a meeting. Not with the Echo leader though. It was time she met Davian Kurcher face-to-face.

Echo vessel Falcata,
Bridge system

The planet of New Haven loomed in their view, a pale celestial body of green pock-marked with tiny blue dots.

Kurcher gazed out at it, although he was actually wondering just why Fischer was standing so close. In fact, he would rather the pirate wasn't in the cockpit full stop.

Break his nose if he insists on breathing so loud, growled Angard.

He's antagonised you throughout this journey, said Frost. *A bit longer won't hurt.*

Fischer had acted like he was in charge for the first few days, until Drake reminded him just who was running the ship. She hadn't needed to beat the shit out of him either. She just glared at him and that was enough.

When they left the *Glaive*, none of them had anticipated that Sally would head to the Bridge system. It was one of the closest inhabited systems to the Expanse and meant that The Kindred had been right on the doorstep of Echo all this time. It was a disconcerting thought. Even more disconcerting was that Bridge was owned by Impramed and it seemed unlikely they wouldn't have noticed the comings and goings to this quaran.

Kurcher moved back to the seat behind Drake, meaning that Fischer was blocking his view of the planet. He didn't care too much though. He'd seen all he needed to and referred instead to the HDU in his hands.

When Impramed took control of Bridge and colonised Dorran, a cold outer planet, they quickly targeted New Haven next. It was more inviting: warmer climate, thick vegetation and land masses interspersed with lagoons of differing sizes. It should have been a veritable oasis and one would have thought a better first candidate than dull old Dorran. However, after the colony of Avalon was built on the surface of New Haven, it wasn't long before the planet revealed a deadly secret. According to Impramed's reports, the colonists succumbed to a rampant disease that wiped them out so fast the corporation didn't have time to send help. It seemed that New Haven had its own way of protecting against intruders, as the indigenous creatures were immune.

All this made for fascinating reading but it didn't make sense that The Kindred then would make this diseased quaran their home, and obviously raised the question of how they would survive on such a lethal world.

'She's definitely down there, right?' Fischer asked Drake. 'On the surface, I mean. She's not just flying around the atmosphere somewhere?'

'Fucking hell.' Drake sounded exasperated. 'How many times do I have to tell you this shit? Sally is right there. Right where Impramed said they built Avalon.'

Fischer shook his head. 'Doesn't make sense.'

'What does these days?' Drake muttered.

'What do you reckon?'

Kurcher realised Fischer's question was aimed at him instead. 'I reckon I go down there and see what's going on. I reckon you stay on the *Falcata*. I reckon I kill any Kindred I find moping around down there. How's that?'

'You're not going down there alone,' replied Fischer. 'Remember why I came along.'

How could we forget? groaned D'Larro. *He mentioned it every day.*

He has a right to see them wiped out, reminded Frost.

After Hewn announced that his second would be joining them on their jaunt, Kurcher had vehemently refused to let Fischer onto the *Falcata*. He of course had no say in the matter and soon all three of them were under way. After their first heated exchange, which took place before they had even reached the jump point in Miller, Fischer explained just why he was there.

It turned out he had lost someone to a Kindred attack a few years back. She had been on the brink of agreeing to marry him after he had asked three times, but was caught up in a terrorist attack during the delivery of goods into Libran space. The transport she had docked with had a stowaway on board primed to blow themselves up, as per their usual process, and she had died in the subsequent explosion. He had been seeking some sort of revenge since then against The Kindred and wanted to be part of their downfall. Turns out the prick did have a valid reason for being there after all.

'It's best I check it out alone first,' Kurcher told him, his tone measured. 'I'll go down with a breathing mask, do some recon and then report back.'

As Fischer opened his mouth to reply, Drake butted in. 'Whatever you decide, do it quickly. Impramed will know we're in Bridge and I don't want them getting in my face, even though we could easily take those pussies.'

Even those pussies have assault ships, said D'Larro.

'We've got a conflector,' Fischer stated. 'We'll be hidden.'

Drake's expression said it all. 'They'll know someone came into their system, you fucking moron. The conflector tech will only garble the jump point data. I'll take us into the upper atmosphere for now and then drop Kurcher off if that's what we decide.'

'*If?*' Kurcher noticed Fischer's smirk. 'I'll need it to be dark down there if I'm sneaking around.'

Drake checked her console. 'The sun's setting over that region right now. By the time we get down there, you'll have all the cover you need.'

As New Haven grew ever closer, Fischer turned to Kurcher, the smirk having vanished. 'Listen, it's no secret that I don't like you. I don't like the way you walk around like you've always been one of us, or like you're better than the rest of us. I don't like that Jaffren chooses you for missions like this or that you've got a lot of enemies who would gladly kill us to get to you.'

Kurcher shrugged. 'You got a point or are you just venting?'

Fischer bit back the angry response. 'Despite all that, you can help us get rid of The Kindred once and for all. If the chance is there on New Haven, tell me and we'll kill these fuckers together. Agreed?'

'Agreed.'

It was easier to keep Fischer happy for now, rather than have him constantly on his back. He wanted to add that the pirate mainly didn't like him because Kurcher got to enjoy Drake's personal attention most days, but that would just undo their temporary truce.

As Drake took the ship first into orbit and then began the descent into New Haven's atmosphere, everything seemed serene. There was a thick layer of cloud cover just below them and the pilot lit a cigarette as she prepared to head further down towards the surface.

'Things could get choppy,' she told them. 'Raining heavy by the looks of it.'

'Should I go strap myself in?' Fischer asked, looking around the cockpit but seeing no third seat.

'Do what the fuck you want,' replied Drake. 'Fine by me if you want to brain yourself on the ceiling.'

As Fischer swore and made a swift exit, Drake shot a mischievous grin at Kurcher. 'That's how you get a dickhead to leave the room,' she chuckled.

There was hardly any turbulence as the *Falcata* emerged from the clouds.

Rain streaked instantly across the screen, however, reducing visibility significantly.

'Can't see shit out there.' Drake turned her full focus to the console data, checking their altitude.

Kurcher didn't reply. He was suddenly feeling that gnawing sense of dread that sometimes ran through him before journeying into the unknown. He had no idea what was actually waiting for him down there and, if this was indeed the base of operations for The Kindred, how many he would encounter.

Maybe they're like a cult, suggested D'Larro. *Replenishing their numbers as others perish.*

Just roll a few explosives into whatever nest you find and burn the bastards, Angard advised.

That wasn't a bad call. He made a mental note to grab some of those useful devices before he left the safety of the ship. They'd helped on more than one occasion.

The smart move is finding their leader, said Santa Cruz. *Take care of that one and the others may falter.*

There was a part of him that just wanted to know who those freaks were. His brief meeting with the falsely named Jenson Cassius on Sullivan's Rest had piqued his interest before. The dubious app tech being used, the lack of humanity in the eyes, the emotionless visage and dirty appearance. Kurcher wanted to finally find out whether there was another power behind the suicide bombers; someone pulling the strings of these brainwashed marionettes.

'Have you gone to sleep or just ignoring me?' Drake's voice cut through his thoughts.

'Just wondering what I'm walking into,' he answered honestly.

'I was saying we don't want to get too close to Avalon so I've located a clearing where I can drop you off. It's next to one of the smaller lagoons.'

'How far is the colony from there then?'

Drake checked her data again. 'Should take about an hour to walk there. As it's you though, probably longer.'

He rose from the seat and approached the pilot. 'I'll go get ready. Don't let Fischer persuade you into dropping him off elsewhere. I've got a feeling he'll try it.'

She looked up at him. 'He can fucking try. I'll hold him here at gunpoint if I have to.'

Kurcher kissed her roughly. He knew she liked it when she responded by biting at his lip. 'There'll be time for that later,' he grinned, heading for the door.

As he gathered his belongings and strapped an ammo belt around his torso, Kurcher considered taking an extra gun just in case. It couldn't hurt. It would though mean having to carry different bullets to those for his revolver, so extra weight.

One gun is usually all you need, noted Frost. *You'll need to move quickly and quietly.*

That made up his mind. He did however grab his knife, in case one of the mute bastards got too close.

As he left his quarters and headed for the small storage room squeezed into one corner of the ship, Fischer caught up with him.

'I read up on the disease that made Impramed class this as a quaran,' the pirate told him as they walked.

'Good for you.'

'The mask should protect you well enough but there were reports of it affecting exposed skin too.'

'Yeah, I read that too.' Kurcher patted his holstered revolver. 'I do prep before a mission, contrary to popular belief.'

When Fischer frowned, he suddenly looked much older. 'What, that doesn't worry you?'

'Not really. I think it may be bullshit. Guess I'll find out shortly.'

'Care to explain?'

'Not really.' He saw the perplexed expression on Fischer's face and sighed loudly. 'Think about it. We find that The Kindred are on a planet in Impramed space in a system that sees regular traffic, and it just so happens to be labelled as a quaran. It seems highly unlikely that Impramed are oblivious to these fuckers living here.'

'So you think they classed it as a quaran to ensure nobody tried to land there and got themselves blown up.'

Kurcher shrugged. 'I vividly recall visiting another quaran in Libran space not so long ago which turned out not to be dangerous at all, apart from the pirates and corp dickheads who tried to kill me. It's a good way to make sure whoever is down there is left alone.'

206

Fischer didn't look impressed at his nod to Tempest. 'If Impramed knew they are here on New Haven though, they would've dealt with them by now.'

'You'd think so,' Kurcher said, heading into the tight confines of storage and leaving Fischer to contemplate this.

He scooped up eight explosives, pocketing them carefully inside his jacket, then one of the breathing masks. It reminded him of the one he had to wear on Rikur when he and Broekow had traversed the stinking sewage works on their way to find Choice, or Maric as he was when they first encountered him.

'I'm not sure it's a good idea you going alone.' Fischer had been waiting for him to emerge. 'If there's any truth in what you're saying, fuck knows what you'll find at Avalon.'

'Exactly.' Kurcher made for the airlock. 'I don't need someone else slowing me down or getting in the way. Look, I know you're a good shot; handy in a fight. You must be good at something to be second to Hewn. I work better alone though.'

'Like on Kharma?' fired back Fischer.

'Very different mission.' Kurcher picked up his pace to try shaking the pirate.

As he entered the airlock and started to close the inner door behind him, Fischer grabbed it and leaned in close.

'If anyone has a chance to get rid of these bastards once and for all, it should be me.'

We've seen that look before, Frost said. *His pain wouldn't disappear if The Kindred did, but it might help ease it somewhat.*

'Starting the descent.' Drake's voice came through loudly in both their ears. 'Prepare to get very wet, and not in a good way.'

With the slightest of nods to Fischer, Kurcher wrenched the airlock shut and put the mask in place.

Why the hell are you so eager to do this? D'Larro asked.

Watching those terrorist fucks burn will be satisfying, Ercko answered.

Curiosity killed the enlister, added Santa Cruz.

Moments later, he found himself standing in the dark, the rain falling almost sheet-like into the clearing. The sound of it hitting the lagoon behind him echoed off the surrounding trees, which was disorientating, and he drew in a deep breath of processed air before heading in the direction of Avalon, or what remained of the colony. He glanced up once into the night sky before entering

207

the thick foliage, glad that he couldn't see the *Falcata*. Drake was clever enough to know when to kill the lights on her ship.

Within five minutes, he was soaked to the skin. The rain was so heavy and persistent that it fell from the canopy like minute waterfalls, which he had no choice but to pass beneath. His route was also blocked frequently by the large vines that wrapped themselves around the smooth-barked trees, forming an impenetrable wall of green that he would have to find a way around.

This will take longer than an hour at this rate, noted Frost.

Kurcher ploughed on, determined that the overgrown forests of New Haven wouldn't defeat him. He lost track of time as he focused on making sure he wasn't heading in the wrong direction.

At least it's not so dark you can't see where you're going, Frost added.

At one point, as he squeezed himself through a tight gap between vines, he was beset by tiny biting insects that had made their home there. They nipped at the back of his neck and he crushed most with his hand, wiping their remains on a nearby tree.

Best hope they're not poisonous, remarked D'Larro.

Eventually, he noticed that the foliage began to thin out and he could move easily through the forest, still avoiding any open ground of course and keeping to the shadows. When he saw a dim light ahead, his revolver quickly found its way into his hand and his steps became wary. It wasn't easy being silent when there was so much ground cover that snapped or rustled, although the rain helped muffle any noise.

He came to a sudden halt when he heard a man's voice call out.

'Tam, you ready yet?'

For a moment, all he could hear was the rain. Then came the reply from somewhere further ahead, this time a woman.

'Nearly. I'll meet you on the ship.'

Are they talking about the lifeboat Sally arrived on? asked Frost.

Kurcher saw the light flicker for a moment as someone passed in front of it. The mask was making it awkward to make much out at that distance, however he thought he caught sight of a man momentarily illuminated before disappearing off to one side. Whoever it was didn't look much like one of The Kindred.

When he crept forward, he could see that the light was one of the basic standing lamps used by the corps when kitting out colonies. They were cheap to manufacture and easy to move. Most of them usually ended up in the scrap heap, burning out after a year or so. Several metres behind the lamp, Kurcher saw one of the exterior walls of Avalon. Some of the vines had already made their home on said wall, seeking out any gaps into the interior.

If he still had his Sight app, he would have found it very easy to follow his target. Corp tech like that did have its benefits. As luck would have it, there was another lamp set up some distance off to his right and Kurcher spotted the man walking swiftly past across much more open ground.

He wasn't surprised to discover the lifeboat from the *Halstead*. It hadn't landed on any designated pad. Instead, it was sitting in a large puddle that had formed in the dirt and brighter light was streaming out from the open airlock.

Kurcher's eyes sought any other movement, although he couldn't see too far beyond the ship thanks to the downpour. If anyone else was lurking out there, he wouldn't find out until he bumped into them. He also looked across to Avalon, which stood as a dark, angular silhouette in the night. From somewhere inside the walls came the glow of more lamps and he was sure he heard a distant voice that was hard to pinpoint.

Best not stand out in the open too long, Frost said.

Maybe get out of this relentless rain, suggested D'Larro.

Kurcher moved quickly to the lifeboat and pressed his back against the cold hull. He could hear the man he followed moving around inside, so cautiously approached the airlock. Over the noise of the incessant rainfall, he heard a sniff followed by fast tapping from inside.

It's the perfect time to take him out, insisted Angard.

Also the perfect opportunity to question him, Santa Cruz pointed out.

As Kurcher made to swing into the lifeboat, revolver raised, he heard the man curse and move again, so returned to his position.

'You really need me in there?' There was a moment of silence. 'For fuck's sake, Tam, you know I don't like being near them. Get Kynt to do it.'

So there were three of them at least. Kurcher guessed there would be more but he still needed to know just who *they* were.

'Alright, alright,' came the exasperated cry. 'Be there in five.'

Kurcher made sure he was hidden as the clearly annoyed man stepped out of the lifeboat and trudged off towards Avalon, again his features and any clue as to who he and his colleagues were disguised by the rain. It had been a chance to grab him from behind and try to determine just what was going on, however Kurcher had noticed the airlock was left open.

When the figure had disappeared into the darkness, Kurcher entered the ship and realised just how wet he was. The water dripped from his hair and ran down his neck, his clothes stuck to him in a very uncomfortable way and his mask had steamed up.

Then it hit him. Whoever that man was, he hadn't been wearing a mask.

'Motherfuckers.' Kurcher wrenched the apparatus off his face and took a tentative breath, shaking his head. 'Lying pricks.'

Could just be they've been vaccinated of course, D'Larro said.

Impramed is a medical corporation after all, stated Santa Cruz.

Kurcher ignored the thought that he may have jumped the gun and instead dropped the mask before heading to a nearby console that was lit up. It was the navigation instrumentation and highlighted clearly on the screen was the Benedict system. Data scrolling on the right hand side gave the coordinates of Summit.

He looked around the rest of the lifeboat, which didn't take long. There were signs that the systems had been tampered with; loose or open panels here and there. Other than that, it seemed ridiculously clean considering one of the unwashed terrorists had been in it for some time. Maybe the open airlock was to let the stench out.

Kurcher returned to the rain with a grimace and decided to circle the colony to see what else he could find. When he came across Avalon's original landing pad on the opposite side to the lifeboat, at least one big question was answered. The much larger transport was emblazoned boldly with the Impramed emblem; the red cross inside the planet.

It was time to head inside Avalon and have a word with these bastards.

~

'We should contact him,' Fischer said, tapping on the arm of the seat. 'I don't like that we haven't heard anything.'

Drake blew a ring of smoke into the air. 'I've learnt that Kurcher gets in touch only when he absolutely needs to. Also, keep tapping like that and I'll cut your fucking hand off.'

'You've never cared much about rank have you, Shannon?'

210

'My ship, my rules.'

'Actually, the *Falcata* belongs to Echo,' he told her sharply.

Drake looked back at him, her eyes stormy. 'Were you born an asshole or did you have to train hard to become one?'

Fischer sighed and shook his head. 'I've just had to take a lot of shit in my life so it's kind of a defence mechanism. I don't wake up in the morning intending to be obnoxious. I want you and I to get along.'

'Oh, I know what you want,' she shot back.

'Can I ask you a serious question?'

It was Drake's turn to sigh. 'If you must.'

'What do you see in Kurcher? If anything, he's more annoying than I am.' He tried a smile to lighten the mood somewhat.

'He's a prick, sure,' she replied. 'But most men are. He has his uses though.'

'Not really an answer,' Fischer mumbled.

She grinned. 'It's the only one you're getting.'

Fischer stood and made his way forward to peer into the darkness outside the *Falcata*. The rain had eased slightly and yet was still torrential. He didn't recall visiting any other world that had quite as much fall in such a short space of time.

'Go on then.' Drake was squinting up at him through the smoke. 'You might as well pass the time by telling me more about the shitty life you've led.'

'You're not interested in that.'

'No, I'm not,' she admitted. 'But do it anyway.'

Fischer gave her a quizzical look. 'I joined Jaffren right at the beginning, when he formed his own smuggling op in 2599. I'd been part of the same convoy as him prior to that, which was a real mash-up of pirates and mercs. Like Jaffren, I lost both parents early on. I heard they got mixed up in some deal that went very bad somewhere in Callyn.'

Drake cocked her head to one side as she regarded him. 'Your parents were pirates?'

'More like mercs really, doing odd jobs for the highest bidder. Jaffren's were part of Fortitude. Did you know that?'

'No. What happened?'

'He said they were being pursued by corp mercs, most likely enlisters, so they left him on Sullivan's Rest for protection. As far as I know, the corp caught up with them and destroyed their ship.'

'Which corp?'

Fischer shrugged. 'Taurus. Nova. One of them. Anyway, we ended up in the same convoy but couldn't have been more different. He'd learnt to handle himself and I was still pretty wet behind the ears.'

Drake stubbed out the cigarette. 'You were a pussy.'

'Fucking hell. If you don't want to know, why ask?'

She waved a hand in his direction. 'Proceed.'

'I got the shit beaten out of me on more than one occasion during my time with the convoy,' he continued with a scowl. 'Jaffren noticed though that I never backed down from a fight, even when the odds were against me. He helped me and I owed him for that; for leading me to a new life in Echo.'

Drake looked confused. 'I thought you said you had a shitty life. It sounds much better than mine.'

Fischer turned his gaze back to the night sky. 'People underestimated me my whole life, Shannon. Just because I'm Jaffren's second, it doesn't mean I'm weak. If anything were to happen to him, I'd be in charge of Echo.'

'Yeah, and there would be a mutiny within days,' she quipped, laughing.

Fischer gave up, knowing there was nothing he could say that she wouldn't take the piss out of. A moment later, Drake suddenly sat up straight and tapped a switch on the console.

'You're on main comms so Fischer can hear,' she said.

'There's a team of Impramed personnel down here,' came Kurcher's hushed voice. 'The fuckers are clearly part of whatever agenda The Kindred have. I'm heading into Avalon to find out more.'

'Wait,' Fischer blurted out loudly. 'Let me come down and help.'

'If you want to help, have the *Falcata* ready to support me just in case any of them try to flee. There's an Impramed transport on one side of the colony and Sally's lifeboat on the other, which is being prepped to go to Summit.'

Fischer shared a look with Drake. 'I can be of use down there.'

'Just be ready and I'll be in touch again shortly.' Kurcher snorted quietly. 'Hopefully.'

With the link severed, Drake powered the ship into action and aimed them for Kurcher's position, albeit slowly.

'Drop me off there,' came Fischer's order.

'He said...'

'I know what *he* said,' snapped Fischer, knowing that interrupting her wasn't the wisest thing to do. 'He's not in charge and I need to see this for myself.'

If Drake was pissed off, she didn't show it. 'You'll stay right here, at least until we know exactly what we're dealing with.'

Fischer jabbed a finger at the darkness outside. 'We're dealing with Impramed. Don't tell me what to do, Shannon. This means too much to me.'

She made to light another cigarette and suddenly decided against it. 'Exactly. Just calm the fuck down and wait until Kurcher reports in again. Don't make me subdue you.'

Fischer swore and stormed back to the seat behind the pilot, muttering beneath his breath. Drake merely smiled as she prepped the *Falcata*'s weapons.

~

The interior of Avalon had a strange energy. It was as though the very air was humming quietly and each step he took felt heavy, not just because he was soaking wet.

Kurcher had made his way into the inner sanctum of the ruined colony, passing some parts open to the elements and rooms containing long-dead equipment. As he had neared Avalon's central hub, he heard the voices echoing through the eerie halls. There were four different people ahead, he decided, although others could've been present and just not getting into the conversation.

He heard the voice of the man he had tracked, this time complaining that he just wanted to get back to the warmth of Impramed's transport. He heard the one called Tam saying the sooner they finished up, the sooner they could leave New Haven and make way for the next team. The other two voices were both male, one hard to understand due to a thick accent and one annoyingly whiny.

'There are only thirty-two left,' remarked the whiner. 'Once the Summit mission is done, we'll be down to the last handful. What are we supposed to do then?'

'Not really our problem to worry about,' replied Tam. 'We're just the tech grunts after all. Let Ziegler deal with the fallout.'

Kurcher knew that name and it took a moment to recall where he had heard it before. Roman Ziegler was the head of internal security for Impramed. He'd never met the man of course and knew next to nothing about him.

'Ziegler doesn't give a shit,' came the whining voice again. 'He's already ordered both devices shipped to Xander once resources here are depleted.'

'He is in charge after all,' the one with the accent said. 'You want to get paid, right?'

'Kynt, the guy didn't bat an eyelid when he ordered our own people blown up.' Whiny was beginning to really grate. 'Don't give me that look. I know it was for the good of Impramed and made the other corps believe we were being targeted just like them. It's just a pretty shitty thing to do.'

'That's why he replaced the usual personnel with long-serving criminals.' Kynt's accent sounded similar to Old Russian, at least to Kurcher's ears. 'Freed up some space in prison.'

'Can we just get this done?' asked the first man nervously. 'They're giving me the creeps in there.'

'Christ, Niko,' Tam sighed impatiently. 'Get a hold of yourself.'

After this exchange, silence had fallen again and Kurcher had continued on to the heart of Avalon. Now he was standing at one of several doorways leading into what would have been the original concourse of the colony; a hub used for socialising. His eyes had fallen first on the four Impramed *tech grunts*, each working at very new-looking consoles that had been pushed together to form a square so they could face one another. Two power generators buzzed nearby, although that wasn't the humming he could hear.

When he craned his neck to peer around an old broken wall just the other side of them, what he saw made a chill run the length of his spine. That didn't happen often. A group of men and women were gathered together, standing still apart from the odd sway. All were dressed in ragged clothes, their hair long and lank, facing in the same direction away from him. Despite the lighting being poor in the hub, the faces he could see were illuminated with a blue glow.

So this was it? All that was left of The Kindred? Whiny had said there were thirty-two left and Kurcher doubted he was talking about bombs or anything else.

Those grenades could take them out, noted Frost.

Or just get the Falcata to blow the shit out of this place, Angard suggested.

Kurcher could see another door that would lead him closer to the statue-like terrorists and quickly peeled back from his position. It only took two minutes to reach the other entrance to the hub, although the doorway was partially covered by foliage that had wound its way in from somewhere above. When he moved it aside, his breath caught in his throat.

He could see every last one of the dirty bastards, their eyes open and staring in the same direction. Every filthy face was blank; no sign of emotion as always. He even spotted Sally standing at the edge of the gathering.

Then he saw what they were so mesmerised by; the source of the blue light. Two strange-looking devices sat inside a clear container that was standing on a raised platform, one almost square and the other conical. They were both made from a dark green material that he didn't recognise, with ridges and unusual patterns all across their surface. The blue light emanated from inside the devices through what looked like sections that had been broken open, with small fissures spreading from the gaps like pale veins. Both looked about the same size as his head, although it was hard to see properly from where he stood.

Hate to say it but those look really familiar, whispered D'Larro.

Similar to parts of the Grail, added Santa Cruz. *That would also explain the gravitational shift in here and the hum in the air.*

'Fuck.' Kurcher didn't know how loud he swore but was relieved to see none of the transfixed eyes suddenly swivel towards him.

He took a moment to compute what he was seeing here on this fake quaran. The Kindred were being controlled somehow by Impramed and used to attack the other organisations, with the smallest of the corps making it look as though the bombings were hitting them too. All this time, the corporation that was mostly overlooked by the rest turned out to be behind the terrorist attacks that had cost the lives of god knows how many people. It was hard to swallow.

So who were these people then? Frost asked. *More criminals they wanted to get rid of?*

Good use for fucking scum like that, remarked Ercko.

Kurcher weighed up the distance between his position, the devices, the frozen terrorists and the four from Impramed. He knew that being able to place his explosives on the devices, or at least on the container, could not only destroy the alien hardware, if indeed that's what they were, but could also put these lost souls out of their misery.

There was also the question of where the fuck Impramed would have got their hands on the devices too, although right at that moment Kurcher didn't really care.

He thought about Drake and Fischer waiting above somewhere. There was

215

no time for him to wait for the latter to get his ass down there. It sounded like the four just the other side of the broken wall would be on their way soon and so too perhaps would The Kindred. No, he needed a distraction of some kind that would allow him to plant the explosives.

Just kill the four of them, Ercko told him.

Risky, said Frost. *Perhaps there's more to discover before blowing them to kingdom come.*

Kill them all, get back on the Falcata and fuck off. Angard was direct as always.

Kurcher's instincts screamed at him to just burn the lot of them and yet there was a huge benefit to knowing more about just what was going on in the dark remnants of Avalon.

He left the hub behind and swiftly retraced his steps back out of the colony, heading out into the rain and making for the Impramed transport. Circling it, he could see a lone figure moving around the cockpit. If he was correct, a transport of that size would have a single pilot and one of the tech team would likely be considered co-pilot, so he was hoping there wouldn't be any more crew on board.

When he had passed the ship originally, he noticed the open airlock and couldn't help but smile when he found that the pilot hadn't seen fit to close it. Most likely, he was expecting the rest of the team any moment.

Kurcher walked cautiously up the ramp and into the transport, his revolver leading the way. Inside, it was a basic layout as expected, with a single central corridor running like the spine of the ship. To his left would be the engines, storage and perhaps a couple of small quarters. His target lay to the right and he soon found his way into the cockpit, which was about the same size as the *Kaladine*'s had been.

This one has that corporation smell though, Frost said.

The pilot was a tall, young-looking man wearing a cap and a jacket that had the Impramed logo on the back. He was whistling loudly as Kurcher entered.

'Nice tune.'

The unknown voice startled the pilot, who spun quickly and found himself staring down the barrel of the revolver. 'Who the hell are you?'

Kurcher shook the rain from his hair to avoid it dripping into his eyes. 'Think I'll ask the questions. You Impramed lot are sneaky fuckers. Turns out you've

216

been behind The Kindred all this time. How're you controlling them?'

The pilot shook his head vigorously. 'Even if I knew, I wouldn't tell you.'

Kurcher's other hand came sharply around the side of the revolver, punching the Impramed officer hard on the nose. Blood quickly ran out of his nostrils and down over his lips as he reeled backwards.

'Tell me what I want to know or you'll die here on New Haven.' Kurcher hit him again before waiting for a response, this time leaving a welt on the man's cheek. 'Where are you taking this ship once you leave?'

The pilot spat blood onto the pristine floor, grimacing when he saw the mess he'd made. 'Stopover at Dorran before heading back to Xander.'

Kurcher pushed the revolver into his face again. 'And Roman Ziegler is behind this?'

The injured officer hesitated, then nodded as he tried stopping his nose from bleeding.

'Why has he attacked all the other organisations?' pressed Kurcher. 'If he wanted a war, all he had to do was ask.'

'I...I honestly don't know,' came the broken reply. 'All I know is that a number of them are being sent on that lifeboat to Summit.'

'Why?'

'To try to kill Morton Hurst after he took over the planet. At least, that's what the others said.' The pilot looked up, his cheek already swollen. 'Why are you doing this? You're not corporate.'

Kurcher smiled. 'I was. Other than the four inside the colony, are there any other Impramed personnel here?'

'No.'

'What can you tell me about the devices in there?'

The pilot gave him a fearful look. 'Nothing really.'

Kurcher gave his nose a hard tap with the revolver. 'You knew all about Ziegler's intentions to kill Hurst, which isn't a bad fucking thing I have to admit. I reckon you know more about this than you're letting on.'

'All I know is that the devices were found here on New Haven by the Avalon colonists.'

Kurcher loomed over the pilot, looking down at the bloodied face and the dislodged cap. He could see in the man's eyes that he didn't know the ins and outs of what was happening here. The others would know more.

'Last question. Who are The Kindred really?'

The officer wiped the fresh blood from his nose. 'I only know what Tam told me. She said they were all that's left of the original Avalon colonists. I don't know any more though, I honestly don't.'

Kurcher tried to take that in. So Impramed were using their own colonists as human bombs? That couldn't be the full story surely.

'Okay,' he said calmly. 'I believe you.'

The revolver cracked the pilot on the side of the skull, knocking him unconscious, and Kurcher stepped over the slumped man to check the data at the helm. It seemed he had been telling the truth as Dorran was locked in as their destination.

'You there?' he asked, activating his comms.

'Course I fucking am,' came Drake's sultry voice. 'What's going on?'

'I'm about to blow the Impramed transport sky high,' he told her, reaching into his pocket. 'I need you to open fire on it once it's burning.'

'Care to explain?'

'You're the distraction I need. Don't tell Fischer but I've got a chance to get rid of every last Kindred down here. I just can't afford to wait for him.'

Drake's laugh was slightly muffled. 'He'll be pissed.'

'Let him be.' Kurcher placed a single explosive on the console and primed it. 'Watch for the flames.'

He ran back through the transport, heading down to the engine room at the rear of the ship. Once there, he placed a second explosive on one of the modern Impramed-manufactured engines. It reminded him of when he had destroyed the *Beck's Fire* on Kismet.

Once back out in the rain, he ran to the same entrance into the main building he had entered by before, stopping for a moment to cast a glance expectantly at the doomed transport. The first explosive went off, blowing out the windows of the cockpit and no doubt killing the unconscious pilot. A few seconds later, the back of the transport burst open as the engine blew and the whole ship listed sideways before crashing to the wet ground.

Kurcher waited to see the *Falcata* appear overhead and was pleased to see the gats kick in immediately, peppering the burning transport. Then, he was heading inside once more towards the hub, eager to finish this particular mission and get the fuck away from Impramed space.

He didn't expect the four tech grunts to appear ahead of him, thinking they would take a more direct route out to see what was happening. They stopped and stared at him for a moment, blinking in the dim light and trying to make out who was standing before them. Niko, the man he had originally followed, shared a look with the only woman in the team, Tam. Kynt, he surmised, was the larger of the other two, which meant the wiry little prick next to him was Whiny.

'Who the fuck...?'

Kurcher's revolver interrupted Kynt as it fired twice in quick succession, the first bullet striking the tall Impramed techie in the shoulder and the second finding its mark in Whiny's stomach. As both men fell, Tam and Niko bolted back the way they came, disappearing through a doorway before Kurcher could open fire again.

As he made to follow, he saw Kynt lifting a pistol slowly. Two more shots from the revolver both took the man in his chest. Kurcher stepped over the body and looked down at Whiny, who was writhing in pain and moaning.

'Please, I haven't done anything wrong,' pleaded the Impramed officer. 'Don't kill me.'

Kurcher glanced at the stomach wound then put a bullet between Whiny's eyes. 'Would've bled out anyway,' he muttered as he headed after the other two, making sure he reloaded. He found Tam at the consoles in the hub, her fingers a blur as she worked and sweat glistening on her face. Niko was nowhere to be seen but Kurcher wasn't taking any chances. He fired a shot that missed Tam and bounced off the surface of the console next to her. She flinched but didn't stop.

'Don't make me kill you,' he shouted, trying to make out he had missed on purpose. 'I need you to step away from there and come with me right now.'

To his surprise, Tam did stop. However, when she looked up, he realised she had accessed an app of some sort as a soft golden glow of data flashed in her eyes. He didn't like it when she then smiled.

'I haven't got time for this,' he growled.

Before he could squeeze the trigger again, he heard the soft scuff of a boot heel behind him and instinctively threw himself to the side. A bullet ricocheted off the edge of the doorway where he had been standing, missing him by inches, and he responded in kind, firing off three rounds in the direction of the shooter.

A grunt told him at least one bullet had found the target and he saw Niko for a split second as the man moved into cover.

Kurcher turned his attention back to Tam, this time feeling confident enough to step into the hub. That confidence drained quickly though as a number of wretched figures appeared around the side of the broken wall, their staring eyes locked firmly on him. The light from the lamps glinted off blades that many of them were now holding.

Kurcher looked at Tam, who had started backing away towards the approaching men and women of The Kindred. The smile was still on her face.

'You couldn't just make this easy for me,' sighed Kurcher, already well aware he didn't have enough ammunition to take out all thirty-two, plus Tam and Niko.

He brought the revolver up and used one bullet that struck Tam just below the throat. Her smile vanished as she let out a gurgled cry before crumpling to the floor.

Were you hoping that would stop them? D'Larro asked.

Kurcher glanced around the large chamber at the centre of Avalon. Not all of the unwitting terrorists were approaching him head on. Some he noticed were disappearing out of other doors, including the one partially covered by vines.

Don't let yourself get cornered, urged Frost.

Heeding the advice, he retreated from the hub. Recognising the connection between the two bizarre devices that held the attention of the mutes and the consoles that the Impramed goons were working on, Kurcher hoped that he could end this nightmare with a few well-placed explosives. It was just getting enough time and space to do so that was the problem.

He headed for where he had seen Niko moments before and wasn't surprised to find the man gone, although there was a clear trail of blood spots showing just where the final member of the team had gone. As he followed, Kurcher was aware of his pursuers moving in the shadows.

Maybe lead them all outside and have Drake gun every last one down, suggested Santa Cruz.

That Impramed bitch set them all on you, said Ercko. *Maybe she's still alive and can call them off.*

Kurcher followed the blood trail outside. The rain had become much heavier, if that was even possible, and the wind was whipping it into his eyes. As he squinted out into the overgrown compound, he saw the lifeboat from the

Halstead starting to rise from the mini-lake it had been sat in.

He reactivated his comms. 'Turn your attention to the opposite side of Avalon. Don't let the lifeboat get away.'

'Understood,' came Drake's abrupt response.

To Kurcher's chagrin, the small ship rose faster than he had anticipated. It seemed Niko was an accomplished pilot as it veered sharply into the rain and accelerated up and away from the colony, nearly clipping the top of a tree. The *Falcata* soared overhead in pursuit, her gats spitting bullets at the escaping ship, and they both disappeared from view.

Kurcher suddenly felt very vulnerable and looked over his shoulder. Several of the brainwashed Avalon colonists were heading swiftly towards him, their hair stuck to their faces as the rain hammered down on them. He spotted some others emerging from a gap in the wall further around the side of the main building.

You're quicker than them, Frost said. *You can get past them and be back in the hub with plenty of time to set the explosives.*

Then you still have to get out again, D'Larro remarked.

He reloaded the revolver again and tried to ignore the quickly emptying ammo belt. Then he was away again, running through the rain. He passed those coming from the broken wall and ended up near the burning transport, stopping momentarily to wipe his eyes. The visibility was so poor that he could hardly even make out the colony, but he could easily retrace his steps back to the other entrance.

As he reached it though, two shabby figures staggered from the haze right in front of him. A knife flashed and Kurcher fell back, slipping on the wet ground. As he landed in the water, he fired repeatedly at the two lunging for him. A spray of red erupted from the skull of one, dispersing quickly in the wind and rain. The other was blown off his feet, falling heavily onto his back.

Kurcher was up and moving again as fast as he could, heading inside. He made his way past the bodies of Kynt and Whiny, finding the quickest route back to the heart of Avalon. When he stepped into the chamber containing the devices, he had already holstered his revolver and was grabbing the remaining explosives from his pocket. As he approached the two devices, he experienced a very odd and yet uncomfortably familiar sensation; a buzzing in his very bones. It was what he had felt on the *Grail* just after the weapon had been

221

activated.

I half expect Santa Cruz to walk in and try stopping you again, said D'Larro.

Oh, I'm here, the commander pointed out.

As he started placing the explosives around the container, aiming to leave one for the consoles nearby, Kurcher used his comms quietly. 'You done?'

Drake's voice came back way too loud in his ear. 'The lifeboat's toast. Who was on board? One of the Kindred fuckers?'

'Niko.' He realised she wouldn't know who the hell that was. 'One of the Impramed team. I need you here now.'

'On our way.'

He couldn't tell whether it was sweat or rain dripping down his face. Probably a blend of both. He nearly dropped an explosive as he clumsily tried to plant it at the base of the platform.

Hurry up, cried D'Larro. *Let's get the fuck out of here.*

Kurcher glanced up halfway through priming them and froze. He hadn't heard the bastards entering the hub. Their soft footwear, or lack of, had masked their approach well. Half of the Kindred had arrived via the doorways he had used himself before and, when he turned, the other half had circled round and come in opposite, making sure there was no easy escape route this time.

'You clever motherfuckers,' he said loudly. 'Not that it's your brains doing the work.'

They moved towards him with sinister intent, rain dripping from their soaked clothing and hair. Most of the emotionless faces were hidden behind the fringes, although the unnerving eyes could just be made out.

Kurcher's eyes searched frantically for a way through. He needed to lighten the numbers. Drawing his revolver once more, he opened fire on a grouping of six who were between him and the nearest exit. He didn't have time to aim properly and expended his ammo in seconds. Only two of the terrorists had fallen, with three others wounded but, as usual, not showing any hint of pain.

Just kill the fuckers, snarled Angard.

He reloaded for the final time and, when he raised the revolver again, he found that the distance between them had closed rapidly. The gun blazed, the first shot giving him hope as it passed through the eye of one man. The other bullets struck flesh and two others staggered but didn't drop.

Kurcher dropped the revolver and drew his knife. Behind him, a ping from one of the explosives reminded him that detonation was imminent. He didn't have time to prime the last couple.

'Shannon?' he called, his voice echoing across the hub.

'Nearly there.'

He shook his head. 'How far did you fucking go?'

'Just hold on.'

Easy for her to say, D'Larro muttered.

Surrounded and with no other option, Kurcher launched himself at the depleted grouping nearest him. One woman with a bullet hole in her shoulder swung her knife at him and he ducked it, slashing his own across her thigh and cutting deep into the muscle. She didn't so much as flinch. A tall, thin man lunged towards him and he managed to narrowly avoid the blade, shoving the weak-looking individual back. Another man stepped in and his knife nicked Kurcher's arm, drawing blood. Kurcher responded by stabbing his knife deep into the man's eye.

Just push through, yelled Frost.

As he went to pull his knife back from the falling man's socket, the thinner one he had shoved and two others grabbed at his arm. Kurcher lost his grip on the hilt and watched helplessly as the body fell and took his weapon with it. Then a burning pain shot through his side and he looked down to see a dirty blade buried deep. The hand holding it belonged to Sally.

How fucking ironic, grunted Santa Cruz.

Should never have come here, groaned D'Larro.

He tried to push past those in front of him but found himself being forced back instead, unable to dodge between the blade and grabbing hands. Another knife found its way through, jabbing deep into his left arm. He felt the surge of adrenaline kick in and delivered a hard headbutt to the face of the one who had stabbed him, smashing the man's nose. He then lashed out and punched a woman square in the face who was trying to wrestle him to the ground.

A moment later, he staggered back against the platform and glanced up at the two devices, then at the explosives flashing their warnings. With blood running from his arm and pouring from his side, Kurcher experienced a sudden moment of calm and his mind cleared.

It's okay, Frost assured him. *You know what to do.*

'Fuck it.' With that, he flung himself into the crowd of approaching Kindred.

223

The explosions tore apart the container, the platform and most of the ceiling above them, sending the terrorists flying in all directions. Smoke and flames rolled across the room, engulfing everything in their path, as the heart of Avalon was demolished.

Kurcher came to, not knowing how long he had been lying in the darkness. His body was numb and his ears were ringing so loud that all he could hear was his own rattling breath as his lungs struggled to cope. There was something heavy on him, yet he couldn't muster the strength to move it. Eventually it seemed to move itself and slid off to one side.

There was a distant light in the darkness suddenly and he realised that he was staring up at the night sky through the drifting smoke. Rain fell through the hole in the roof of the colony and hissed as it landed in the flames.

Kurcher started to feel something in one of his arms and, when he managed to turn his head slightly, he saw that his limb was on fire, the skin blistering and raw. He couldn't move to try putting it out though. His eyes wouldn't focus properly and he thought he saw something protruding from his shoulder.

As the smoke continued to disperse somewhat, he tried to lift his head but a sharp pain lanced through his skull and his vision swam. He vomited and choked as he was unable to spit the bile out, his throat burning.

He knew he was dying. He had been too close to the explosion this time and didn't have a human shield like he had on Warren. No doubt he looked a real mess. He didn't care. He didn't have to care about anything any more.

There was movement to his right and his head flopped to the side so he could try to make out what it was. Six blurry figures were standing watching him. He could tell that two of them were women and one was a hulk of a man, standing much taller and wider than the rest. They didn't look like members of The Kindred.

One of the women approached him, seemingly unaffected by the smoke and flames all around them, and knelt at his side. As her face came into view, something happened that he hadn't experienced for a long time. Tears ran down his blackened face and he felt his chest heave as an overwhelming feeling of guilt and regret struck him.

Don't worry any more, Frost told him, smiling. *It's time to let them go.*

Kurcher again tried to lift his head but failed. He gazed up into the pilot's eyes and saw only peace there. Maybe there was also pity too.

When he looked past her at the other five, he saw them clearly then. Angard, D'Larro, Ercko, Santa Cruz and Trin. They all acknowledged him in their own unique way before turning and vanishing into the shadows.

You're on your own now, Frost said, still smiling.

Her image dissipated, as though she had been part of the smoke all along. In her place appeared several bleeding figures, some dragging broken legs and some carrying wounds that would have killed any normal person. All of them had knives in their hands, their glazed eyes turned towards him. He couldn't move though and could only watch as they loomed over him.

Muffled gunfire came from somewhere and Kurcher saw bullets tear through the Kindred. Their bodies fell next to his and he heard a voice call his name, however he couldn't make it out clearly.

Two more figures appeared, a woman running to him and looking down with a look of horror on her familiar face. The man behind her was holding a gun of some sort, the barrel of which frequently lit up as he fired it into the smoke.

'Fuck,' he saw her mouth.

There was a moment of clarity as he recognised Drake and Fischer, but he couldn't say anything and could only slightly move his head. She called out something to the pirate, who glanced down, grimaced then made to drag her away. Drake yelled at him and pushed him back, then crouched down and began studying Kurcher, her expression making it obvious just how bad it was.

Something caught his eye and he looked down. A dark green shard was protruding from his chest. He saw more pieces of the same material lodged in other parts of his body; his stomach, his legs, his arms. Some were tiny fragments, whereas some were almost as long as the blade Sally stabbed him with. That was when he realised he also had pieces embedded in his head, their sharp edges just showing in his peripheral vision. Was there even one lodged in his temple?

Clearly those fucking devices didn't survive the explosions either, he realised. That was one good thing to come from what had happened, as well as the end of The Kindred. He hoped.

As Drake tried to call to him, her voice still unclear, Kurcher noticed the approaching darkness all around him. This wasn't like the smoke. It was the darkness of oblivion and he knew this was it. The voices in his head had stopped talking to him and he no longer heard the screams of the dying or the pleading of those on Cobb. For the first time in years, he was at peace.

That was, until he realised there was something in the dark waiting for him. Shapes moved around him suddenly, partially hidden by the encroaching void. There was a flash of blue, stark against the blackness, followed by glimpses of silver. The shapes writhed and coiled, foul tendrils suddenly unfurling from hellish alien forms. They were many and yet they were one.

'Holy shit,' he uttered.

When the darkness rushed forward to envelop him, Kurcher drew one last sharp intake of breath and his heart finally gave in.